THE HERO, A HAG,
and
Foggle-Nogger

The Race for Croggerpooey

❖ J. FUREY HOPKINS ❖

To Grace, Vivian,
and Thomas,
Hope you enjoy
the adventure!
Thanks,

For Lisa and Henry and Sofia.
Of course.

And a special nod of appreciation
to a primitive painter
named DC.
Cheers.

CONTENTS

THE HERO, A HAG, and Foggle-Nogger

PROLOGUE

"**H**alt! Who goes there? Rone?"

"No. It is Sir Ambrose." A tall man strode into the flickering light cast by the castle's sconces. "Relax, my boy. I have come to relieve you for the night."

The guard—who was no boy, but still much younger than the legendary Knight—replaced his sword in its sheath and bowed. "Then the rumors must be true. Horrible Rick is afoot, perhaps lurking in the shadows. King Urabus is taking every precaution. Why else send a Knight of your stature to act as guard?"

Sir Ambrose surveyed the round room. The thick, leather-bound Book lay upon a pedestal under a locked dome of glass and steel. The rest of the room was empty. "The Book of Coded Spells, the King's most prized possession, must never leave Castle Neede. If the wrong person ever deciphers its magic…." The Knight shook his head.

The guard said, "I was expecting Rone."

"He is outside Croggerpooey recruiting Knight prospects."

"Guess the current crop is getting up there in age."

Sir Ambrose cocked a white eyebrow.

"Sorry, sir. I meant no offense."

The Knight chuckled, "None taken. Good evening."

PART ONE

CHAPTER ONE:
Stop Playing With Your Snot

"Who said it?" yelled Bulldog, stomping off the school bus. All the kids did whatever it took to stop laughing. Some held their breath. Others hit themselves in the leg. A few squeezed their faces shut. But no one spoke up, and no one made eye contact with the cursing, purple-haired, dirty finger-nailed, pimple-farm of an eighth grader. They were too afraid. And she knew it.

"WHO SAID IT?"

Bulldog's gaze locked onto Samir in the back of the crowd. "Was it you?" Samir nearly wet himself. His throat dried up. "It *was* you. You little twerp." Bulldog pushed through the group. She shoved a seventh grader named E.J. into a seventh grader named Liz who fell into her big brother Rafael who rammed into his buddy Hunter who crashed into a seventh grader named Dennis Ponder who stumbled forward and sideways and stepped on Bulldog's foot. She fell flat.

Which, of course, was very funny.

Instantaneous laughter infected everyone. Some spit forth giggles. Others chuckled tears. A few winced with side aches, failing to catch their breath. Dennis tried fighting the urge, knowing too well the price paid for laughing at Bulldog. But something burst out of him. It sounded like a donkey choking on helium.

The laughter roared louder.

From the ground, Bulldog glared up at Dennis, whose giggling died quicker than a hiccup.

Not again, he thought.

"You tripped me," she growled.

"I-I didn't mean to."

Bulldog's eyebrows wrinkled into one.

And Dennis took off, darting down the sidewalk, shedding his book bag before his third stride. He hustled as if a hungry hyena raced in hot pursuit. He dashed as if a swarm of stinging killer bees buzzed his way. Bulldog loved the chase, and Dennis never could outrun her. But this time he had gotten a pretty good head start. *Maybe, just maybe. This will be the time. One more block. Almost there.*

But then he looked back.

Bulldog was gaining on him.

I'm-not-gonna-make-it, I'm-not-gonna-make-it, I'm-not-gonna.... And like an escaped balloon making funny fart noises, Dennis ran out of gas.

OOMF!

She tackled him like an All-Pro linebacker. A crowd of excited kids caught up and surrounded them. Dennis wriggled free and spotted his best (and only) friends, Kimberly and Samir, squeezing through the bloodthirsty mob.

Samir shook his guilty head. His wide eyes puddled with fear. He bit his lip until a thumbnail took its place.

Bulldog's punch to Dennis's gut doubled him over.

"That's for tripping me!"

Samir found his voice, "Wait, I—!"

A wallop on the chin staggered Dennis.

"That's for runnin'!"

Kimberly yelled, "Stop it!"

But Bulldog pounced. She threw Dennis onto his head and pinned him beneath her. She jackhammered a knuckle onto Dennis's chest, punctuating each syllable, "And Don't Ev-Er Laugh At Me A-Gain!" Then her hard sniffle snort began the grotesque victory celebration routine. She made The Noise. It started deep within her throat and grew louder in thick scratchiness until she hocked up a healthy helping of phlegm. It was Loogie Hanging Time.

"No…wait…please," begged Dennis.

Bulldog leaned so low it seemed the blackheads bulging from the ball of her nose might shoot Dennis in the eye. A yellowish-green blob oozed from her puckered lips. It hung about two inches long and swayed there a bit over Dennis's face. She slurped it up.

"Eww!" the crowd moaned.

"Stop!" screamed Kimberly again, shaking her violin case over her head.

Bulldog oozed the glob from her mouth again, longer this time, letting it sway until gravity pulled it free. The loogie plopped just above Dennis's right eyebrow.

"EWW!" the crowd moaned louder. Their faces contorted with disgust.

She stood over her victim, turning and glaring at each and every spectator, and completed her victory celebration by flexing her biceps.

Dennis wiped off his forehead, blinked, and discovered Bulldog's blue jean-covered rear end hovering above him as she flexed. He pulled his knees into his chest and aimed. If he shot his legs out straight, he could send Bulldog tumbling through the air all the way to the sidewalk. He imagined her yelling "Whoa!" and flailing her arms and landing halfway across the street. It would be glorious! He'd be the hero! The whole school would know his name! But Dennis froze; he knew better. He'd had enough pain for one day.

Bulldog strutted across the street to her house, grunting like a successful Olympic powerlifter.

The show was over. One kid pointed at Dennis and giggled. Another shook his head. Most just shrugged and headed home. Samir and Kimberly helped Dennis to his feet.

"I can't stand her! She's such a…." Kimberly stomped her foot instead saying a bad word.

"You okay?" asked Samir. He brushed some dirt off Dennis's shoulder and smiled. "Thanks."

"It's okay," Dennis said.

"No, really. She would've killed me. Thank you."

Dennis smiled. In a weird way he was glad he had accidently saved his friend.

"You're welcome, Sam. But keep your voice down next time. You're always so loud."

Kimberly said, "For a second, I thought you might make it home this time."

"Almost," Dennis grinned. "Maybe I'm getting faster."

"Will you be okay?"

Dennis nodded and wiggled his jaw. "Got a headache, but no blood this time."

"Well, I have to get ready for soccer practice," she said. "See you guys tomorrow."

"I've got to go, too," said Samir. "You know how my mom gets when I'm late. Sorry about all this. Really. I'll try to talk quieter. Thanks again. You're a good friend, Dennis. See you later."

Dennis fetched his backpack. It wasn't until he got home that he felt his empty pocket. No key. He slinked to his side yard and wondered what he had done in a past life to deserve living right across the street from Bulldog. With a throbbing head and a runny nose, Dennis leaned against the chained link fence and fantasized all sorts of ugly ways to exact his revenge. Common decency prevents the highly inappropriate, atrocious, appalling, horror movie-like specifics to be detailed here. But these fantasies vanished when Dennis wiped his nose with his sleeve and smeared a huge, gooey booger on his shirt. It looked like a mutilated garden slug. He pinched and stretched the slimy goo between his finger and thumb.

His mind wandered, and he started thinking of his friend. Samir Mourtada, the only seventh grader in the whole school with a decent mustache, was shorter and thinner than Dennis. Bulldog taunted Samir a lot, and had beaten him up once. It was on a cloudy Saturday afternoon. Dennis remembered taking Samir home and being surprised at how his friend's dad reacted. Mr. Mourtada had always been a cold, serious person. Dennis had never seen him smile. But that day Samir's father hugged his sobbing son and whispered in Arabic into his ear. Dennis recalled Mr. Mourtada mouthing the words "Thank you" at him with a wink. Walking home that day, Dennis recalled wiping away a few tears of his own and somehow feeling sad and proud and envious all at the same time.

Dennis had not seen his own father in a long time. But that was okay. Dennis did not miss *his* dad; he just missed having *a* dad. It was hard to explain.

He absentmindedly continued rolling and stretching the mucous glob until a familiar high-pitched, gravelly voice startled him.

"Stop playing with your snot."

"Huh?" he rubbed his hand against the grass. "Mrs. Goodwyn, I… I wasn't playing with my snot."

"I may be old, Dennis Ponder, but I'm not blind." She noticed his stretched out of shape shirt and messed up hair. "Bulldog again?"

He nodded.

"Feeling sorry for yourself is best done privately indoors."

"I'm locked out," said Dennis. "Forgot my key again."

CHAPTER TWO:
Old Enough, But Not Yet Too Old

"**C**ome on," Mrs. Goodwyn said. "You can borrow mine. And if I'm ever gone, remember I keep my spare house key underneath the green flowerpot by my door. Just let yourself in."

"Okay, thanks."

"I baked some chocolate chip cookies. Better wash up."

Mrs. Rosie Goodwyn was old. Very old. For as long as Dennis could remember she had been old. But she wasn't sickly old. She tended her garden daily. Her flowers grew bigger and brighter than any others in the neighborhood. Mrs. Goodwyn's short silver hair framed her tanned and wrinkly face. A few white hairs protruded from a mole on her chin, but Dennis rarely noticed them. Samir once said she looked like a cartoon witch. But she was not witchy.

"Thank you." Dennis grinned as his neighbor set down a plate of cookies with a glass of milk beside stacks of white, blue, and red poker chips. They had been playing poker the day before, and the chips remained exactly as they were when they had stopped.

"Here." She handed him an icepack and began shuffling the deck of cards to continue the game. Dennis's headache vanished before the cards were dealt. He always felt better inside her home. He looked at his cards, made a small bet, and shared the details of his latest humiliating Bulldog defeat. Mrs. Goodwyn called his bet, placed more poker chips into the pile, and said, "It was noble of you to protect Samir. But don't you think it's time to end Bulldog's bullying?" She flipped over a ten, a king, and a six for the next round of betting.

They did not help his hand at all, but he tried hard to keep his expression normal and not give anything away. "Wish I could end it. If you have any bright ideas, I'd love to hear them." He peeked again at his face down cards and decided to raise the pot a hundred. Looking up at Mrs. Goodwyn, he continued, "I don't even know why Bulldog picks on me."

"Because she can," Mrs. Goodwyn said. "And she will continue until she gets bored or someone makes her stop." She stared at Dennis, trying to find a clue about his cards. "I call your raise."

Mrs. Goodwyn dealt the four of diamonds face up. Dennis looked at her. She had a great poker face and never showed any excitement or disappointment while playing cards. He decided to gamble. "Raise. Two-fifty."

She called his raise and flipped over the last card.

The six of hearts didn't help his hand at all, but she didn't know that.

"Raise six hundred." He slid the chips into the pot.

Dennis focused on breathing normally and keeping his expression blank, even though his heart raced. Mrs. Goodwyn stared at his face and really made him sweat it out before folding.

He exhaled and smiled as he dragged all the poker chips towards him. "What'd you have?" he asked.

She showed a pair of tens. "What did you have? Two kings?"

"No, I bluffed you!"

"Well," she feigned anger. "You little stinker. Got me again. I used to be able to tell when you were bluffing. I'm down to 450 in chips. So that means you have...?"

"9,550. Sure wish this was real money."

Mrs. Goodwyn set aside the deck of cards. "Back to Bulldog."

"I don't know how to make her stop," he shrugged. "I can't really bluff her."

"What would happen if you stopped running from her?"

"She'd kill me that much sooner, that's what."

Mrs. Goodwyn shook her head. "Well, if you want things to get better, you need to make some changes. Take a karate class or something."

"Mom can't afford it."

"You know, there's strength in numbers," Mrs. Goodwyn said. "Maybe if you and all your buddies stood up to her."

"Umm, all my buddies? You don't exactly see a line of kids outside begging to play with me. Except for Kimberly and Sam, nobody else at school even knows my name. I'm just that guy who Bulldog beats up. Besides, she can take on all three of us at the same time."

"Well, you better think of something. Don't give up. Giving up can be habit forming, which is why I never let you quit a Sudoku." Dennis struggled with those number puzzles. But he'd rather work on one at Mrs. Goodwyn's than sit alone at home waiting for his mom.

After they each ate another cookie, Mrs. Goodwyn said, "You know, like I've told you before, I could help."

"No. Please. I don't want you to."

"Well, then maybe it's time for your mom to speak to Bulldog's parents."

"No. The only thing worse than getting beat up is having my mom fighting my battles. I'm definitely too old for that."

"Oh, so grown-up for an eleven year old."

"I'm twelve," Dennis corrected her.

Mrs. Goodwyn's eyebrows jumped. "You're twelve years old?"

"Yep"

"I thought you were eleven." She pursed her lips in thought.

"Nope. Nearly twelve and a half," smiled Dennis.

She said slowly, "Twelve years old." Her attention shifted beyond the window. "You're old enough, but not yet too old."

"Hmm?" he asked.

"Well, you better go and do your homework," she brushed him to the door. "I just realized I've got some important calls to make."

"Okay. See you tomorrow. Thanks for the cookies."

At the door, Mrs. Goodwyn placed her hands on his shoulders. "Listen kiddo. You are destined for greatness. This Bulldog business won't last forever. Tomorrow will be a better day. Here's your key."

Dennis gave his neighbor a quick hug and said, "Tomorrow's Career Day."

"Oh? Good." She nodded slowly, as if trying to think of something. "Who knows, maybe you'll discover a Bulldog solution."

"At Career Day?" Dennis asked. "I doubt it."

"Well, sometimes solutions hit us when we're not really looking. You'll see."

CHAPTER THREE:

Never Mind

Dennis and his mom finished eating dinner and discussing their days. Once again he managed to hide his bruises and keep the latest Bulldog incident a secret. He decided long ago that with her work and everything, his mom had enough on her mind; he didn't want her to worry about him. Dennis cleared the dishes and started his homework in his room.

As he tackled a math problem, a quick shuffling noise disturbed his concentration. Dennis's eyes darted between his wastebasket and the dirty clothes on his bedroom floor. His inside-out socks, crumpled underwear, and dropped t-shirts lay like clumped islands on the floor. A topographical map of a far away, stinky archipelago. He returned pencil to paper before the same sound again stole his focus. Something shot across the floor! He lunged over his bed to get a better look.

A long rat cowered in the corner, covering its face with tiny dark brown rodent hands.

Dennis stared at it with his mouth wide open. It wasn't really a rat. Maybe a small weasel. Its light brown furry long body sat up on its hind legs. It uncovered its face and stared back at Dennis.

It blinked.

Dennis blinked.

Its nose twitched.

"How can I trap it?" whispered Dennis.

And he thought he heard "You can't" as it dashed under the bed, over the dirty clothes, and down the hallway. Dennis ran after it, crashing into his mother and knocking an armful of folded laundry to the floor.

"Slow down!" she said.

"Mom, I just saw… did you see…?"

"See what?" his mom asked.

The strange rodent was gone.

"I don't know. You didn't see it?" The boy blinked and twisted his lips in thought.

"See what?" she asked.

"Never mind."

She knelt to pick up the clothes. "Stop messing around and finish your homework. It's getting late and the trash still needs to be taken out." She looked past him at the clothes on his floor. "And it would be nice if you put your dirty clothes in the hamper *before* I did the laundry."

"Sorry." Dennis bent down to help her.

He returned to his bedroom and leaned against the shut door, his heart racing like a drum roll. *Did that thing really talk? Maybe I thought it more than heard it. But….* Dennis scratched his head and blew out a long sigh. *How did Mom not see it run right past her?*

CHAPTER FOUR:

Career Day

The fidgety seventh graders at Ernest Q. Klibzowski Middle School huddled in homeroom to read the lists of Career Day speakers. They were told to choose two presentations. Dennis and Samir made their way to Kimberly, who stood closer to the lists taped on the wall. Dennis skimmed the occupations and considered his options.

POLICE OFFICER, RM B-8 *Too dangerous.*

FIREFIGHTER, RM B-11 *Way too dangerous.*

DENTIST, RM B-12 *No way.*

FAMILY DOCTOR, RM B-15 *Pass.*

ELECTRICIAN, RM B-22 *No.*

CHIROPRACTOR, MR B-24 *Could be cool.*

Dennis skipped to the second page.

CARTOON VOICE ARTIST, RM B-26 *Maybe.*

CLOTHES DESIGNER, RM C-2 *Not if you paid me.*

BAKERY SHOP OWNER, RM. C-5 *Free samples?*

SCHOOL PRINCIPAL, RM C-23 *Are you kidding me?*

Hair Stylist, Graphic Designer, and Bank Loan Officer concluded the unappealing list.

Dennis wondered, "Why couldn't they get better people? Where are the game designers, MMA fighters, pro skateboarders?"

Kimberly wished they had a coroner or a mortician.

"What about assassins and spies?" Samir asked. "Or stunt men and prison guards? Or pirates?"

"I've always liked pirates," said Dennis.

"Really?" Samir said. "I've always been more of a spy kind of guy, myself."

A third boy with glasses said, "I wish they had a wizard."

"Wizards aren't real, stupid bonehead," scoffed a lanky boy with an over-sized Adam's apple.

"And pirates are?" mumbled the boy with glasses.

Another voice chimed in, "It'd be cool to have a hypnotist."

Dennis, Kimberly, and Samir nodded at each other.

"Which should we go to first?" Samir asked.

"I'm going to the firefighter," said Kimberly.

"No way, not me," said Dennis. "Have fun. How about cartoon voices?"

"Okay, cartoon voice first," said Samir in a weird attempt at sounding like a cartoon. "Then let's do the chiropractor."

"Sure, sounds good," agreed Dennis.

The school bell rang and hundreds of seventh graders poured out of their homerooms. They pushed and bumped, thrashed and jostled their way toward their desired presentations. Presentations were deemed closed as soon as all the classroom desks were taken. The meanest teachers roamed the hallways to keep the chaos to a minimum and swept those who lagged behind into the rooms with fewer students. The last thing Dennis wanted was an adult to sit him down in front of the clothes designer.

But alas, Dennis's bladder didn't cooperate; he needed a pit stop.

Samir told Dennis he would save him a spot and jogged across the quad. Dennis flew around the corner towards the Boy's Restroom and crashed into somebody.

"Watch out!" snarled Bulldog, shoving him onto the seat of his pants. "Look where you're going."

Dennis rolled to his feet and scampered into the Boy's Restroom.

"Ugly purple-haired dragon!" Dennis called from inside his sanctuary. It would have sounded more powerful if his voiced hadn't cracked.

She pounded against the closed door. "You're dead, Ponder!"

Dennis relished the safety of the yellowish-tiled fortress of urinals, toilets, mirrors, and sinks. He assumed not even Bulldog dared violate its borders.

He was wrong.

"Whatcha gonna do now?" she sneered.

Dennis ran into a stall, but before he could slam the door, Bulldog rammed into it. Dennis fell back onto the toilet.

"Hey!" a man's voice echoed throughout the restroom. "Knock it off right now." It was Coach Davis, the P.E. teacher. Dennis was saved! He ordered Bulldog to get to a classroom or else he'd haul her into the office. He waited patiently outside for Dennis to tend to his original business.

Coach Davis, from behind his ever-present sunglasses, said in a calmer tone, "Okay, Ponder, get yourself to a presentation. Pronto."

Dennis mumbled a thank you and fast-walked his way to Room B-24 where Samir waved from a desk in the back. He had managed to save Dennis a seat. "The cartoon lady was packed," Samir told him. A life-size model of a spinal column rested on the table in the front of the classroom. Mr. Bones, the life-sized plastic skeleton from the science lab, hung on a rack next to the table. A pot-bellied middle-aged man who could have used a comb waddled into the room. His necktie was crooked and part of his shirttails needed a tuck. Slouching in front of the mostly disinterested students, the disheveled man began, "I'm Dr. Binder. I am a chiropractor." The guy twisted the rubber spinal cord and talked about 'making adjustments' on patients.

Both Samir and Dennis frowned.

"We should've made an 'adjustment' and gone to the firefighter with Kimberly," Samir whispered a little too loud.

A monotone voice droned from the school's intercom. "Please excuse the interruption. Would Dennis Ponder please report to room C-61 immediately."

"Hmm. Wonder what that's about," Dennis said, rising from his desk.

Samir looked perplexed. "What? What are you doing?"

"Going to room C-61." Dennis pointed to the intercom speaker. "They just called me."

"No, they didn't," Samir shook his head. "You're hearing things."

"You need to clean your ears. Have fun with Dr. Bonecracker here. Hey, where's room C-61 anyway?"

"C-61? I don't know."

"I'll find it. See you later, Sam."

Coach Davis accosted Dennis as soon as he reached the outdoor lunch tables. He squatted down to the boy's level, "Ponder, what is with you this morning? You have a pass?"

"No sir," Dennis blinked. "They called for me over the intercom. Didn't you hear it?"

"No, I did not." Coach Davis grabbed the walkie-talkie from his belt clip and confirmed no one had summoned Dennis.

That's weird, thought Dennis. "I'm supposed to go to Room C-61."

Coach Davis leaned down until the bill of his cap nearly touched the boy's forehead. "C-61? There is no Room C-61 at this school. Follow me, I'll find you a presentation."

CHAPTER FIVE:

Just Follow the Script

Dennis hurried to keep up.

The coach poked his head into Room B-21. Even the bank loan officer's class was full. That was a very bad sign. Down the hall, several teachers struggled to corral the students overflowing from the cartoon voice lady's classroom.

An odd looking gentleman poked his head out of the classroom at the opposite end of the hall and beckoned Coach Davis. "I have one empty seat in here if hyou need to rid hyourself of that laggard."

Coach Davis grunted, "He's all yours" and strutted off.

Dennis entered the room. Nobody else was in there.

"Hello there hyoung man," the gangly character extended his hand and cleared his throat. Before Dennis shook his hand, the man withdrew it to wipe tiny beads of perspiration from his oversized forehead. He wore a short-sleeved collared shirt with a striped necktie and wrinkled dress slacks. The greenish-gray stain on his tie dismissed any hope of credibility. One of his brown shoes appeared a darker shade than the other. He had a prominent nose, a weak chin, and a mouthful of straight and long yellowish-brown teeth. Dennis examined the man's noodle-thin arms and narrow shoulders and wondered about his career. "Let me introduce myself," he extended his hand again. "My name is Mr. Daffulion."

"Dandelion?" asked Dennis, shaking his sweaty palm.

The odd man snickered, "Close. Daffulion. Mr. Daffulion. If hyou say it five times while looking at me, hyou will never forget it."

Dennis wasn't sure he wanted to remember it. He wiped his hand on his pants and looked around at thirty-four empty desks. "Where are all the other kids?"

"There aren't any others. Just hyou, Dennis. It is Dennis, isn't it?"

"Mm hmm," Dennis squinted one eye. "But you told Coach Davis you had one empty seat."

"I do. This one is empty. Please sit down."

Dennis sat. "But they're all empty."

"Of course they are," chuckled the man, flinging an arm through the air. "Do hyou really think I'm here for those others? Frankly, hyoung man, most of hyour schoolmates are, well, to be somewhat diplomatic about the whole thing, most of the students here are, uh, lacking."

"Lacking?"

"Oh, hyou agree? Yes, lacking, to put it mildly." Mr. Daffulion nodded his head for several long seconds as if he knew a great secret. "Now, Dennis Ponder, I have quite a presentation for hyou." The man opened a briefcase and began fumbling through some papers.

Dennis asked, "How do you know my name?"

Mr. Daffulion froze, and without looking up, cleared his throat and hiccupped, "What was that?"

"You called me Dennis Ponder, but I never told you my name."

The odd fellow stared at the boy for several...uncomfortable... moments. Judging by the sweat beads forming on his forehead, those moments stretched much more uncomfortably for Mr. Daffulion than for Dennis. Finally, the man blinked and said, "Oh, umm, from the sign-up sheet."

Dennis shot a glance at the door, wondering if he should make a break for it. "I didn't sign up for this."

"Hyou didn't? Are hyou sure?" The man grinned so widely his ears disappeared. "Here is my paper. And here is hyour name—and only hyour name—clearly written." He waved the paper inches from Dennis's face.

"That's not my writing," said Dennis. "I didn't sign up for this."

The presenter spit out a quick laugh. "Of course! How could hyou? But neither did hyou not sign up not to attend. Did hyou?"

Dennis, certain he was the butt of someone's joke, pulled on an ear and glanced around the room. He scooted in his seat, preparing to bolt. "No, I did not NOT sign up for anything."

"Good," the man jutted his finger in the air for emphasis. "Then hyou must be in the right place. Someone else signed hyou up for hyou. Someone has done hyou a fabulous favor of the highest degree!"

"Really?" asked Dennis, sitting back a bit.

"Certainly." Mr. Daffulion licked his lips and wiped the sweat from his sweeping forehead. The disgusting yellow grin flashed again. "Let us begin then. Welcome to Room C-61. Today...."

"C-61?" interrupted Dennis. "This is Room C-61?"

"Y-yes," stammered Daffulion as his eyes shrunk behind his grin.

Dennis leaned forward in his desk, "But there's no Room C-61 at this school."

"There isn't?" Mr. Daffulion looked about the classroom with uneven eyebrows. "I am quite certain of where I am." His boney finger pointed to the 'C-61' stenciled on the door.

"But Coach Davis said—"

"Coach Davis said 'He's all hyours' and so hyou are, that is, all mine. For now. So, hyoung Mr. Ponder, let me try once again to begin. I am here as a representative to alert hyou to the possibilities of," he paused to nervously clear his throat as he searched his mind for the right words, "wonderful, umm, a tremendous opportunity," he cleared his throat once more, "to, umm, let's see, how should I put it?"

Dennis groaned and slouched his head into his hands. He thought of Samir learning to twist people's spines.

The odd man again shuffled through some more papers in his open briefcase. "I am here as a representative from Croggerpooey to represent to hyou a most spectacular proposition of opportunity and wonder and, umm, daring, and mmm," another throat clearing, "adventure, yes! Adventure," he flung his limp arms into the air, "and, umm, possibly death."

"Death?" Dennis's shot out of his seat to make a run for it. But the excited speaker grabbed him by the shoulders.

"Yes! Hyou may very well perish in the line of duty!" He guided Dennis back into his desk and continued in a more subdued manner. "Of course everyone dies eventually. And the odds actually are more favorable that someone else—not hyou—dies first. Or they continue their horrific existences. Hmm, existences? Existenci? No, I was right, existences. Their horrific existences. Completely dreadful. Unless hyou," the boney finger tapped Dennis's chest, "do the right and correct and courageous and heroic, and correct deeds, indeed." The man raised his eyebrows with pride and nodded. "Hyou must do good well."

Dennis cocked his head and asked, "What career is this?"

"Yes," Mr. Daffulion cleared his throat, rolled his eyes, and swallowed. "It is a wonderful opportunity." He searched the papers in his briefcase. "I, hmm, let's see. I, yes, I am here as a, umm, representative to… offer hyou quite the unique opportunity for a great chance to be someone important. If hyou are willing and able and ready and willing to undertake the most rigorous of training."

"Training for what?" asked Dennis.

Mr. Daffulion pounded his head in his hands. "I'm supposed to present it to hyou exactly like the script."

"What script?"

"I can't find it!" he bawled. "I had it. Honestly, this morning. I was practicing, but now… I don't know."

"Just tell me what it is," Dennis said.

Mr. Daffulion sucked in a deep, whistling breath through his large nose and beamed with a huge yellow smile and extended arms, "Knight School!"

Dennis blinked. "Night school?"

"Yes! One must attend Knight School if, uh, one is to…."

"Night school?" Dennis blinked twice more. He felt exactly the same as that time he stepped in dog poo on his way to Samir's house.

"Yes," Mr. Daffulion cleared his throat, "I wish to extend to hyou the very precious and exciting opportunity...."

"No. Umm, listen," Dennis rose from his desk and started toward the door. "I go to school all day. I'm not going at night, too."

"Night? Oh no!" Mr. Daffulion wrapped his skinny arms around his head. "I've done something terribly wrong." He cleared his throat yet again. "Oh, where did I put it? 'Just follow the script,' that's all I had to do. Wait a sec, please! Mrs. Goodwyn thought...."

The boy froze in mid-step. "Mrs. Goodwyn? What does she have to do with this?"

"Why, this was her idea. She signed hyou up."

For night school? She must think I'm stupid. Looking like he had burped up something bitter, Dennis pushed open the door and left.

Mr. Daffulion leaned back against the wall and exhaled long and hard. "Oh no. No no no," he muttered to himself, wiping his perspiration with his necktie. The stain caught his eye, and he scratched at it. "I really mussed things up this time."

CHAPTER SIX:
The Silent K

That afternoon Mrs. Goodwyn stopped pruning her roses to call out, "How was school today?" But Dennis just faked a smile and made his way inside his house. A couple hours later, enthusiastic knuckles knocked on his door.

"Who's there?"

"Dennis Ponder, is that hyou?"

Dennis stretched himself taller to see out the peephole. The distorted image of Mr. Daffulion's already distorted face stared back. "What…what do you want?" the boy called through the closed door. "I'm not interested in night school. I'm only in seventh grade."

The man coughed. "Please, Dennis. There has been a huge misunderstanding, I'm afraid. Entirely my fault. And I'm dreadfully sorry for it. Perhaps hyou could let me in to explain all this."

"Nobody else is here."

"Oh, that's wonderful! Simply perfect!" Mr. Daffulion clapped his hands. "Then we won't be disturbed."

"No, you don't understand. I'm not allowed to have anyone in the house when I'm here alone. I can't let you in. Go away."

The visitor persisted. "I made or, umm, caused a misunderstanding. Now hyou can see how these misunderstandings can confuse and, umm, lead to, uh, confusion. And misunderstandings."

Dennis couldn't help but laugh. "If I could, umm, if I could just, err, maybe we could see hyour neighbor?"

"You really know Mrs. Goodwyn?"

"Yes! Of course! We're old frr… well, acquaintances. Perhaps she can fix what I, uh, have, umm, well, mussed up. Don't give up on me quite yet, hyoung man," he begged.

"You're not going away, are you?"

"No, no, not until I fix what I mussed up so badly. I owe hyou that much."

Dennis rolled his eyes, opened the door, and started towards his neighbor's house.

Mr. Daffulion lingered on the doorstep.

"Aren't you coming?" Dennis called to him.

Mr. Daffulion coughed. "I, uh, I think it would be best, or at the very least, better if I, umm, stayed put. Here. I want to stay here, now, because of, well, hyou know, perhaps it would be best."

"But I don't know what to say to Mrs. Goodwyn," he protested. "I don't even know what's going on?"

Just then Mrs. Goodwyn opened her door. "Dennis!" she called out. "I baked oatmeal cookies. You want some?"

Dennis glanced back. Mr. Daffulion dropped to his hands and knees and crawled around in two circles before crouching behind some bushes. Dennis, looking as though he couldn't comprehend an important test question, stared at his weird visitor trying to hide. Mr. Daffulion gestured for Dennis to go on. The boy scratched his confused head and walked next door.

Inside, Mrs. Goodwyn again asked about his day.

"Career Day was a waste of time."

"It was?" her head cocked with confusion. "Why?"

Dennis searched for the right words. "Night school? That's what you think of me? That's the big solution? Really?"

"Night school, huh? Night school is the term he used?" she chuckled.

"What's so funny?"

"Listen, I think I understand. Mr. Daffulion forgot his script, didn't he?"

Dennis nodded.

"Silly guy. His heart is in the right spot," she said. "It's not night school he offered you. It was Knight School, the Knight Academy."

"Night school, night academy, whatever."

"No," she leaned closer to him. "Listen carefully, Dennis Ponder. You are being invited to the Knight Academy." Mrs. Goodwyn had a way of saying things. Dennis smiled. He had heard the silent K.

CHAPTER SEVEN:
Be the Grape

"The Knight Academy," he said. "You mean I'm really going to be a Knight?"

"Quite possibly, yes," she nodded. "If you excel at The Sir Ambrose Academy of Knightly Acts for Noble Causes. But it won't be easy."

Dennis blinked, "What do Knights do?"

"Knights do good things well." Mrs. Goodwyn gave him a cookie and winked. "I've been preparing you for this with our talks and our games. And yesterday I realized my work is almost done."

"But why me?"

"Because Knighthood runs in your family. On your father's side."

"My father? Come on, Mrs. Goodwyn, my father's not very knightly."

"No, he isn't. Sometimes greatness skips a generation or two. But your father used to be a good enough man."

"A good enough man doesn't abandon his family," said Dennis, looking down.

Mrs. Goodwyn placed a comforting grip on his shoulder and said, "No, a good enough man does not. Your father is battling his own demons. And until he conquers them, you are better off without him. But Dennis, your father is not an evil person. He prioritizes the wrong things, but you mustn't let that interfere with your dreams and goals."

"If my father wasn't a Knight, does that mean Grandpa was?"

"No, it is your grandfather's father, your great-grandfather, Ambrose Ponder, who is among the most valiant and exceptional Knights ever in Croggerpooey!"

"Croggerpooey? Why didn't Mom ever say anything to me?"

Mrs. Goodwyn's eyes widened, and even though she knew they were alone, she glanced about the room and leaned closer to Dennis and whispered, "Your mom doesn't know."

"I've never heard of Ambrose Ponder. Tell me about him, please."

"Well, The Sir Ambrose Academy of Knightly Acts for Noble Causes is named after him. They don't name prestigious academies after so-so people," she said. "Your great-grandfather is kind and giving. And exceptionally brave."

"You talk as if he's still alive," Dennis said.

"Oh, I've said enough."

"No," Dennis said. "Tell me more about him? Did you know him?"

"Yes, but it has been a long time since…. I first met Ambrose when I was no older than you are now. His younger sister, Lisseve, and I were best friends. We used to play and talk and laugh all day. It was Ambrose who introduced me to a fine young man named Fred, my future husband. But that's all for now. The important thing is, you can do this. You have Knight's blood in your veins!"

"So did my father," said Dennis, rolling his eyes.

"Yes, but you are not your father."

"People say I look like him."

"There is a resemblance, but grapes and olives resemble each other, too. And they are very, very different," she explained.

Dennis scrunched up his nose, "I don't like olives."

"Then be the grape," Mrs. Goodwyn winked. "Listen, this is not happening by accident. You are exceptionally special, and, if I do say so myself, I have done a superb job preparing you for what lies ahead. You have the potential to do great things."

"Me?" Dennis beamed, "Great things?"

"You are full of potential." Mrs. Goodwyn gave Dennis's shoulders another squeeze and suggested he go speak with Mr. Daffulion, who was still hiding in the bushes. "He can provide you with all the details. If you're not careful, one day you may be a real live hero."

Hero. Dennis liked the sound of that. A brave Hero stopping bullies like Bulldog, helping those in need, and making the world safer for democracy. The Action Hero. Like in movies. Dennis Ponder, Super Hero. He liked it. But as he walked back home, excitement and doubt clashed like cymbals in his head. How could he be a Knight Hero when he can't even protect himself from Bulldog?

"I forgot to tell hyou something very important," said Mr. Daffulion, crawling out from behind the bushes.

He warned Dennis everything about The Sir Ambrose Academy of Knightly Acts for Noble Causes should not, could not, and must not be shared. "Hyou mustn't tell anyone—not hyour mother nor hyour friends—what hyou are up to." When asked why, Mr. Daffulion referenced some official memo regarding the dangers of ridicule and doubt subverting the training. Dennis did not understand, but nodded with a smile anyway and promised to keep quiet. Then, with the greatest degree of urgency, Mr. Daffulion ordered, "But hyou mustn't lie."

Like most children, Dennis had lots of experience not telling the whole truth without technically lying.

Later in the evening when his mom asked about his day, Dennis put some of his experience to work. "At Career Day I was offered the chance to attend night school." Dennis took care to keep the K silent. "It's not really at night, just an extra class on achieving my potential. I want to try it. Mrs. Goodwyn recommends it."

"Mrs. Goodwyn? How does she know about this class?"

"Oh, well, she knows about a lot of stuff. I think she's friends with the teacher or something. You can ask her. I'm not exactly sure when or where the class is, but I'll find out. It's free and I really want to do it. Okay?"

With suspicious eyes she said, "I'm not sure you should take on more work with your current grades."

"Mom, I'll be fine. The school year's almost done. It will give me something to do over summer. Besides, you said you wished I'd get interested in some extracurricular activities like flag football or chess club or something. Remember? And you are always telling me I'm getting older and I need to start making more decisions on my own. I think it will help me. And Mrs. Goodwyn thinks I should. Please. I'm asking politely." Then he threw in the clincher: "I cleaned my room."

Parents don't know how to react when their children use their own words against them in an argument. It confuses them.

"If Mrs. Goodwyn thinks it will be good for you, I suppose so," she relented. "But I can't take off work to drive you. Can you ride your bike there?"

"I guess so," Dennis said. "Thanks, Mom."

At bedtime Dennis found a little yellow note on his pillow.

DeAR PRospecTive KNighT StudeNt,
TRAiNiNg sTARTs TooMoRRow. I
wiLL meeT you AT The hi skooL TRAck
immeediATeLy AfTeR skooL.
Do NoT be LATe!

He looked around and wondered if somehow this note and that weasel were connected. Something told him Mrs. Goodwyn would know.

Dennis awoke the next morning excited and smiling. It was a sunny day.

CHAPTER EIGHT:
Being and Becoming

Dennis fidgeted by the bleachers. As high school students jogged around the track, he sweated in the sunshine and wished he were home playing video games. He had no idea what to expect at The Sir Ambrose Academy of Knightly Acts for Noble Causes. Dennis imagined his Knight Trainer with a long white beard, pointy cap, and magic wand demanding Dennis's focus by shooting lightning bolts at his rear end. Or maybe his Trainer would be a well-built middle-aged retired Knight wearing a silver whistle in his teeth, and when Dennis struggled to do things right he would spray spittle-ridden insults at him. Or perhaps his Trainer would be more understanding and sympathetic. Maybe he would be a little green man with big ears and a raspy voice.

"Stand up straight, Dennis."

The low voice startled him. He hadn't seen the two middle-aged men walk up. They were identically short, but with bodies stretched thin. One wore thick glasses. They stood with their teeny arms crossed and noses twitching. Both had long, stiff whiskers shooting straight out from their fuzzy cheeks. The one with glasses wore a tight-fitting blue sweatsuit with white stripes down each side. The other wore a red one of the same style. They both quickly chewed on something unseen inside their mouths.

"Up straight," the man in the blue outfit repeated, nervously darting his eyes about the scene.

Dennis wondered if a ventriloquist hid nearby because the low and nasally voices did not match these men. An underwater tuba came to mind. Dennis stood tall and offered his hand to be shaken. But the men, an inch or two shorter than Dennis, just stared at him.

"Nice to see you again," said the one dressed in red.

"Again?" asked Dennis.

The one in red covered his face with little brown hands, then pulled them away.

"Oh." Dennis's jaw dropped. "The weasel!"

"Weasel? I'm not a weasel!"

"Neither am I!" said the one with glasses.

"Oh," Dennis blushed. "Sorry. What are you?"

"We're what happens when a witch doesn't like your attitude," said the one in red.

"Or foul mouth," added the one in blue.

"Or practical jokes," said the one in red.

"Really?" said Dennis, trying unsuccessfully to make sense of it all. "What are your names?"

"I'm Glenn," said the one in blue, adjusting his glasses on his small, twitching pink nose. "His name's Frank."

The men stared at Dennis, evaluating him. Dennis stared back, examining them.

"Are you my Trainers?" Dennis summoned the nerve to ask.

"No," Frank blinked twice. "We are messengers."

"And deliverymen," nodded Glenn, looking about. "Follow us."

The men walked towards the parking lot. Without looking over his shoulder, Frank asked Dennis, "Are you absolutely committed to becoming a Knight?"

Dennis said, "I think so."

The two men stopped. Frank turned, "No. No, no, no, no. That is not good enough. Listen carefully." He peered up into Dennis's eyes. His low voice rumbled, "Are you one hundred percent fully committed to becoming a Knight and doing good things well for King Lewis Urabus?"

The sun felt hotter.

Dennis squinted. "Umm, yep. One hundred percent. I really want to be a Knight."

"Oh goodness gracious," Glenn shook his head.

Frank jumped in, "Hey, I didn't ask if you wanted to *be* a Knight. I asked if you wanted to *become* a Knight. Being and becoming are very, very, very different things."

Glenn echoed, "Very, very different."

Dennis tugged his ear and frowned, "Huh?"

"Many want to *be*," started Glenn.

"But," his counterpart jumped in, "*becoming* is too much work. So they give up."

"Well," Dennis said. "I'm pretty sure I want to become a Knight."

"Oh, for crying out loud!" Frank slapped his forehead.

The one in blue spoke with his eyes darting about. "Come back Monday at the same time. We'll ask you again."

And before the child could respond, the small men in their tight-fitting sweat suits ran off. They were fast.

A heavy lump filled the boy's throat.

CHAPTER NINE:

Like Hearing a Giraffe Meow

Dennis pedaled his bike home. It took him longer than usual as a growing mass of doubts slowed him down. Mrs. Goodwyn stopped tending her garden when Dennis reached home. She brushed the soil from her knees, removed her gloves, and waved him over. "How did it go?" she whispered.

Dennis opened his mouth but no words came out.

The old woman gave him a gentle squeeze and escorted him into her kitchen. "Wash your hands and have a cupcake," she smiled. "Want to work a crossword or try to take the rest of my poker chips?"

When he finished recalling his afternoon, Dennis said, "I'm not Knight material. I should probably forget the whole thing. I can't do this. I can't even stop Bulldog."

Mrs. Goodwyn cupped his face in her warm hands. "You *are* Knight material. You *can* do this. You are Sir Ambrose's great-grandson. I've done all I can to help you along. You're ready. This is your shot at greatness. I will be disappointed if you don't try."

The boy's weak smile betrayed the fact he was not convinced.

"An invitation to The Sir Ambrose Academy of Knightly Acts for Noble Causes is difficult to come by and should not be declined lightly. You have the weekend to consider it. Come Monday, I trust you'll make the right choice."

Dennis finished the cupcake and left biting his lip and full of indecision. As she closed the door, Mrs. Goodwyn coughed.

Even the most familiar sounds, when unexpected or out of context, can shock the senses. For example, we have all heard a rooster crow, but we look twice if a pig cock-a-doodle-doos. It's like hearing a giraffe meow. Dennis jumped when he heard her cough. He reached the sidewalk before realizing he could not recall Mrs. Goodwyn ever coughing, sneezing, or sniffling before.

Dennis stared at the television all afternoon. His mind focused not on the shows—cartoons he had seen at least seven times before— but on the future. To be or not to be a Knight? Or as the fuzzy men put it, to become or not become? Could he live up to his great-grandfather's legacy? It sounded so hard. Should he just forget about all this knighthood stuff? How do you go to the bathroom wearing a suit of armor? Would he get to use all sorts of cool weapons? It might all be worth it if he could use the weapons on Bulldog. If nothing else, he should learn enough to make her leave him alone.

Sunday night after dinner Dennis found another yellow note taped to his dresser.

> DeAR Boy,
> DoN'T foRgeT To meeT us AT The TRAck by The feeLd MoNdAy (TooMoRRoW) AfTeR skooL.
> YouRs TRueLy,
> FRANk ANd GLeNN

How do they do that? Dennis looked around and bent down to check under his bed. He found only abandoned toys.

The little yellow note was the first thing Dennis saw Monday morning. He had fallen asleep with it in his hand. He read it over again, crumpled it up, and threw it at his wastebasket. He missed.

As he left for school, Dennis expected to see Mrs. Goodwyn out gardening. It was a warm, sunny morning. But Mrs. Goodwyn wasn't outside. He realized he hadn't seen her all weekend.

Nevertheless, Dennis couldn't wait to come back and tell her all about his afternoon at The Sir Ambrose Academy of Knightly Acts for Noble Causes. He biked off to school that morning with every intention of becoming a Knight. His excitement pushed his pedals harder. He arrived at school early, as he imagined all good Knights should.

Samir showed up a few minutes later. Dennis jogged over to him.

Hyou mustn't tell anyone, he recalled Mr. Daffulion command. Dennis shrugged and tried to stop smiling. He bottled up enough of his Knightly excitement to appear normal for a Monday morning. But his grin kept pushing out.

However, first period's challenging math problems bit off a significant chunk of Dennis's excitement. Next, forty minutes of history notes chewed up a bit more of his Knight Academy enthusiasm. A large dose of PE embarrassment swallowed up even more. And then a confusing flood of participial phrases in English class washed down nearly all of his remaining Knightly aspirations. Nearly all. For Dennis's attention still wandered enough in class to keep a few sparks of The Sir Ambrose Academy of Knightly Acts for Noble Causes allure glowing.

Then came lunch.

Bulldog squished his banana until it oozed from its split peel. She poured milk over his head and strutted off laughing. And thus, the rest of his happy thoughts of becoming a Knight evaporated into thin air like steam from a cup of hot chocolate.

Dennis skipped his after-school meeting at the track, and instead pedaled straight home. At his door, he realized he had once again forgotten his house key. As Dennis walked past Mrs. Goodwyn's garden, he spotted a tall weed among her flowers. It was like a seeing a skyscraper in the ocean.

Dennis hesitated at Mrs. Goodwyn's door. He realized he had never knocked on her door before. She always had it open for him. Dennis knocked. He rubbed his hands against his pants. All was quiet inside. Dennis knocked again. He stretched his toes up inside his shoes. He rolled his tongue around inside his mouth. He made little popping noises with his lips. Dennis put his ear to the door and heard Mrs. Goodwyn coughing. He felt bad for disturbing her and wanted to run. But it was too late. The door opened.

CHAPTER TEN:

I Guess That's It Then

mrs. Goodwyn coughed at the fresh air. Dennis explained he needed a key and asked if she was feeling all right.

"I've a bit of a cold or something is all," she forced a smile. "You're early. Does this mean you have declined your invitation to the Academy?"

Dennis mumbled and stuttered something about wanting to do other things instead.

"I see. Well, can't blame me for trying. I'm sure you will be just fine." She sniffled and dabbed an eye with a tissue. Handing him a key, she said, "Well, I guess that's it then. Thank you, Dennis. Please take care." Mrs. Goodwyn closed the door. Dennis heard another thick cough.

He went home, slouched on his couch, and tried playing a videogame. But for the rest of the day her words replayed in his mind: *Well, I guess that's it then. Thank you, Dennis. Please take care.* "Why'd she say that?"

Tuesday morning he found another yellow note in his underwear drawer.

DeAR PupiL DeNNis,
We will be AT The TRAck by The feeLd
AfTeR skooL. TooDAy. You shouLd go There. IT
Is IMPoRTANT!
YouRs TRueLy,
F And G

He glanced about his room, but did not expect to find anyone. Dennis tossed the crumbled note at his wastebasket. He missed.
Then he ripped a piece of paper from his notebook and grabbed a
pen. Dennis took his time to write his neatest. He placed the note on
his floor so even the shortest person could see it.

Dear Frank and Glenn,
I do NOT want to be a Knight anymore. Please leave
me ALONE now!
Dennis

On his way to the bus stop, Dennis stopped in front of Mrs.
Goodwyn's house. Two more weeds thrived among the wilting flowers. Her garden needed watering. The dirt was hard and cracked. He
bent down to yank out one of the weeds. The root snapped off. He
pulled another, but its root also broke off. The closed door failed to
muffle Mrs. Goodwyn's thick, hard coughing. Dennis stared at her
door, but decided against knocking. He didn't want to miss the bus.

Thoughts of coughing and weeds occupied him throughout
math, social studies, English, and science. After school, he spent
about an hour in her front yard digging out weeds, pruning dead
flowers, and watering. Because Mrs. Goodwyn never came outside,
and Dennis did not hear any coughing, he assumed she was sleeping.

In the middle of the night, bursts of red lights flashed through
his bedroom window. They penetrated Dennis's dreams and woke
him up. He peeked through his blinds and saw an ambulance outside Mrs. Goodwyn's. He ran next door. His mother, already there
in her bathrobe and slippers, caught him at the sidewalk. They both
watched Mrs. Goodwyn rolled from her house on a gurney. She wore

a plastic mask over her nose and mouth. The doors in the back of the ambulance slammed shut and off she went.

"Is she…will she be all right? What happened?"

"She was having trouble breathing," his mom said. "That's all I know. I'm sure they'll monitor her and run some tests. She's in good hands."

Dennis was sorry he hadn't hugged Mrs. Goodwyn after their last talk. He wished he had watered her garden sooner. The thought of her looking out at dying flowers chewed at his conscience. He couldn't go back to sleep. He tossed and turned remembering the games they played together.

The next evening, Dennis pelted his mom with a bunch of questions as soon as she walked through the door.

"So you saw her at the hospital?"

"Yes."

"Is she okay?"

"She's stable."

"What does that mean, stable?"

"She isn't getting worse, but she isn't getting better yet, either."

"But she will, right?"

"The doctors don't know for sure." She watched her son swallow and blink back the tears. "Oh Dennis, listen, it's harder for older people to bounce back from illness. But we know how strong she is."

"She was totally fine the day before yesterday. What happened?"

"Probably a virus. She will be in the hospital for a few days at least. Maybe longer."

They sat down for dinner, more out of habit than due to hunger. Dennis pushed his peas around the microwaveable tray.

"Elbows off the table," his mother said.

"Remember the after-school class I told you about?" Dennis asked.

"The one Mrs. Goodwyn recommended?"

He poked at his floppy turkey. "Yup. She really wants me to do it. But I kinda gave up on it, and now it might be too late. I feel like I let her down."

"You seemed pretty excited about it before. What changed your mind?"

Dennis shrugged, "I dunno. It seems hard. Too hard. It'd just be easier not to."

"It's always easier, dear, not to do something. But I bet Mrs. Goodwyn was right when she said this would be good for you. She probably thinks you'd earn an A+. She is a very wise lady. Maybe you should reconsider, if it's not too late."

Dennis never unzipped his book bag that night. Homework did not matter.

He yawned into his bedroom, closed the door, and rubbed his eyes.

And jumped back!

A stranger sat on his bed.

CHAPTER ELEVEN:

But I Don't Believe in Fairy Tales

"**H**ello Dennis," said a trim, smiling man. He looked like a darker-skinned President Obama, but with more muscle and smaller ears. He wore a faded blue, untucked t-shirt. And the friendliest eyes. His hair was full, but graying. He needed to shave. The man folded his hands in the lap of his well-worn jeans. "I understand you are confused about attending The Sir Ambrose Academy of Knightly Acts for Noble Causes. Let me help you." His brown eyes, smiling as big as his grin, gazed into Dennis's. "You should go."

"Wait. What…who are…? How'd you…?"

"My name is Mister Doctor Rone." He stood and extended his hand. The wrinkles around his eyes and his white whisker stubble contrasted with his well-conditioned physique.

Dennis blinked and shook the man's hand. A comforting calm flushed over the boy, as if he had stepped into a warm bath. "Mister Doctor?"

"Yes. I have a Ph.D. in Deliberate Moral Thinking. But I was a mister long before I became a doctor. Mister Doctor Roger Whee Rone." He almost sang his middle name.

"Whee?"

"Yes. Whee with an h and two e's. It's fun. Like riding a bicycle downhill. Or a roller coaster."

"I don't like roller coasters."

"That's okay," the uninvited, but polite guest winked. "So I'll send my friends to pick you up right after…."

"No, hold on," Dennis shook his head. "Why me?"

"You are Sir Ambrose's great-grandson. And Rosie believes in you."

"You mean Mrs. Goodwyn?"

"Yes. She is a dear friend, as was her husband. Rosie has done a fine job preparing you. So can I count on your commitment to The Sir Ambrose Academy of…?"

Dennis interrupted, "You knew her husband?"

Mr. Dr. Rone nodded, "Yes. Fred Goodwyn was my best friend. We endured lots of laughs and enjoyed some tough times together." Dennis wasn't sure he heard correctly.

"And Mrs. Goodwyn's best friend, Lisseve?"

"Yes, I knew Queen Lisseve. May she rest in peace."

"Queen?" asked Dennis.

"Rosie didn't tell you that part, huh? I guess she doesn't want you to get a big head. Yes, Lisseve was King Urabus's wife and Sir Ambrose's sister. Your great-great aunt. That makes you related to the King, somehow or another. Now, about your enrollment…."

"Tell me about the King, please."

Mr. Dr. Rone rolled his eyes with a grin, "King Lewis Urabus is a great man. If you play your cards right, you may earn Knighthood and protect the kingdom of Croggerpooey from the King's enemies. Especially Horrible Rick."

Dennis said, "Croggerpooey? Horrible Rick?"

"Didn't Mr. Daffulion or Rosie tell you anything?"

"No, not much."

"Well, I guess you should know."

Mr. Dr. Rone sat down and told about the King's eldest son. "He wasn't christened Horrible Rick, of course. But he wasted little time earning his nickname. Rick was an awful baby."

"Did he cry a lot?"

"No. In fact, he hardly cried at all. Horrible Rick was more of a glarer."

"A what?"

"Glarer. As an infant, he glared at people whenever he didn't get his way—even at his own mother. Can you imagine a pudgy-cheeked baby with angry eyebrows? It was, well, horrible. And he only got meaner as he grew older. He tortured his younger brothers miserably. Spitting in their food and pouring honey on their heads. Pushing them off swings and sticking gum in their hair. One time he even glued their clothes on. When I was assigned to tutor him, Horrible Rick pretended he couldn't understand English and spoke gibberish. He put tacks on my chair and refused to complete his lessons. He once filled my shoes with peanut butter. And I'm convinced he drove his mother—that kind and gentle and beautiful soul—to an early grave. Whenever she or his father disciplined him, Horrible Rick just giggled. See Dennis, he is not merely mean, but also a little batty."

"Batty?"

"Not quite right in the head," Mr. Dr. Rone swirled a finger by his ear. "Doing mean things amuses him. He used to go to the farmers' markets and jab his thumbnail into the apples. Every one of them, so nobody would want to eat them. And he's always seeking approval, asking if we like what he'd done. By the time Horrible Rick was eighteen, the King had had more than enough and disowned him. Oh, but enough of this. About your Academy commit—"

"Where's Horrible Rick now?"

"He lives in a small castle in the farthest Eastern Down territory, surrounded on one side by the Twisted Gray Forest with its winding River of Snakes, on another by the rugged coast of the Sea Churn, and on the third side by the pimpled and pockmarked cliff known as the Caves in the Wall of Wards. Before the King expelled him from Castle Neede, Horrible Rick stole a chest full of gold. We caught him soon thereafter stealing the King's most prized possession, the Book of Coded Magic Spells."

"Magic spells?" asked Dennis.

"It holds all kinds of magic secrets, including the exact portal location and the words necessary to pass into and out of Croggerpooey. The King wrote the Book in code and riddles for security reasons. The day King Urabus expelled Horrible Rick, Fred Goodwyn died protecting the Book and preventing it from being stolen. I have never forgiven him for killing my friend." Mr. Dr. Rone pulled a handkerchief from his jeans pocket and wiped his nose.

"Over the years, Horrible Rick has built alliances with all sorts of lowlifes, like witches and ghosts. Twice they have made pathetic attempts to overthrow Castle Neede. The King's superior army swatted them away, much like a child swats an annoying mosquito. But Horrible Rick's forces are growing stronger. His army may now outnumber the royal forces. Our spies tell us he is plotting another attack.

"This is why you have been asked to train for Knighthood, Dennis. King Urabus needs young Knights to protect the Kingdom and keep the King's Book of Coded Magic Spells safe, especially now that Horrible Rick has Prince Zotch the Itchy on his side. But I have rambled on long enough. Can I count on you?"

"Wait, Prince who?"

"King Urabus's second son. Prince Zotch the Itchy has inexplicably grown close to his older brother. I believe it's because of a witch's spell, although Prince Zotch has always been a bit rebellious. However, their youngest brother, the good and ugly Prince Unfeeo remains true to the King. Because of that loyalty, Horrible Rick has thrown Prince Unfeeo in prison. The whole situation saddens King Urabus very much."

"Why doesn't the King's soldiers break the youngest son out of prison?"

Mr. Dr. Rone shook his head, "No one escapes from the Caves in the Wall of Wards."

Dennis's gaze narrowed into concentrated thought, and the older man paused to let the boy's mind absorb the tale.

Dennis broke the silence with, "This all sounds a lot like a fairy tale."

"Well, of course it does," Mr. Dr. Rone chuckled. "You want in?"

Dennis bit his lip and confessed, "But I don't believe in fairy tales."

"Really? All of them? Well, how interesting. And sad. If you don't believe, there's no point in continuing."

Dennis looked as if he had tried to swallow something too large. "Mr. Dr. Rone, no offense or anything, but I don't think I'm the right guy. I'm not hero material. I have my own problems, you know."

"I am well aware of the challenges you face."

"And you still think I can be a Knight?"

"I think you should try," said Mr. Dr. Rone. "You know, Sir Ambrose, a good friend and your great-grandfather, wasn't exactly hero material when he first started. Heroes are made when circumstances collide with their other plans."

"How far away is this Academy?"

"It's closer than you think," Mr. Dr. Rone grinned. "Ever hear of a parallel universe? Well, the Academy's in a perpendicular one. If you're not careful you'll run right into it. Frank and Glenn will take you. They know all the shortcuts."

"What's it like?" asked Dennis. "Do we ride winged horses or play any flying sports?"

Mr. Dr. Rone laughed. "Dennis, The Sir Ambrose Academy of Knightly Acts for Noble Causes isn't a school for wizards. I can tell what books you've read."

"Oh, I didn't read the books. I saw the movies."

"At the Academy, you will practice all the Knightly skills. And you'll learn enough boxing, martial arts, and wrestling to keep yourself out of trouble. We have the best instructors. And I think you will like the other boys."

"Do the other boys also have Knight ancestors?"

"Each was recruited for his own special reasons. But most won't make it to Knighthood. You might not, either. Dennis, your family history only gets you the invitation. Your actions determine your worthiness. It's a competition not everyone will win. But the winners will be provided the opportunity to achieve greatness beyond imagination. Greatness." Then he shrugged, "But most will fall short."

If it was possible to feel both encouraged and intimidated, Dennis found himself mired in that very mix. The word competition made his stomach feel like he was getting on a roller coaster ride. Greatness, on the other hand....

Mr. Dr. Rone stood and asked, "How many push-ups can you do?"

"Push-ups? Gee, I don't know. Not a lot," his embarrassment proving his sense of inadequacy. "About six or seven, I think. I'm not really sure. Maybe more if I try hard."

"Well, no point in trying if you're not going to try hard. Let's see you do twenty."

"But I said I can only do seven."

"Yes, I heard you." The man kicked aside some dirty clothes to clear a space. "Seven in one try. But if you try enough times, you can do twenty. Give it a try. Go ahead."

Dennis rubbed his hands together, dropped to the floor, and pushed out not seven, but eight decent push-ups.

"Ah, not too bad. Now watch me." Mr. Dr. Rone dove to the floor and pumped out push-up after push-up, up and down, commenting as he did so, "It's all about technique. You need some work perfecting yours. It's far better to do ten push-ups with good technique than twenty sloppy ones."

Dennis stared at Mr. Dr. Rone performing one perfect push-up after another.

The man continued, "And don't hold your breath. Breathe as normally as you can."

Mr. Dr. Rone kept pushing, up and down, up and down.

Dennis wished he had been counting.

Mr. Dr. Rone jumped up into a standing position, neither red-faced, nor out of breath. "That felt good!" he swung his arms about, hugging himself.

"How'd you do so many?" Dennis blinked his eyes.

"I can do so many because I've done so many. After you have done so many, you'll also be able to do so many. The only difference is the number of times you stop in between. Okay. Now it's your turn again. Do more and more until you've done twenty. It's all mathematics, my boy!"

Somehow this inspired Dennis, who took his turn and squeaked out six more push-ups.

"That makes fourteen!" smiled Mr. Dr. Rone. "Wonderful!"

Then Dennis did three more. And three more again. He stood tall. "I really did it."

"Of course you did," Mr. Dr. Rone placed a hand on Dennis's shoulder. "You are capable of a lot more than you think. Start doing push-ups regularly. And sit-ups, too. You never knows when a gooblin might cross your path and smack you in the gut with his staff."

"What's a gooblin?"

Mr. Dr. Rone shook his head, "The disgusting consequence of goblins and goons doing things together they should never do. The darker regions of Croggerpooey are crawling with them."

"How far away is Croggerpooey?" asked Dennis.

"Depends on how you travel. Let's get you to the Academy first. It's much closer. So, what do you say? Want to give it a try?"

Dennis let out a long breath and looked into Mr. Dr. Rone's warm brown eyes.

"Okay," he smiled back. "I want to become a Knight."

"Great!" Mr. Dr. Rone shook the boy's hand to seal the deal. "Well then, young man, you better start believing in fairy tales. They can be quite fun. And scary."

"Like a good movie," Dennis grinned.

"Or a good book," said Mr. Dr. Rone as he began to open the bedroom door.

"Wait! My mom will see you," said Dennis.

The man in the faded t-shirt and worn jeans glanced back and winked, "No she won't."

CHAPTER TWELVE:
Closed For Renovations

Dennis did not have to wait long at the high school track.

"Come with us," Frank and Glenn said. Dennis followed them to the parking lot. They stopped at a dented, old, rusty and primer-spotted brown '74 Dodge Dart.

Dennis pulled at the rear door handle three times before it opened. Inside smelled like a pet store. Thick industrial tape patched holes in the lumpy seat. Wires twisted out from under the dashboard where a radio used to be. The car started up and they shot down the street, past a honking horn. Dennis reached for the seatbelt. There wasn't one.

Another car horn blared as the Dart's tires squeeched into a turn. Dennis bumped his elbow against the car door.

They soon roared past a road sign advertising a nearby amusement park. Dennis braced himself through many zigzagged lane changes by grabbing the back of the front seat.

"Are we going to Dizzy Whirled?"

Glenn, who was not driving, turned to the boy and smiled, "Why yes, we certainly are! The Land of Whirling Cartoon-themed Thrill Rides!"

Frank, who was driving (and sitting on a stack of thick cushions to help him see over the steering wheel) added without turning to Dennis, "Home of the World Famous Ultra Spinning Coaster!"

"I don't like the Ultra Spinning Coaster," Dennis said, looking flushed. "I get sick on fast rides."

Glenn looked back at Dennis, "Oh, you won't be going on any rides."

"Then why are we going there?" Dennis asked.

Another car horn screamed at them. The boy noticed thick wood blocks taped to the gas and brake pedals so Frank's feet could reach them.

"You'll see," Frank said with a grin.

"Oh yes you will," giggled Glenn. "You certainly will."

As Frank slowed into the line of cars before the parking booth, Dennis caught his breath and swallowed until his stomach calmed. Frank flashed a silver shiny pass at the attendant who promptly waved them in. The tiny man parked in the employee section and the three walked briskly toward the entrance turnstiles. Frank and Glenn's shiny passes allowed all three to enter without waiting in line or paying. Dennis jogged through hotdog and cotton candy aromas to keep up with the fast fuzzy men. They negotiated the crowd until Frank and Glenn sneaked Dennis underneath a tarp hanging next to The Mystical Mole Hill ride. Above them a faded red and brown sign read 'The Grub Burrow—Closed For Renovations.'

Inside an invisible cloud of men's cologne overpowered the senses and made Dennis sneeze. A beast with wide, flaring nostrils and green eyes stood guard beside double-doors. Its whole body was out of proportion; its legs were much shorter than its arms, and its forearms thicker than its thighs. The guard's large and rounded shoulders resembled bowling balls, and a thick jaw protruding from a narrow forehead formed its pear-shaped head. The creature's skin was gray and smooth. Its huge hands gripped seven chains leashed to seven enormous, bad-breathed Rottweilers, one of which was incessantly scratching itself.

Frank and Glenn petted the dogs and winked at their silent master. The dogs' wet noses sniffed and wiped against Dennis's legs and arms and poked him in places we shouldn't discuss. Dennis squirmed while Frank and Glenn snickered. Finally, the guard gave the chains a quick jerk to stop the dogs' abuse, and Frank and Glenn led Dennis through the double doors.

The small men yelled, "Goodbye!" and shoved Dennis onto an escalator shooting down into the shadows. Dennis collapsed against the steep steps. He bit his lips together as his stomach shot into his throat. At the foot of the escalator, Dennis lurched head first onto his belly. He landed in a thick blackness. He could not see his hands in front of his face. His heavy breathing and pounding heartbeat echoed through the darkness. He stood and stepped forward, walking like Frankenstein's monster with his hands out in front to keep from banging into a wall. For several minutes, Dennis felt his way down a narrow passage, through left and right turns, more straight passages, and more turns until he stumbled out of the dark maze and blinked at the sudden brightness of the sunshine.

He found himself in the center of a large grassy clearing littered with obstacle courses, hanging ropes, balance beams, and a row of bullseye targets. In the distance, a thick wall of very tall trees surrounded it all.

There was no hint of the maze's exit.

A bunch of boys milled about, but none paid any attention to Dennis.

"Welcome to The Sir Ambrose Academy of Knightly Acts for Noble Causes," smiled Mr. Dr. Rone.

"Where'd the maze go?" the boy asked. "Did you do that? Was that your magic?"

"Magic's one way of explaining things you can't understand or do yourself."

"But you are a magician or wizard or something, right? Like Merlin?"

"No," Mr. Dr. Rone chuckled. "Merlin was a true legend. You've read Sir Thomas Malory's *Le Morte d' Arthur*?"

"Huh?" asked Dennis.

"The adventure book of King Arthur and the Knights of the Round Table? With Merlin?"

"Naw, but I saw an old movie on TV." He took a look at the crowd of boys.

"Again with the movies. Nobody reads anymore," Mr. Dr. Rone sighed. "Dennis, go introduce yourself to your fellow Knight prospects?"

CHAPTER THIRTEEN:
Just Dennis

Dennis immediately spotted a tall, athletic boy with yellowish blond-haired pulling himself up a hanging rope.

"Who's that?" he asked.

Mr. Dr. Rone's eyes twinkled. "Sebastian! I want you to meet someone!" Then, in a quieter aside to Dennis, "He's a very impressive young man. Look how he climbs! And he can run like a cheetah. And he's so polite. He just may become an ideal Knight."

As the man-boy Sebastian jogged over with his chin held high and chest out, Dennis scratched his elbow and wondered aloud, "How many push-ups can he do?"

"Many," answered Mr. Dr. Rone, grinning. "And wait until you see him throw rocks!"

"Throw rocks?"

"Yes. Excellent skill for thumping gooblins in the head. The lad is extremely accurate at both long and short distances. He is amazing!"

"Good afternoon, Mr. Dr. Rone." Sebastian was one big smile. "Good to see you again."

"Wonderful to see you, young man," Mr. Dr. Rone shook the teenager's hand. "Sebastian, this is Dennis. I'd like the two of you to pair up in training as much as possible." Dennis detected a subtle change in the smile as the boy, half a head taller, looked down at him.

"Hi," Dennis offered a handshake.

"Nice to meet you, Denny."

"It's Den—," Sebastian crushed his hand.

As Mr. Dr. Rone and Sebastian walked off together, Dennis rubbed his throbbing hand and bumped into two boys.

"Sorry."

"No problem. I'm Justin. And he's Donald." They looked ordinary enough to be Klibzowski Middle School students.

"Nice to meet…." A pungent stink punched Dennis in the nose. "Eww!"

Justin laughed and covered his nose. "Not again, Donald!"

"Guess I'm a little nervous or something," the offender shrugged with an uncomfortable grin.

Backing into cleaner air, Dennis thudded into a padded wall, which, when he turned around, discovered was not a wall at all, but a big man. Dennis's eyes scaled up the big, tall, and wide man. But it wasn't a big man gazing down at him. It was a baby-faced giant with curly light hair. Dennis hiccupped, and the largest person he had ever seen said in a much higher voice than expected, "You all right?"

"Mmm hmm," he nodded. Dennis checked out the other prospects. One guy was quite short and couldn't stand still, as if he needed to pee very badly. Another was a somewhat pudgy boy whose lower lip trembled so violently it made noises. When he noticed Dennis looking at him, he broke down in tears.

"Listen up!" interrupted an important looking man with perfect posture and a perfect mustache. He stood tall and muscular and carried a clipboard. His perfectly shaved face complimented his perfectly trimmed hair. His perfectly fitted dress shirt tucked perfectly into his perfectly creased slacks. He wore shiny black shoes.

"I am Rinbombo! Welcome to The Sir Ambrose Academy of Knightly Acts for Noble Causes! Line up shoulder to shoulder, facing me, starting here!"

"Yes Sir!" they yelled, forming a line. Dennis took his place at the end.

"Aren't there any girls?" someone asked.

"Not in this group," said Rinbombo. "But we've trained some before. There are some pretty tough girls out there." He glanced at Dennis who did his best to shake Bulldog's image from his brain.

Rinbombo walked to the first young man and commanded, "Tell us your name and a helpful skill you possess!"

"I'm Miguel." His smile stretched across his face. "I'm pretty good at kicking footballs."

Rinbombo looked him over from head to toe, glanced at the clipboard, and announced, "Boys, this is Miguel the Eager!"

They repeated his new title in unison, "Miguel the Eager!"

Next, the short boy who couldn't stand still, bounced in place. He nibbled on a fingernail and pulled on his ear.

"I'm Brooks and I sing."

Rinbombo consulted his clipboard and introduced, "Brooks the Fidgety!"

"Brooks the Fidgety!" the boys yelled.

The introductions continued. Justin said something about the value of doing good things well and earned himself the title of Justin the Wise. Vance the Grinning and Tom the Huge were christened for obvious reasons. As were Matt the Mumbler, Ziggy the Tearful, and Donald the Flatulent.

When it was Sebastian's turn, he stood tall and looked straight at Rinbombo's eyes. "I am Sebastian and I excel at every sport."

Rinbombo moved his nose within a fraction of an inch of Sebastian's. "Is that so?"

Sebastian did not flinch. "Yes, sir. Every one I've tried."

Rinbombo stepped back and jutted out his lower lip. "We shall see," he said with a nod. "Gentlemen, Sebastian the Bold!"

"Sebastian the Bold!" they shouted back.

After all the others, Dennis stumbled forward half a step, and rolled his tongue around inside his mouth. He admitted, "I'm Dennis and, well, I'm not sure what helpful skills I have."

Rinbombo stepped back and rubbed his smooth chin. "Don't be modest, son. It's okay."

"I…I'm not being modest, sir," Dennis blushed. "I don't know."

Carlos the Quick and Dylan the Dutiful rolled their eyes.

Josh the Distracted wasn't paying attention.

Buddy the Enterprising muttered something to Carter the Clever and the two snickered.

Rinbombo shot them a stern, silencing look. He rubbed his chin again and put his hands on his knees to get closer to Dennis. "Well," Rinbombo lowered his voice, "there's got to be something. Play any sports?" he asked.

"I've tried baseball and soccer."

"Soccer. Great, okay," nodded Rinbombo. "Score any goals?"

Dennis's eyebrows pinched up. "Well technically, I scored twice. But only one counted for my team."

The others erupted in laughter. Rinbombo turned his back, and Dennis detected a quivering of Rinbombo's perfect shoulders. Dennis bit his lip and blinked. His cheeks grew redder.

Rinbombo turned back around. "How about baseball? Get many hits?"

"Only foul balls."

"Hmm. Okay, let's see. Dennis the...umm," Rinbombo double-checked the clipboard and evaluated the boy, who stood before him shifting his weight from one foot to the other. "Dennis the... hmm. Just Dennis!"

"Just Dennis!" the boys repeated.

"Umm, you mean Dennis the Just?" he asked.

Rinbombo's shook his square jaw. "No, Just Dennis!"

"Just Dennis!" they all shouted again.

"Okay boys, jog over to those benches. The instructors are eager to meet you." But as the boys took off, Rinbombo stopped Dennis. He put his hands on his knees again and tried his best to speak with an understanding tone. "No offense son, but how exactly did you get here?"

"I think I space traveled or something."

"No. How did *you* get invited to The Sir Ambrose Academy of Knightly Acts for Noble Causes?"

Dennis shrugged.

Rinbombo blew out a long, whistling breath and re-examined his clipboard. "Son, I am afraid there may have been some mistake."

"Excuse me," Mr. Dr. Rone stepped up and whispered a few words into Rinbombo's ear.

Rinbombo's perfect eyebrows shot up. He looked back at Dennis who immediately looked down. "Is that so?" Evidently, Rinbombo was incapable of whispering.

"That's right," Mr. Dr. Rone winked.

CHAPTER FOURTEEN:
Thus Began Knight Training

An assortment of instructors took turns demonstrating their areas of expertise.

First up was a Mr. Rollin Bowns, a small man with a tight tummy and round shoulders. He showed off his tumbling somersaults, handstand push-ups, and flying leaps through flaming hoops. After the boys stopped cheering, he grabbed Josh the Distracted and Jay Obie the Attentive for volunteers. Mr. Bowns quickly taught them a few basic moves they demonstrated by running, diving head first through a hoop, and landing in a forward roll. Of course, their hoop was not on fire.

Sir Sugar Joe Dempsey, a man with a flat nose and a confident swagger, shadowboxed, skipped rope, and worked a speed bag with his fists, forehead, and elbows. He chose Miguel the Eager, who had frantically raised his hand, to enter the ring. The fighter laced some boxing gloves on Miguel the Eager and challenged him to land a punch anywhere above the waist. Despite the volunteer's enthusiasm, Sir Sugar ducked and slipped each swing.

A tall and slender woman, Mistress Melissa Sabre, was next. She wore a long black dress with a belt and held a polished cutlass in one hand and a longer, shiny steel broadsword in the other. She had Matt the Mumbler and Brooks the Fidgety toss a series of apples, peaches, and cantaloupes toward her. Mistress Sabre swung and flicked her blades at each flying fruit, slicing and dicing them before they hit the ground. And not one bit of fruit ever touched her. She asked for a volunteer to sit with a watermelon between his knees, but no one—not even Jack the Willing—raised his hand.

Master Bruzely, dressed in what looked like loose white pajamas, warmed up by swinging his arms in big circles and hopping about. The martial artist asked Sebastian the Bold and Carlos the Quick to hold up some pieces of wood that he punched in two with a loud yell. He spun his body through the air and kicked a Jack-o-lantern off Ziggy the Tearful's head. Master Bruzely ended his demonstration by elbowing a cinder block in half!

The barrel-chested Dr. Andres Trangler next demonstrated his wrestling prowess by taking on Eric the Quiet, Justin the Wise, and Tom the Huge at the same time. He flung and twisted the poor boys around the ring. Even Tom the Huge was no match. They each tapped out.

Miss Ekwa Libbreeum pranced along a thin beam several feet above the ground before lifting herself into a one-handed handstand atop a swaying post. To everyone's relief, she never asked for volunteers.

Dr. Nolan was next. He stood with wide shoulders and arms that seemed a little too long. He chose Dylan the Dutiful, Clayton the Smooth, and Dennis to set up various targets both near and far. Dr. Nolan than threw a series of rocks and nailed every single target dead center.

A squat man with a wide handlebar mustache was introduced. Sir Ascendenscale climbed up and down a fifty-foot wooden pole. Then, in perhaps the most impressive demonstration of the day, he challenged Vance the Grinning to a race up a thirty-foot rock wall. Sir Ascendenscale gave Vance the Grinning a ten-foot head start before standing on his head and scaling the rock wall upside down! He beat the Knight trainee by six feet.

Dennis wondered why his school's Career Day couldn't be more like this.

And thus began Knight Training, which wasn't anything like Dennis had imagined. The boys didn't wear suits of armor or joust each other off horses. In fact, there weren't any horses around to ride. The whole thing seemed more like a school recess than a formal training routine. The boys spent most of their time competing against each other in contest after contest. Mr. Dr. Rone and all the instructors watched each competition, offering encouragement and advice, applause and playful boos. Once in a while, an instructor pulled a boy aside for a brief, private lesson.

They ran races, jumped on and over things, and darted through obstacle courses. "You never know what you'll have to escape!" roared Rinbombo.

They threw rocks at a variety of targets. "Twist your whole body and keep your eye on the target!" shouted Dr. Nolan.

They practiced tumbling with Mr. Rollin Bowns so they knew how to land safely if ever knocked off a wall or tossed aside by a giant beast.

All the while, Mr. Dr. Rone cheered louder than anybody.

The boys worked on their boxing footwork, stiff jabs, punching combinations, and head movement as Sir Sugar Joe Dempsey spat out quick demands such as, "Hands up!" and "Bend your knees!"

They wrestled, trying on each other again and again the tricky holds and escapes the thick-accented Dr. Trangler had showed them.

They balanced on seesaws and shaky platforms. They walked across thick ropes. "Tuck in your bellies and focus straight ahead," Miss Libbreeum instructed. "Slow breaths."

Sir Ascendenscale taught them how to climb limbless tree trunks and rush up rock walls without losing their grip or footing.

Rinbombo recorded every result on his clipboard, sometimes smiling and sometimes shaking his head.

Dennis most enjoyed the tree climbing competitions. He often placed in the top half of the group and was not surprised to see himself doing well. After all, he had had to shimmy up a tree more than a few times to escape Bulldog. And he often climbed the old pine tree behind Samir's house. "Climb higher with me," Samir would beg while disappearing into the dark needles. But Dennis was content to sit on the lower branches. He was not fond of heights. At the

Academy, Sir Ascendenscale fortunately did not require Dennis to climb up very high. At least, not yet.

Rock throwing was Dennis's worst skill. In the distance throwing competition, Miguel the Eager hurled his stone so far the little flag marking its landing looked like a mere speck on the horizon. Sebastian the Bold chucked his at least as far. All the other boys took their turns jogging up to the line and throwing their rocks down the field. The marker flags dotted the field's horizon anywhere from forty to sixty yards from the line. Nobody could tell for certain who was in first—either Sebastian the Bold or Miguel the Eager—nor who was in last.

But then came Dennis's turn.

CHAPTER FIFTEEN:

Just Den-nis! Just Den-nis!

He picked up a fist-sized stone and bounced it in his hand. He trotted sideways to the line as he saw the others do, and trying hard not to stumble, heaved his rock as far as he could with a grunt.

His stone skidded into the dirt, rolling to a stop well before the sign marking twenty yards.

Sebastian the Bold laughed the loudest. Most of the others politely turned away or at least tried to stifle their laughter. Dennis bit the inside of his lip, trying to hide his humiliation.

Next the Knight Prospects threw rocks at three bowling pins arranged in a triangle on a platter about ten yards away. But there was a catch. The Knight Prospects had to hurl their rocks through a swinging hoop. A test of both timing and accuracy.

Vance the Grinning was the first to knock all the pins off the platter. Carlos the Quick did it, too. Buddy the Enterprising knocked off two. Jay Obie the Attentive clipped one. Tom the Huge's rock made it through the hoop, but sailed above the pins. Sebastian the Bold somehow managed to send the three pins flying and knock the platter from its pedestal!

And then came Dennis's turn.

First the rock slipped out of his hand and dropped behind him as his arm flailed forward. The other boys couldn't help but snicker. Dr. Nolan gave him another shot. Dennis rubbed his hand against his shirt and picked up the stone. He watched the swinging hoop's rhythm, took aim, and threw.

His rock did not hit any pins.

His rock did not even make it through the hoop.

His rock shot way off target and smacked Dr. Nolan in his side!

This time genuine concern for Dr. Nolan kept the others from laughing. But Sebastian the Bold flashed a wide grin while shaking his head.

Dennis got his first private throwing lesson right after Dr. Nolan returned with an ice pack wrapped to his ribs. Dennis learned to reach his arm way back and take a step while throwing. Both his accuracy and distance improved. Keeping his eye on the target helped, too.

Sebastian the Bold never lost a contest, although Miguel the Eager almost won the rock-throwing contest. And Carlos the Quick barely missed beating him in a race. But Sebastian the Bold made it look easy. Everyone else competed for second or third place. Soon the second place finisher was congratulated and celebrated as if he had won.

Dennis never finished above sixth place in any of the contests. He often got pulled aside for personal tutoring.

Then Miss Libbreeum upped the ante on a balancing test.

"No more balancing only a few feet off the ground," she announced. "This time you will scale this twenty foot pole all the way up to that platform."

All the boys craned their necks to gaze up at the tiny square. Dennis got dizzy and had to lower his chin in order to swallow.

"On the flat edge you will stand and raise one foot at least ten inches." Miss Libbreeum demonstrated how it should look. She posed perfectly still like a ballerina with her chin up. Her raised leg extended straight out to her pointed toes. "Stay like that as long as you can. We will be timing you."

Dennis's heart hammered into his twisted stomach.

Heights.

Sweat poured from his forehead.

Maybe, he thought, *if I run to the bathroom they won't miss me and....*

"Just Dennis!" called out Miss Libbreeum. "You're first!"

Dennis tried to steady himself with a deep breath, but it didn't work. He coughed. He rubbed his clammy hands dry and grabbed the pole. Climbing up the pole was no problem. Because he didn't look down, it was kind of fun. When Dennis reached the platform, he froze with his legs wrapped around the pole and his hands and chin resting on the platform.

"Pull yourself up!" commanded the trainer.

Dennis did not move.

"Can you hear me?" she yelled. "Pull yourself up and plant a knee on the platform!"

Dennis did not move.

Mr. Dr. Rone yelled, "You can do it!"

"Come on, Just Dennis!" Jay Obie the Attentive cheered him on.

"You can do it!" yelled Jack the Willing.

Dennis did not move.

"Aw jeepers," Miss Libbreeum shook her head. "Tom the Huge, help him down."

The very large boy with a baby-face grabbed a ladder and retrieved the humiliated failure. Tom the Huge smiled as he patted Dennis on the back.

"Don't get too comfortable," Miss Libbreeum said. "You have to try it again."

Buddy the Enterprising practically ran up the pole and balanced on one foot for forty-three seconds! Sebastian the Bold balanced for an unbelievable one minute and fifty-two seconds! When he returned to the group, Dennis noted the lack of perspiration on Sebastian's lightly freckled face.

Justin the Wise incredibly lasted one minute and thirty-nine seconds!

"All right, Just Dennis. Give it another go," ordered Miss Libbreeum.

Dennis blew on his hands and reached up the pole. Again, climbing was the easy part.

At the top, he paused with his legs wrapped around the pole and his hands and chin resting on the platform.

"Now pull yourself up!" called Miss Libbreeum, trying to sound encouraging. But Dennis heard more than a tinge of exasperation in her tone. He managed to wiggle himself up enough to get his hands beneath his elbows. He took three big breaths and tried his best not to look down. From there Dennis pushed himself up to where he leaned forward across the platform with his elbows out. He straightened his arms and squeezed a bent leg onto the board. The pole pitched forward, or so it seemed as Dennis glanced down and got dizzy. He closed his eyes. Sweat dripped off his nose. He tried to get his other leg up, but it would not move. Sweat tickled the side of his face. Somehow he willed himself up into a crouching position. He looked like a baseball catcher atop the tiny platform.

"Great!" Miss Libbreeum cheered.

Mr. Dr. Rone shouted, "Now stand up, my boy!"

"You can do it, Just Dennis!" hollered Carlos the Quick.

All of the Knight Prospects (but probably not Sebastian the Bold) along with Mr. Dr. Rone started chanting, "Just Den-nis! Just Den-nis!"

He closed his eyes and exhaled loudly. *Come on. I can do this. I can do this.*

He stood up a few inches at a time with his arms extended to his sides for balance.

"Just Den-nis! Just Den-nis!"

He looked straight ahead.

"Just Den-nis! Just Den-nis!"

His feet seemed glued to the wood.

After several moments of not being able to budge his foot off that unsteady platform, Dennis overcame sweating palms, shaking knees, and dripping sweat to balance on one foot for a grand total of four and a half seconds!

"Just Den-nis! Just Den-nis!"

Once he had both feet back on the ground, Dennis lifted his chin way back and looked straight up at the top of the pole.

He smiled.

And fainted.

CHAPTER SIXTEEN:
That Was Make-Believe

After his first day of Knight training, Frank drove him home. The violently erratic ride was a constant blaring of car horns, but Dennis was too tired to be concerned for his safety.

"Mom, I'm home," he called out. But she wasn't. The microwave clock read 4:03 PM.

"That's weird," he said to himself. *School ends at three, and training took about three hours.* He groaned loose a gigantic yawn and stretched out on the couch. *More of Mr. Dr. Rone's magic, I guess. What have I gotten myself into?*

The next day was Friday. Dennis hurried home from school, hoping Mrs. Goodwyn would be all better and back from the hospital. But no one answered when he knocked on her door. Dennis considered watering her flowers. It seemed like the right thing to do.

Bulldog's door slammed before Dennis turned on the garden hose. He had somehow managed to avoid her for a whole week. She spit before yelling, "Coach Davis ain't here to save your butt!"

Dennis stood silent.

"Whatcha call me, when you ran into the toilet stall?"

Perhaps it was the gloomy mood set by the wilting flowers.

Perhaps it was his one whole day's worth of Knight Training.

Or perhaps it was temporary insanity.

Whatever the reason, Dennis sneered and shouted back, "Ugly! Purple! DRAGON!"

Have you ever seen a wild beast attack its prey? When the predator struck without hesitation or remorse before the poor victim knew what hit it? If you have ever seen such an attack on television, there's no need to describe what unfolded at blinding speed next to Mrs. Goodwyn's dying garden.

But here's how it ended.

Bulldog squeezed a chokehold around Dennis's neck. His hands flailed about with no effect. He couldn't breathe. As things darkened, he recalled Mrs. Goodwyn's words, *"You have to make her stop."*

Bulldog threw him to the ground.

"Make her stop."

Dennis gasped for air, folded his upper lip in determination, and got up. He tightened a fist, closed his eyes, and let it fly.

He missed.

Dennis opened his eyes.

Bulldog was not there. She wasn't anywhere.

Where'd she go? Dennis rubbed his sore neck. *What's happening?* He scratched behind his ear, backed his way toward his front door, and after blinking several more times, wandered inside to his room.

"Ready?" Glenn popped up from behind the bed.

Dennis jumped back and bit his tongue. "Ready? Now?"

Frank, who had been behind the door, answered, "Yes." He walked past the boy and opened the closet.

Dennis made funny faces due to his bit tongue. "Is there a magic passage way in the back of my closet?" he asked.

Glenn's nose twitched. "The back of the closet?"

Frank's eyes stopped darting about long enough to roll in exasperation.

"No," answered Frank. "That was make-believe. Can't always believe what you read."

"I didn't read it," said Dennis. "I saw it in a movie."

65

Frank gestured at the closet and said, "Just grab another shirt. Bulldog ripped that one."

"You saw? What happened? She disappeared!"

Glenn, with eyes darting and nose twitching said, "We, umm, took care of her for you. We really should go now."

"Right now," Frank emphasized.

"Took care of her? What'd you do?"

"She'll be all right," said Glenn. "We only escorted her home."

"But next time," said Frank, "I suggest you keep your eyes open."

"It's easier to hit something you can see," Glenn nodded.

Frank shoved Dennis into the back seat of the Dart.

And off they raced to Dizzy Whirled.

CHAPTER SEVENTEEN:
Cut and Gone

They flashed their shiny passes and made their way to the side of The Mystical Mole Hill where that odd beast with wide, flaring nostrils and strong cologne guarded the double-doors under The Grub Burrow's red and brown sign.

The dogs once again roughly sniffed Dennis and when the double doors opened, Dennis jumped onto the very fast escalator without being pushed. He again fell on the seat of his pants and clumsily made his way through the pitch-black maze. He emerged into the brightness to find Mr. Dr. Rone standing in the center of the grass.

The man noticed the redness around Dennis's neck.

"The neighbor and I got into a little, uh, scuffle," the boy said, looking down.

"Yes," Mr. Dr. Rone replied. "I know."

"Do you know how Mrs. Goodwyn's doing?"

"She's the same. I suspect she'll get better when you do better. Here."

"Really?"

"Yes. Now, before we start, tell me what you've done today to improve yourself?"

"Umm," Dennis scratched his head and rolled his tongue around in his mouth, "I don't know. My ordinary, normal stuff."

Mr. Dr. Rone slapped his forehead and began talking with his eyes still closed. "As a Knight prospect, you must do good things well. Be your best. Your ordinary, normal stuff won't make this any easier."

"Yes, sir," Dennis smiled.

"Ready for Day Two?"

"I'm pretty stiff. My legs hurt like a gooblin bashed me with his stick."

Mr. Dr. Rone chuckled and said, "Now Dennis, first off, it's a staff, not a stick. And how in this world—or any others—do you know what it feels like to be bashed with a gooblin staff?"

The boy shrugged with blushing cheeks and a silly grin.

"Listen, don't be alarmed now, but six of the Knight prospects you met yesterday won't be continuing at the Academy."

"Why's that?" asked Dennis.

"A couple quit. The others have been dismissed."

"What about their special reasons for being recruited in the first place?"

"Special reasons alone won't make someone a Knight. Like I told you before, this is a competition not everyone will win. Some will still go on and do other great things in life, I'm sure. But the others," Mr. Dr. Rone shrugged. "Such is life. Remember, your actions determine your worthiness."

Dennis nodded without really understanding. How could some have been dismissed already? Nearly all those guys had done better than he had. Dennis looked around, eager to see who was missing. He counted twelve Knight prospects, including himself and Josh the Distracted who stood off to the side with his shoes untied, picking at an elbow scab. Cut and gone were Donald the Flatulent and Ziggy the Tearful.

"No big surprise," Dennis heard Miguel the Eager say to Vance the Grinning. "But I can't believe they cut Tom the Huge."

What? Dennis thought. *If he's not Knight material, how the heck am I?* It didn't make sense. He was so big and strong and nice.

Matt the Mumbler muttered something to Justin the Wise, but Dennis couldn't make it out.

Dennis heard Jack the Willing ask Dylan the Dutiful, "Where's that Bold guy? Surely, they didn't cut him."

"Nope," said Dylan the Dutiful, pointing.

Sebastian the Bold jogged into line. Of course, he was still here. Dennis's shoulders sagged. Memories of yesterday's crushing handshake and Sebastian laughing at Dennis's rock throw stung like a poke in the eye. But deep down, Dennis admired his arrogance. *I wish I was more like him*, he admitted to himself. *But at the same time, I'd hate myself if I were* exactly *like him.*

Brooks the Fidgety and Buddy the Enterprising? Gone. And so was Carlos the Quick. After you-know-who, he was easily the fastest runner. His absence chilled the remaining prospects, except Sebastian the Bold, who wore a satisfied smirk. He seemed to find the diminishing number of Knight prospects amusing.

The activities of the second day of training at The Sir Ambrose Academy of Knightly Acts for Noble Causes went much like the first. The experts kept demonstrating and correcting and challenging the young prospects. But the mood seemed thicker. The boys feared a quick dismissal if they made a wrong move or didn't improve enough after an instructor's tutoring.

Dennis managed to improve in each and every skill—especially his rock throwing accuracy—but he still never came close to winning a single competition. The highlight of his day was coming in third place in a tree-climbing contest. But overall Dennis again struggled to keep up with all the remaining athletically superior Knight prospects.

And all the others still struggled to keep up with Sebastian the Bold.

He pushed more push-ups and sat more sit-ups than anyone else. He jumped farther, climbed higher, and balanced longer than any of the others. Sebastian the Bold made all of his boxing and wrestling matches look easy. He never lost a race or rock-throwing contest. His sword skills were incredible. Dennis caught himself begrudgingly admiring the jerk more than ever. Even Rinbombo couldn't hide his admiration for the prized pupil.

"Excellent work today, Sebastian the Bold!" beamed Rinbombo at the end of the day. "Superior, simply superior!" He gave the young man a congratulatory pat on the back.

"Thank you, sir." The young man wiped his forehead with his sleeved bicep. "See you tomorrow, Just Denny," he added as he jogged off.

"It's Dennis. Just Dennis."

CHAPTER EIGHTEEN:
The Epic Brawl

Dennis stared at the ground and made little circles with the toe of his shoe.

Rinbombo's perfectly manicured hand lifted Dennis's chin. "What troubles you, son?"

"I can't compete with these guys, especially Sebastian the Bold. He's so much stronger and faster than I am."

"Yes he is. But there is more to Knighthood than physical abilities." He tapped Dennis's heart. "In many ways, you have passed more tests than Sebastian the Bold. Time will reveal if he has what it takes. Time reveals everything."

"So what should I do?"

"Just keep going," Rinbombo said. "Persevere. Listen, a long time ago, back when Knights battled dragons on a regular basis, we had a Knight Prospect named Alec the Clumsy. During his first full year of training, he fought and lost 738 consecutive baby dragon fights."

"Every single one?" Dennis asked.

"Yes. After his 738th defeat, Alec the Clumsy crawled over to me and said, 'I give up. I've failed.' I told him, 'You only fail if you stop trying. If you would rather go fishing, chase pretty girls, or ride horses through daisy fields, go ahead and quit. But you will never be a Knight or anything else worthwhile.' That's what I told him."

"So what happened?" Dennis asked.

"He persevered. He did not allow the doubts in his head over-power the desires in his heart."

"Did he ever defeat a baby dragon?"

"He did."

"Did he become a Knight?"

"He did."

"And then what? Did he ever slay a real dragon and become a great hero?"

Rinbombo shook his head, "No."

"Did he save damsels in distress or stuff like that?"

"No."

"Well, what happened to him?"

Rinbombo's stiffness gave way to a shoulder shrug. "Wolzelles ate him."

"Oh," hiccupped Dennis.

Rinbombo wagged a kind finger at Dennis. "You listen to me, son. Your great-grandfather never quit."

"I'm not my great-grandfather. I'm not exactly impressing the heck out of everybody here."

"Sir Ambrose did not initially impress everyone either," Rinbombo said. "It was quite surprising to some when he succeeded on his first mission. Refreshingly surprising."

"What'd he do?"

"He allowed a giant to pound on him for three and a half days. How is that for perseverance and courage?"

"Why'd he do that?"

"Hermit dwarfs."

"Hermit dwarfs?"

"Yes. The giant had kidnapped nearly all of the hermit dwarfs. He used them as playthings, like dolls or toy soldiers. He forced them to battle hungry dogs or swim all the way across Lake Duckspit. Sometimes the giant forgot to feed the dwarfs. He kept them in drawers without beds or blankets where they shivered through cold nights. And hermit dwarfs detest living close together, so their crammed imprisonment heightened their torture. Once King

Urabus heard of their plight, he asked a young Sir Ambrose to rescue the poor little fellows.

"Sir Ambrose knew strength alone could never defeat the giant; his endurance was his only chance. He needed to distract the giant long enough for the hundreds of hermit dwarfs to sneak away. The best way to do this, he thought, was to fight him."

"For three and a half days?"

"The battle had to last long enough for all the hermit dwarfs to escape and run far enough away to avoid being recaptured. By rolling with the giant's lumbering blows and robbing them of their full force, your great-grandfather frustrated the humongous ogre to the point of exhaustion."

"The giant didn't even hurt him?" Dennis asked.

"I did not say that. Occasionally the giant walloped Sir Ambrose."

"Did my great-grandfather ever hurt the giant?"

Rinbombo answered, "He did. Armed with a heavy club, he belted the giant's feet and legs with a couple thousand blows. When the giant could no longer stand, he rolled onto his side. He rested his weight upon one arm as he took swipes at Sir Ambrose with the other. This allowed the Knight to target the defenseless arm as well. Eventually, Sir Ambrose jumped up and clubbed the giant's head. Of course, the gallant Knight did all that while withstanding the giant's own relentless attack. It all boiled down to endurance and mental determination."

"How'd it end?" Dennis asked.

"After about eighty hours without stopping, the giant summoned every ounce of energy left in his limp, fatigued body and took one last ferocious slap at the Knight. Sir Ambrose—also exhausted and riddled with bruises, lumps, and bumps—ducked the giant's mighty swing. Legend claims the gust of wind created by that swipe blew nine grown hermit dwarfs tumbling off in bouncing somersaults! They found them down the road tangled atop a eucalyptus tree!

"After the giant whiffed, Sir Ambrose swung his club and clobbered him on the side of the jaw. The giant stiffened to his feet and fell over backwards in a heap, obliterating his table and three chairs, and causing an earthquake felt all the way to Castle Neede! The epic brawl finally ended.

"The giant rubbed his sore jaw, spit out a dislodged tooth, and passes out for two months. A river of drool flooded the east wing of his castle. He awakened so dehydrated that he gulped down half of Lake Duckspit. And it took Sir Ambrose just as long to fully recover."

"Wow," whispered an awestruck Dennis.

"Yes. He is one tough and courageous man."

"And fearless."

"Only drunken fools are fearless," Rinbombo explained. "Your great-grandfather set aside his fears to help the hermit dwarfs. It was a noble cause. Sir Ambrose did good well."

Dennis whistled with pride. "And the whole thing lasted eighty hours?"

"It would have been shorter, but many of the hermit dwarfs stayed around to enjoy the bloody action instead of running to freedom. They love a good brawl."

"Wow," Dennis sighed. "So he beat up a giant and survived."

"Sir Ambrose always survives. At least thus far."

CHAPTER NINETEEN:

Kind of Familiar Somehow

Friday night, Dennis woke up in the middle of the night. His bedroom light was on. And Mr. Dr. Rone sat in a chair next to the bed.

"Hmm," the boy squinted at the brightness. "What's going on? Is Mrs. Goodwyn all right? What time is it?"

"It's either really late or really early. Mrs. Goodwyn is the same. I need to tell you something."

Dennis sat up on one elbow and yawned. "What is it?"

"Horrible Rick has stolen King Urabus's Book."

Dennis rubbed his eyes. "The Book? The magic one?"

"Yes. If Horrible Rick deciphers its coded spells," Mr. Dr. Rone paused and shook his head, "he will rule Croggerpooey. King Urabus has summoned me to the Kingdom. I'm off to steal back the Book. But I wanted to see you before I left. To say goodbye. Wish me luck."

"Good luck," said Dennis. "Be careful."

"Of course," the man winked. "And you, my boy, take care of yourself. And do good well at the Academy. I have faith in you and your Knightly destiny." The two shook hands. "Okay, I guess that's it then. Bye bye, Dennis."

Mr. Dr. Rone flicked the light switch off as he left the room, but Dennis could not fall back asleep. Their conversation had sounded kind of familiar somehow, like one of those déjà vu moments, but different. He couldn't quite shake out in his mind whether Mr. Dr. Rone downplayed the dangers of being summoned to Croggerpooey and taking on Horrible Rick. Mr. Dr. Rone had made it sound easy: 'I'm off to steal back the Book.' Or was he really saying goodbye for good?

CHAPTER TWENTY:

So This Is How It Happens, Huh?

Dennis bit his fingernails Monday at the high school track. He couldn't wait to ask Frank and Glenn about Mr. Dr. Rone. He hoped Mr. Rinbombo had some kind of update on how the weekend went in Croggerpooey. Or maybe Mr. Dr. Rone would be back already and welcome Dennis at the Academy with those twinkling eyes and bright smile.

Dennis checked the time. Frank and Glenn were nine minutes late. They had never been late before. He looked in the direction of the lot and listened for honking horns. He expected the old Dodge Dart to come swerving around the corner any second. Dennis looked up at the sun. He fidgeted. And waited. And started thinking up all kinds of reasons why Frank and Glenn would be late. A car accident seemed most likely. Flat tire? Ran out of gas?

The hot almost summer sun beat down on Dennis. He wiped some sweat off his eyebrows. A car horn in the distance grabbed his attention, but the driver wasn't honking at the weasel-like men. Dennis checked the time again. They were now twenty-three minutes late. Something was wrong. A feeling of dread fell over Dennis like a scratchy wool blanket on a hot day. Another eight long minutes took their time strolling by.

Wait a sec. Maybe they're waiting for me at home. Dennis started jogging home. He walked when he needed to catch his breath, then he jogged some more. All the way home, he searched the hot neighborhood streets for that rusty Dodge Dart. He found no sign of it. Not even in front of his house.

So this is how it happens, huh? They don't even have the decency to tell you to your face? He doubted the others would be surprised by his dismissal. They probably expected him to be next and wondered how he had lasted this long. Dennis sniffled and wiped his nose with his sleeve. He thought of Mrs. Goodwyn.

She would invite him over and offer him cookies or brownies or something. They'd play poker or work a crossword puzzle. She wouldn't let him feel like a failure. She'd say just the right things to make him smile.

But she was not around.

As he fell onto his bed, Mrs. Goodwyn's words shook loose from his memory: *You can do this. This is your shot at greatness.*

Then Mr. Dr. Rone's words echoed inside the boy's head: *I have faith in you and your Knightly destiny.*

"Guess you were both wrong. I failed."

PART TWO

CHAPTER TWENTY-ONE:
King Urabus Needs You!

Knock-knock KNOCK knock-knock.

"Hello? Hello in there?" Dennis recognized that voice. And the nervous throat clearing that followed. "Are hyou home, hyoung man?"

KNOCK. KNOCK.

"It's Mr. Daffulion. Do hyou remember me? Open the door, if hyou would, please."

KNOCK knock-knock-knock KNOCK

Dennis opened the door a bit. "Yes, I remember you. From Career Day."

The man poked his large nose through the small opening. "Yes, Career Day. That's right. Is hyour mother at home?"

"Nope," Dennis answered.

"Good," he slipped in sideways and pushed past the child. "I really need to talk with hyou."

"Hey, wait a second. You can't just barge into my house," Dennis protested. "My mom's not here." He noticed the man's brown shoes still didn't match. An ink spot blotted the chest pocket of his beige short-sleeved collared shirt. The clumsy fellow collapsed into a chair at the dining room table. His face glistened with nervous moisture. He slammed his briefcase onto the table and fumbled with the rolling numbers of its combination lock.

"Come here and take a look at this."

"You're not supposed to be in here when my mom's not home."

"I know," he confessed and dabbed some sweat from his elongated forehead with a handkerchief. "But I really do need to discuss hyour future with hyou. For it is hyour future and hyour future only that we need to discuss and since hyou are here alone, I really *am* supposed to be here too. Please sit down." Mr. Daffulion tapped the seat of the chair next to him and fumbled with the lock some more.

"But didn't you get the memo or whatever?" Dennis asked. "I've been dismissed from the Academy. Dropped. Frank and Glenn never showed up today."

"Oh, Dennis. No. Dropped? Well...yes, I guess hyou have. Everyone has. The Sir Ambrose Academy of Knightly Acts for Noble Causes has closed."

"Closed? Then why are you here?" asked Dennis.

Mr. Daffulion showed his long yellowish-brown teeth in an unconfident grin and asked, "Why wouldn't I be here?" He still worked at the combination lock. "I can do this just as well as anyone else." He shook the briefcase and pounded it twice against the floor. It finally opened. "There!"

Dennis rubbed his head. "Why did you knock on my door?"

"Why? To see if hyou were home, of course. And if hyou stop with all hyour questions, I'll begin. Here, take a look at this." Mr. Daffulion removed a scroll from his briefcase. He unrolled it across the dining room table delicately with raised eyebrows.

Dennis examined the parchment. It was a map of some sort with scribbles, doodles, and writings on it. Much of the writing was not in any language Dennis knew.

"What's this?"

The yellowish-brown grin returned as he said, "A map. Of Croggerpooey. We thought hyou might need it for hyour trip."

"My trip?"

"To help the Honorable Mr. Dr. Roger Whee Rone. Hyou remember the Honorable Mr. Dr. Rone, don't hyou?"

"Of course. Is he okay?"

"Umm, well, I don't know. Probably not."

"WHAT?"

Mr. Daffulion wiggled a finger into the ear Dennis had just yelled into. "He needs hyour help."

"*My* help?" asked Dennis. "But...."

The odd fellow turned his face towards the door and shouted, "Okay guys!"

Instantly Frank and Glenn entered, dressed in their red and blue sweat suits, respectively. They grabbed Dennis by his arms to escort him outside. "Come on, we gotta go now," twitched Frank.

"Yep, gotta go," repeated Glenn.

Mr. Daffulion interrupted, "Umm, don't forget the...."

Dennis shook loose and yelled, "Wait a second! I'm going to Croggerpooey right now?"

"King Urabus needs you," said Frank.

"To rescue Mr. Dr. Rone. Retrieve the Book and save the Kingdom," said Glenn, adjusting his eyeglasses.

"Me?" asked Dennis. "I can't do that! Get Sebastian the Bold."

"Ah, Sebastian," said Frank, shaking his head.

"We sent Sebastian the Bold," said Glenn, biting his lower lip.

"He vanished," said Frank.

"Terrible shame," Glenn said. "Probably imprisoned. Or killed."

"Killed?" Dennis's voice cracked. "What? No. What about my great-grandfather?"

"If you see him," Glenn said, "tell him I said hello."

"He'd be a great help," said Frank.

Mr. Daffulion interrupted again, "But wait, uh, don't forget...."

"Now *you* have to rescue Mr. Dr. Rone," Frank said. "And the Book. And Sebastian the Bold, too, if he's still alive. Which I doubt."

"Yes, Sebastian the Bold, too. That would be nice," nodded Glenn.

Mr. Daffulion yelled, "Get the Book, Dennis! King Hurabus needs hyou!"

Dennis blinked twice and continued his protest. "Me? You guys are crazy! If Sebastian couldn't do it, how can I? I'm not bold. Get someone else!"

The two fuzzy men glanced at each other and twitched.

"We tried," Frank said.

Glenn shook his head, "But it seems Dylan the Dutiful has a broken leg."

"Football injury," shrugged Frank.

"And Jack the Willing," offered Glenn.

"Broken arm. Terrible luck," Frank shook his head.

"Pie-eating contest, somehow," Glenn said.

"What about Miguel the Eager?" asked Dennis. "He'd be good."

"He really wanted to, but…." Glenn shrugged. Frank shook his head.

Dennis counted on his fingers, "So I'm your fifth choice?"

"That was Josh the Distracted," Frank said.

Glenn nodded, "But he's ineligible. Poor grades."

"And Justin the Wise," said Frank.

"In bed with a 102 temperature, poor fellow," Glenn explained.

Dennis rubbed the back of his neck. "All these things happened to these guys over the weekend?"

"Weird, isn't it?" Frank said.

Dennis rubbed his face with both hands. "So I'm your what… seventh choice?"

Frank and Glenn glanced at each other once more.

"I'm not your seventh choice."

"Well, there was Jay Obie the Attentive," Frank nodded.

"And Vance the Grinning," Mr. Daffulion interjected.

Frank said, "You are actually our ninth choice. But not our tenth or eleventh. There are other options, less worthy than you. Remember Donald the Flatulent?"

"Much less worthy," added Glenn. "And Ziggy the Tearful? *You* are our ninth best choice!"

"Because hyou are hyou," said Mr. Daffulion.

"Indeed!" clapped Frank. "We need you, Dennis!"

"King Urabus needs you!" Glenn exclaimed.

"And Mr. Dr. Rone needs hyou," said Mr. Daffulion.

"Me, huh?" smiled Dennis.

"There you go!" clapped Glenn. "Mrs. Goodwyn will be proud!"

"Might just save her," Frank whispered.

"But," Dennis said, "I can't do this by myself."

"Sure, hyou can!" grinned Mr. Daffulion.

"How long will this take?"

"Longer there than here," said Frank, pushing him out the door.

"Don't forget the…." Mr. Daffulion waved the map.

"Shouldn't I leave a note for my mom?" asked Dennis.

Glenn pulled the boy's arm and winked, "We'll take care of that for you."

"Just save Mr. Dr. Rone," said Frank, opening the front door.

"And the King's Book," Glenn said.

"And one last thing," said Frank. "Do not get killed."

"Killed?" squeaked Dennis.

Mr. Daffulion nodded and yelled from the house, "I told hyou hyou could die!"

Glenn said, "Do good well. You can't help anyone if you are dead."

Mr. Daffulion cleared his throat and said, "Please remember to take the…."

"But how will I get back home?"

"Mr. Dr. Rone knows how," Glenn answered.

"It's in the Book," said Frank as he opened the car's back door.

Dennis got in the car before asking, "What if I can't find Mr. Dr. Rone or the King's Book?"

Glenn said matter-of-factly, "Then I guess you won't come back."

Frank slammed the car door.

Mr. Daffulion called from the doorway, "Wait! Hyou forgot the…."

But it was too late. The Dodge Dart swerved away, leaving a trail of white exhaust smoke. Mr. Daffulion held the map of Croggerpooey in his hands.

"Well, hmm, that just got more challenging," he muttered with a shrug.

CHAPTER TWENTY-TWO:
Then It Got Worse

Frank and Glenn and Dennis made their way through Dizzy Whirled in determined silence. They walked quickly through the crowd to the Mystical Mole Hill. Dennis reached the odd beast with wide, flaring nostrils guarding the double-doors under The Grub Burrow sign before Frank and Glenn. Dennis again recognized the cologne on the guard, whose big hands still held the seven chains leashed to the seven large, ugly, bad-breathed dogs. One Rottweiler scratched itself, but Dennis couldn't be certain it was the same one as before. Frank and Glenn again winked at the guard and petted the dogs. The dogs once again sniffed Dennis, poking him rudely in the same places we probably still shouldn't discuss. The double doors opened. This time they all turned right and jumped onto a different escalator Dennis had never noticed. This one went up as steep as it was quick. Frank and Glenn held Dennis up so he didn't fall backwards.

At the top of the escalator, they reached an elevator. Dennis asked, "Sure you can't come with me?" The two little men shook their fuzzy heads. Glenn wiped a tear and Frank gave a short sniffle. Dennis shook their hands and exhaled as the door opened with a pleasant ding. He stepped inside and pushed the only button. It was red with a sideways double-ended arrow on it. The doors closed on Frank and Glenn.

An unfamiliar—though not entirely unpleasant—tingling jolted Dennis. Things sped up and the temperature dropped. Dennis shuddered and wrapped his arms around himself. His ears ached as if he had dived to the bottom of a deep pool. He squeezed his eyes shut as his entire insides pressed upwards towards the throat. It didn't feel like the elevator was going up as much as it felt like it was going out.

Then it got worse.

The elevator shook and swayed. Dennis bounced like a racquetball against the walls. The elevator lurched forward and sent Dennis crashing onto his knees and elbows. When the floor dropped in what felt like a free fall, Dennis bopped his chin against the carpet. He struggled to keep his last meal in its place.

The elevator stopped. Ding. The doors opened.

Dennis regained his feet, took a deep breath, and stepped—

"WHOOOAH!!"

CHAPTER TWENTY-THREE:
Welcome to Croggerpooey

"**W**HOOOAH!!" (continued)

Somewhere, somehow, Dennis had lost his clothes. As bare as a shaved Chihuahua, he splashed into the slimy, black Croggerpooian swamp. The filmy water was armpit deep. All around him swamp bubbles burped out a sharp stinkiness, like rancid lasagna drizzled with spoiled milk. Dennis scrunched up his nose. The smell stung his eyes as he scanned the horizon. Green, black, and brown trees stretched from the gunk in every direction. In Dennis's mind, their shadows morphed into distorted faces. A big-eyed face within some tall shore grass seemed to peek his way, but when Dennis glanced back there was no such face. The swamp was abuzz with the chirps and clicks of bugs. Some zoomed by as big as hummingbirds. Dennis flinched under each flyby. Droopy trees loomed in front of him, beyond the dry land. The thick muddy bottom sucked at his feet.

Dennis tried dogpaddling through the stagnant muck, keeping his nose as far as possible from the gucky water. He looked like a drowning T-rex. The clicking and chirping, zooming and buzzing grew louder. Eerie shadows, bubbling burps, and imagined faces whirled around him. Panic pounded his heart.

Somehow Bulldog flashed into his thoughts. He wondered if one of her humiliating beatdowns was worse than slogging through a slimy swamp in Croggerpooey.

It wasn't long before he knew the answer.

Something brushed against his naked bottom.

He screamed, "Aaah!"

Something slimy swam between his legs.

He peed.

Two large yellow eyes glided along the surface towards him!

"AAAH!"

The alligator's (or crocodile's) powerful tail created an enormous wake behind it. Dennis reached for a low hanging branch, but it was just beyond his grasp. His attempt to jump only pushed his feet deeper into the putrid, cement-like mud. Dennis was stuck.

The yellow eyes closed in!

The mighty jaws growled open!

All he could see were teeth!

Dennis covered his head.

"AAAAAHHH!"

A hard, smooth inner tube-like thing rolled into Dennis's legs, knocking him sideways and freeing his feet.

A massive coiled snake rose from the swamp! The serpent struck like lightning behind the crocodile's (or alligator's) open jaws. Its powerful tail thrashed, forcing waves to crash over the swamp's edge. Dennis tumbled with the current to the swamp's edge. He scratched and crawled like a toddler who drank too much espresso up the slippery embankment. The snake's thick body twisted itself about its prey, constricting the life out of those stunned yellow eyes.

Black mud coated Dennis's arms and legs. Before him lay a path that wound away from the swamp and into the drooping trees. But before he could stand, a darkness passed over the scene, like fast rainclouds blocking the sun. A bird larger than some airplanes swooped down and plucked the monstrous snake out of the water like it was nothing more than an earthworm! Half of the dead alligator (or crocodile) hung out of the serpent's mouth. The giant bird's talons carried the snake up and away, disappearing with an echoing squeal. Dennis fell back against wet grass as Fear and Relief fought for control of his heart and mind. He thought aloud, "Welcome to Croggerpooey."

A slight chuckle bounced from somewhere within the bushes.

Dennis jumped to his feet.

Another laugh shot out.

Dennis ran.

Our soggy, naked boy darted down the path.

He dashed around mud puddles and between twisting trees.

He scurried through the creepy forest surrounding the swamp and its bizarrely vicious wildlife.

He sprinted clear of the trees, across a grassy field, through a cloud of thick blue-gray fog, and up and over a small hill.

And he never once glanced back.

Dennis slowed to a jog only when his body demanded. He jogged as far as he could before stopping to catch his breath. The crispness of the clean, fresh air kind of stung his lungs.

It was in a flower-covered meadow dotted with trees drooping full of leaves as round and wide as basketballs that Dennis finally paused a moment to take in his surroundings. Extreme yellow, orange, and red flowers popped from the green field. The warm sun shone in the bluest sky Dennis had ever seen. Everything burst so bright and fresh. It reminded Dennis of an old movie where the girl leaves her black-and-white house and steps into a techno-colored land of little people. But there were no little people here. Completing the picture, birds sang a glorious melody. The whole scene was beautiful, but hardly relaxing. Even after catching his breath, Dennis couldn't stop his knees from trembling like a low, steady earthquake.

He wiped off the swamp guck and dark mud and used some long grass to tie some large round leaves around his waist. Briefly he thought of all the other boys Frank and Glenn preferred over him, sitting comfortably at home, fully clothed, playing games.

It was noble of you to protect Samir, Mrs. Goodwyn had said. "Well, he's on his own now," he whispered. "Hope he'll be okay. Finding and protecting Mr. Dr. Rone is sure going to be tougher than keeping Samir safe from Bulldog." He wished he could somehow turn around and go back home. "Getting beat up and teased is better than this—alone in this weird land with giant snakes and huge birds. I've never even gone camping before."

Had Dennis run in the right direction? It wasn't like he really had a choice. He could only go away from that swamp. But now what? He didn't know where to go. Dennis remembered glancing over Mr. Daffulion's map, but of course couldn't recall any details. Dennis shook his disappointed and frustrated and worried head. He trudged on.

The path before him bisected the vast meadow and crashed into a blue-green pine forest. As he trudged down the path to other side of the meadow, Dennis flinched at every odd bug or bird twitter, hiss, and click. The warm sun shined lower in the blue, cloudless sky; it was clearly getting late.

A marbled stone no bigger than Dennis's palm grabbed his attention. He examined it. Dennis liked rocks. If he had a pocket, he would have taken that rock with him. Instead, he dropped it. Thud-thud-thud sounds like giant raindrops plopping on a roof or an impatient teacher drumming her fingers on her desk rumbled from somewhere not too close. Dennis searched all around for its source. The rolling thuds grew louder and faster.

THUD,THUD,THUD,THUD,THUD,THUD,THUD,THUD.

A group of tiny, fuzzy men—resembling Frank and Glenn but without the sweatsuits—rushed from behind. Fifteen to twenty Weasel Men dodged and weaved past the stunned boy, as if he was nothing but a bump of road kill.

"Wait!" Dennis shouted after them. But they disappeared into the forest ahead without the slightest hesitation. Dennis knew of only three reasons why people (or animals) run. One, for exercise. Two, because they are late. And three, to escape something scary. He doubted the Weasel Men were exercising. Dennis worried about something scary chasing the Weasel Men away, but if so, that scary something lagged far behind, out of view. He concluded the Weasel Men were literally running late. Where they were headed, he of course had no clue. But he supposed it might be someplace nice. Why else would they be in such a hurry?

Dennis looked up at the tall pine trees shooting straight into the sky. He was not thrilled about going in there, so he sat on clump of grass. After hiking so long, he did not know if he had accomplished anything. *What if I can't find Mr. Dr. Rone? Or the Book? How will I get back home? Will I ever get home?* Dennis thought of his mom. And playing poker with Mrs. Goodwyn. And Mr. Dr. Rone sitting somewhere, expecting help. Awaiting *his* help. Every so often an animal's call or a bird's squawk startled him. His knees still vibrated. And he couldn't shake the odd sensation of being watched.

Something rustled behind a tree.

CHAPTER TWENTY-FOUR:

Ah, Foggle-nogger!

Dennis ran, the best his exhausted self could, inside the shade of the forest. Here the path forked in two directions. Arrows painted atop a signpost offered two destinations.

The arrow pointing left read KING URABUS'S GLORIOUS CASTLE NEEDE. That path wound safely along the forest's edge.

The arrow pointing straight up read THE WILEY OLD HAG'S LAIR. That path disappeared into the dark trees.

The Wiley Old Hag, thought Dennis. *That doesn't sound good.* Dennis scratched his head and wondered which path the Weasel Men took. He couldn't see any little footprints.

He preferred the safety of the King's Castle and started that way. But he stopped. A memory popped into his head of Mrs. Goodwyn challenging him to tackle a logic puzzle. *Think, Dennis. The answers aren't always obvious or comfortable. What do you know for sure?* The only thing Dennis knew was Mr. Dr. Rone was in danger somewhere in Croggerpooey. Then it hit him: *It makes more sense that the farther Mr. Dr. Rone is away from the King, the more danger he's in.* So Dennis decided on the scarier path—the one neither obvious nor comfortable—through the forest toward the Wiley Old Hag.

Even in the shade of the forest, the colors tickled Dennis's eyes. He had never seen such green greens and brown browns. The ground was flat and soft, making the walk easy and pleasant on Dennis's bare feet. Birds sang and squirrels collected nuts. Butterflies drifted by.

The path took him to the side of a wide pond. Dennis searched the water for swimming bumpy logs with yellow eyes and found none. Four or five slender white birds with black heads and tipped wings glided and dived, soaring and searching for a fishy meal. These birds whistled a constant dwee-eee-eee. A deer across the pond bent down for a drink. Dennis had never seen a real deer before. Dwee-eee-eee. He took in a deep breath that grew into a yawn. It was getting late.

Night fell suddenly and the full moon painted the path and trees silver. It remained warm. Stars twinkled big and bright between the treetops. Songbirds, invisible in the trees, whistled a smooth chip chipshee, chip chipshee. Dennis fought against falling asleep, really struggling to keep his eyes open. *Who knows what's out here? Keep walking...just keep walking.* He staggered on like a zombie, clinging to the last slippery sliver of being awake, too tired to be bothered by occasional footsteps heard from somewhere in the dark. *Probably another deer*, he reasoned. *Just keep walking.* Chip chipshee, chip chipshee. When he realized he had been walking with his eyes closed, Dennis rattled his head and slapped his face. He was afraid to sleep. *Just keep going.* His head pounded from exhaustion, and he recalled Mrs. Goodwyn saying, *Feeling sorry for yourself is best done privately indoors.*

"What I wouldn't give to have a private indoors," he said to himself and bit his lip to stay alert. And to keep from crying. *Keep walking...just...keep...walking.*

Dennis woke up curled against a tree. The sky was a vibrant blue and the sun was bright. He did not remember falling asleep or covering himself with a blanket of ground moss. *It wasn't a dream,* he thought after a few drowsy and confused moments. He sat up, stretched, and rubbed his eyes.

And started down the path. He walked a long time.

His stomach growled loud enough to scatter some birds pecking at the dirt ahead of him. *Oh, I wish I had a big bowl of frosted flakes with milk. No, scrambled eggs and toast. And orange juice. Maybe a banana.* Some bushes spotted with red and blue and yellow berries caught his eye. They looked juicy, but…. *They might be poisonous? What else can I eat? I don't know how to trap an animal. How would I cook it, anyways?* None of his questions had any good answers. So Dennis sat on a fallen log, plopped his head into his hands, and listened to his tummy complain. He looked around and tried not to think.

Dennis tried so hard not to think that he did not realize he was staring directly at someone or something behind the trees staring back at him.

His stomach grumbled again. He had to take a chance with the berries. As Dennis walked into the shadows of the tall trees, birds and squirrels scurried out of sight across dry leaves and twigs. Something obviously larger than a squirrel snapped twigs and crumpled leaves behind a nearby tree.

Dennis froze.

"Who's there?"

Nothing answered. Dennis took a step toward some yellow-berried bushes and listened. After two more steps, something somewhere giggled.

"Who's there?" demanded Dennis, who armed himself with a rock. But when nothing answered, he plucked a yellow berry.

"Don't eat that!"

Dennis fell backwards while throwing his rock into the plants.

"Missed me!" giggled the same voice. "Those berries give you the collywobbles."

"Where are you?" asked Dennis. He got no answer. Dennis searched his surroundings. "Who are you?" Nothing. "What are you?" Among the leafy branches dotted with red berries, Dennis spotted two blue eyes. They blinked. "I see you!"

"Ah, Foggle-nogger!"

CHAPTER TWENTY-FIVE:
Bad Things Started Happening

Dennis grabbed another rock.

"Heehee! You found me, heehee." A short, chubby man with white hair and a beard skipped out of the bushes, laughing. He dressed like a woodsman, but wore a large red bowtie. He stuffed a book into his canvas sack. "Now you hide."

Dennis raised his rock. "Hide?"

The chubby man brushed off his clothes. "Don't aim that stone at me. That's not how you play the game."

"Game?" Dennis dropped the rock, "What game?"

The chubby man smiled his blue eyes into a squint.

"Hide and seek! Heehee! And I am winning," he spoke in quick bursts.

Dennis blinked and asked, "Winning?"

"But I must confess," the man continued, "there were times it felt more like seek and hide. Heehee! When you ran off, oh you are so fast, it took me some time to catch up, but I did. I caught up. I found you, but I was supposed to be the hiding one. But you turned the tables on me, you sure did. Heehee! So I sought you, yes, I found you, and now you have found me! Heehee!"

The man took a knee and kept laughing and laughing. Dennis blinked.

"So it is your turn now. This is such fun. Go ahead and—"

"I'm not playing a game," said Dennis.

"But you were! It was so much fun, too!"

Dennis shook his head and sighed. "Come here. What's your name?"

The odd little man removed his hat and gave Dennis a deep bow, exposing a wide shiny bald spot, as smooth and bare as a newborn's rear. "I am Clamant Contubbnal Farshtinker the Fourth," he announced. Dennis noticed several black and gray hairs shooting forth from the little man's ears, like exploding fireworks.

The two shook hands and Dennis said, "Nice to meet you, Clement Contubbner Farstinker."

"Heehee, close enough," the man winked. "Foggle-nogger!"

"Foggle-nogger?"

"Yes. Please. Call me Foggle-nogger. All my friends do."

"Foggle-nogger," Dennis repeated it. "It kinda sounds like a bad word. I thought you were cursing or something."

Foggle-nogger shrugged, "Sometimes I am."

Dennis asked, "Have you been following me since the swamp?"

"Yes. Was that bad? Heehee-hee. Sometimes I do bad things."

"What were you doing in the swamp?" Dennis asked.

"Waiting for you, or someone, to appear like before."

"Before? When?" asked Dennis.

"A little long while ago. Not a big long while, but a little long while ago. He dropped out of the sky. Just like you. Heehee! Plopped down right into the Black Burp Swamp!"

Dennis put his hand on Foggle-nogger's shoulder. "What did he look like?"

"Muddy! Heehee! Heehee-hee!" giggled Foggle-nogger. "Covered in mud. That is all I can say for that is all I know. He did not want to play with me. Heehee! He ran away like you did. But I couldn't keep up with him. Heehee! He ran off in all his nakedity. Heehee! I watched his mud-covered bottom disappear across the meadow. Heehee! I couldn't keep up!"

"I bet that was Sebastian the Bold," grinned Dennis. "If he ran across the meadow, we ran the same direction."

Foggle-nogger nodded his head.

96

"Do you know which way he went when he reached the sign?"

Foggle-nogger shook his head.

Dennis blinked. "Do you think you can help me find him?"

Foggle-nogger smiled and said, "Find him? Yoicks, so you *do* wish to play with me!" He quickly removed a book from his satchel, thumbed to a specific page, and scribbled a few words.

"Listen, Mr. Foggle-nogger?"

"Mister is not part of my name."

"Okay, but this isn't a game. You seem like a fun guy, but this is serious."

Foggle-nogger stopped grinning and listened carefully as Dennis laid out his dilemma. He told how he had been sent to find and rescue Mr. Dr. Rone. How Horrible Rick had stolen King Urabus's Book. How he couldn't go home unless he returned the King's Book. How Sebastian the Bold had been sent to Croggerpooey before him and disappeared. And during his lengthy explanation, Foggle-nogger stared intently into Dennis's eyes.

"So, can you help me?"

Foggle-nogger put his journal away, nodded slowly, and said, "This is quite a zugzwang. I hear bad things about Horrible Rick. He's crazy and mean. Boy, I'm glad I'm not you. Heehee. But I will help you. It'll be fun!"

"I wonder if Sebastian the Bold went this way instead of going toward the Castle Neede."

"Oh, he went this way, heehee," said Foggle-nogger.

"Are you sure?"

"Don't be such a dwiddler. Of course I think I'm sure. First, I saw the boldless Sebastian run this direction. Second, if he had run the other way toward Castle Neede, King Urabus's patrol guards certainly would have probably found him by now, and he would no longer be disappeared. So, let's keep going, heehee."

Dennis moved his lips in thought, trying to make sense of his new companion's logic. He gave up and said, "Okay, but first can you help me find something to eat?"

"Well, braid my back hair! Your yapness has finally caught up with you. I'm hungry, too. I've been wondering how long you'd go without eating." And he opened his sack and handed Dennis a bundle of real clothes. "I knew you would need them, since the other one was naked, too." The clothes smelled like musty tree bark, but Dennis jumped into them. They were soft and comfortable. Even the shoes fit. The boy looked like Robin Hood's son.

Foggle-nogger led Dennis through the trees to a small stream of crystal-clear water. As Dennis drank and washed up, Foggle-nogger gathered a hatful of small green fruits and a few pink and yellow berries speckled with blue flecks. He thought they looked safe enough to eat. He also dug up some orange mushrooms and grabbed a few nuts. After eating, the two carried on down the trail.

They walked for half an hour or so through the pleasant woods. A soft breeze cooled them while they entertained themselves by imitating the whistling birds. Even the squirrels didn't seem to mind having them around.

Then bad things started happening to Dennis.

He rubbed his eyes and stared at his hands. "My hands look funny."

He grew dizzy and fell to his knees. "My feet feel funny."

"You just need more food and sleep. Eat these." Foggle-nogger handed Dennis a few more nuts. "Food and sleep are what we need. Sleep and food cures everything." He opened his satchel and spread out two blankets. Dennis lay down, watched the world spin a few times, and passed out. Foggle-nogger pulled out his journal and took advantage of the quiet time to do more writing.

CHAPTER TWENTY-SIX:
I Think Much More Than I Know

A short while later, Dennis's groans woke up Foggle-nogger, who had dozed off. "Ugh, I feel awful. I must have eaten something bad."

Foggle-nogger sat up and combed his white beard and the sides of his head with his fingers. "Got the collywobbles, huh? Tummy cramps?"

"Umm hmm," Dennis hugged his middle.

"Do your knees ache?"

Dennis rubbed his legs. "They do."

Foggle-nogger shook his head and rubbed his front teeth with his tongue. "Do your eyeballs feel like they are about to explode and splatter all over?"

Dennis squeezed his eyes closed and nodded. "You aren't helping. What's wrong with me?"

Foggle-nogger lit his pipe. "Well, tummy cramps, achy knees, exploding and splattering eyes. I'd say you are correct. You must have eaten something bad. Something very bad. You must have eaten those berries speckled with blue flecks."

"Of course I did," moaned Dennis. "You said you thought they'd be okay."

"Well, yes I did," he straightened his red bowtie. "But I think a lot of things, which doesn't mean they are right."

Dennis asked, "How're you feeling?"

"Oh, I feel tip top. Heehee. Couldn't be better." Foggle-nogger began to write again.

"But didn't you, ooh, didn't you eat the berries?"

"Oh, I didn't touch those berries. I only *thought* they seemed okay. But I didn't *know* they were okay so I didn't eat any. They were a weird pink and yellow, don't you think? And something about those blue flecks didn't seem quite right to me. Heehee. I ate the mushrooms and nuts. Delicious. Now stop quibbling. What's done is done. You should be just fine. I don't think those berries will kill you."

"You don't think?" Dennis grimaced.

"No I don't. You didn't eat but a handful or two. I think a boy your size would have to eat at least double that amount to die. Aren't you glad I didn't pick more? Heehee."

Dennis winced and asked, "How long do you think I'll be sick?"

"Let's see. Judging by the size of the berries, I think you will be moaning in great agony for at least another five hours and forty-two minutes."

"Five hours and forty-two minutes?" An odd noise escaped from inside him. "Is this something you *think* or something you *know*?"

"Both. Heehee. But I think much more than I know. Heehee Hee."

"This isn't funny," Dennis convulsed. "Mr. Dr. Rone needs us. We can't just sit around for five hours."

"Five hours and forty-two minutes," corrected Foggle-nogger. "And no we can't. I suppose I must carry you until the berries run their course." He put away his writing and began gathering his things. After Dennis staggered into the trees to vomit, Foggle-nogger exhaled, bent at the knees, and grabbed Dennis. "Up you go." And the good man hoisted the queasy boy over his shoulder.

We cannot be certain exactly how much time passed before Dennis truly felt better, because neither he nor Foggle-nogger wore a watch. But it did seem awfully close to five hours and forty-two minutes. Of course, poor Dennis took several puke breaks. And Foggle-nogger also needed several breaks to catch his breath, so they did not make much progress on their journey. Once Dennis felt better, they did their best to pick up the pace in the afternoon.

When the trail opened to a wide clearing amidst the trees in the early evening, they decided to stop for the night. Dennis's head still throbbed and Foggle-nogger was exhausted from carrying him. After eating some nuts and orange fruits, both gathered soft leaves to make a nest under their blankets. Dennis watched as Foggle-nogger shook a small leather pouch around his makeshift bed.

"What's that you're sprinkling?"

Foggle-nogger spoke as he shook the pouch. "A little powder ground from willo nuts and disphrensia blooms, of course. I do not wish to die out here tonight."

Dennis's eyes widened and he asked, "What do you mean?"

"The salesman said this keeps wolzelles away."

"Wolzelles?"

"Oh my, vicious wild dogs. Jaws like traps. Quite fast and nimble."

"How does it keep them away?" asked Dennis. "Are they allergic to it or something?"

Foggle-nogger laughed, "Heehee, can you imagine a wolzelle sneezing? Heehee." He wrinkled his forehead. "Hmm, maybe it doesn't keep wolzelles away after all. Come to think of it, maybe he said gooblins. Either way, it works, that's all I know."

"How do you know it works?"

The question surprised Foggle-nogger, who took a second to think. "Don't be such a snog swallower. I know it works because every time I've used it I woke up the next day without being eaten or clubbed or killed in any way."

Dennis blinked and nodded. "Can you please sprinkle a little over here?"

CHAPTER TWENTY-SEVEN:
A Favor, a Flower, and a Compliment

They got off to another early start. The sun had just begun to paint the dark sky. Foggle-nogger and Dennis continued down the path back into the forest of tall trees where a fork in the trail forced a decision. This time no posted signs helped clarify the situation. To the left the trail swooped down across the stream and disappeared into the darkness. To the right, it climbed over a sunny, rocky pass. Foggle-nogger guessed Sebastian the Bold must have traveled to the right.

"Why do you think that?" asked Dennis.

"The trail to the left is too dark. It's too scary down there, don't you think?"

"I don't know."

"Well, I do. It is too dark and scary. Trust me. Whenever you have a choice between down and dark or up and light, choose up and light."

"Okay, but how can we be sure Sebastian the Bold reached the same conclusion?"

Foggle-nogger stared at Dennis. "Because if Sebastian went down and dark, the gooblins would have killed him and eaten his brains."

"Gooblins live down there?"

"I have no idea where they live," Foggle-nogger winked. "Heehee! But I am quite sure gooblins would not want to live where the sun shines. Besides this trail goes to the right, so how could it be wrong?"

"Huh?"

"It cannot be both right and wrong. That doesn't make sense. So if it is right, the other way is wrong. Let's go!"

Dennis, unwilling to argue with such logic, followed.

The two hiked for well over an hour. After the rocky climb, the trail's slight decline through the trees' cool shadows was smooth and pleasant. Birds sang. Various nuts offered themselves as snacks. Foggle-nogger lit a pipe and enjoyed blowing blue smoke at the curious chipmunks. Dennis caught himself smiling at his companion's antics. They soon reached another fork in the trail. Once again, there was no signpost.

"They look the same," said Dennis. "Neither one gets darker or lower. Which way should we go?"

Foggle-nogger peered down both paths and said, "If we were right to go right before, then would going left now still be wrong? Or what if going right really was wrong? Should we go left now to be right? But I thought two wrongs don't make a right. Or maybe they do. Oh, what do I know? This is your journey. You should decide."

The boy scratched his elbow and said, "What if I make a mistake?"

"Then we go down the wrong path."

"Exactly!"

"If we realize we're headed in the wrong direction, we'll turn around and come back." Foggle-nogger scraped dirt from under a fingernail.

"That may take a lot of time," Dennis said.

"Or maybe we won't realize we're on the wrong path until it's too late and—"

"Oh, stop it. Maybe we should flip a coin?"

"Flip a coin? Well, trim my ear hairs! Oh Dennis, we have no time for that."

"Do you have a coin?"

"As a matter of fact I do. Heehee. A very special coin." Foggle-nogger reached into his satchel and fetched a bright silver piece, quite larger and much shinier than any coin Dennis had ever seen. A deep L-shaped scratch marred the surface of the heads side. "A long time ago when I was just a little Foggle-nogger, I got this from Lady Lisseve herself. Before she became Queen."

Dennis decided not to take the time to explain his family heritage to the funny, little man. "Why'd she give it to you?"

"I sold her a favor, a flower, and a compliment. Not that she ever needed to pay for a compliment, of course. Heehee. I threw it in for free, really, heehee. But she paid me with a smile. Ooh, quite a lovely smile. Then, with twinkling eyes and full red lips, Lady Lisseve leaned close to me—her chocolate-colored hair brushed against this very cheek right here—and she whispered the three sweetest words we all long to hear."

"I love you?" asked Dennis.

"Ah, Dennis, that's so thoughtful of you, but…."

"No! I don't love…. Did she whisper 'I love you' in your ear?"

"What!" Foggle-nogger grabbed his sides. "Heehee Heehee! You sifflewang! No, she said, 'Keep the change' and so I have. Heehee, 'I love you,' heehee."

"Okay, okay, it's not that funny." Dennis held the thick coin in his palm. "It's so heavy. Is it pure silver? Must be worth a fortune if it is."

"I'm afraid the scratch diminishes some of its value. Anyway, its true worth lies more in what it can do, rather than what it can buy."

"It's sure a neat coin," said Dennis. "Anyway, heads we'll go to the right, tails we go left."

"What? Heehee. Don't be foolish."

Dennis flipped the scarred silver piece in the air. As if filmed in slow motion, the coin rolled over and over as it ascended to the heavens. The coin's shininess flashed in the sun. Up it floated, smaller and smaller, until it was too high to see.

"Unbelievable!" yelled Dennis. "I've never seen anything like that."

"I tried to tell you. It's a special coin. You really should try listening more closely next time," Foggle-nogger sounded genuinely annoyed.

Dennis searched the sky and said, "Sorry. I didn't know. Should we wait here for it to come back down?"

"Don't be an izzleflog. That coin will not return to us anytime soon or anywhere near. Around here, a good coin flip may take months. Months! Or maybe less. Who can say for certain? I fear it's lost to me forever."

Dennis felt terrible and apologized again. After a few silent moments spent staring into the sky, he asked if it was really gone forever.

"Could be, but maybe not. Probably is. Who can say for certain? Maybe it will land sometime when you need a coin. I once got hit in the head by that very same coin after I flipped it weeks earlier. Weeks! It hit me on the head right when I needed it. Knocked me out cold. When I came to my senses, I saw it next to me on the ground. It was tails. I won the flip."

"What did you win?"

Foggle-nogger wrinkled his forehead. "I don't recall."

"Well, we still need to decide which path."

"Oh right," Foggle-nogger glanced down both paths while sucking on his pipe. He blew out a thoughtful blue smoke ring that drifted to the right. "Let's go this way."

And they did.

CHAPTER TWENTY-EIGHT:

How Can You Be Nowhere If You Are Somewhere?

About two or three miles down the path, Dennis stopped for a brief rest. Foggle-nogger skipped ahead a bit, humming. As he stepped over a patch of yellow grass, Foggle-nogger stopped humming and started giggling. It was an odd, nervous giggle. Dennis looked up and noticed Foggle-nogger slowly growing taller.

"Whoa, heehee! Heehee Heehee! Dennis!" But Foggle-nogger was not growing taller at all. He was floating into the air. "Whoa, heehee. Hey!" Dennis ran to a tree adjacent the yellow patch of grass and pulled himself over the first limb.

"Grab the tree!" Dennis called up.

Foggle-nogger seized a crooked branch, but it did not stop his flight straight up. His feet kept rising until Foggle-nogger hung upside-down. Dennis shimmied up the tree trunk to the next limb strong enough to support him. The branch in Foggle-nogger's hand snapped off. Up he went, right side up again. Finally Foggle-nogger's pants snagged themselves on a thick branch. He grabbed hold of another below it, so Foggle-nogger remained suspended some fifty feet in the air, his bottom hoisted slightly higher than his top.

"Oh Dennis, help me!" He no longer laughed.

Dennis climbed higher up the tree. "Hold on. I'm coming." Eventually a sweaty and trembling Dennis reached his suspended companion. It took some effort to unsnag the pants and pull Foggle-nogger to him. Once freed, Foggle-nogger quite easily climbed down the tree to safety. He looked back at Dennis, who remained high up in the tree.

"You okay?" Foggle-nogger called up to him.

"I don't like heights!" Dennis shouted.

"Come on, now."

"I'm coming. Please don't rush me." As most know, climbing down a tree is often scarier than climbing up. Dennis slowly and cautiously descended the tree. Several minutes later, he jumped to the ground, his forehead sweatier than an orangutan in a sauna.

"You saved me!" Foggle-nogger hugged Dennis. "Why, you're all out of breath."

"Yep," he panted. "I'm afraid of heights. Give me a second."

"And still you climbed up so high to rescue me!" grinned the still-hugging Foggle-nogger. "I owe you one. A big one. You make my feet warm."

Dennis smiled, "That's okay. I just don't like heights. What happened?"

"That, my good friend, is a Pit of No Pull." Foggle-nogger clapped his hands, "Anything or anyone who crosses over it goes up. I've heard of them, but that's the first time I've ever ridden one. Wow, it was kinda fun! Want to do it again?" He started back to the patch of yellow grass.

Dennis took him by the arm, "No. Once is enough for me. It's dangerous."

"But fun, too! What are you afraid of?"

"Falling," Dennis admitted.

"Oh, heehee," Foggle-nogger giggled. "The falling part is fun. It's the landing part that hurts."

Dennis guided the excited Foggle-nogger along, "You may be right, but we have important things to do. Come on. I'm beginning to think you're as crazy as Horrible Rick."

"Crazy? Me? Hmm, you are not the first one to say that. Heehee, maybe I am. But not the same crazy as Horrible Rick. He tries hard to be mean. I try harder to be nice."

"Yes, you do."

The two traveled through the woods. Distant odd grunts and howls from unseen animals put Dennis on high alert. He kept his eyes trained on the thick brush and trees on both sides of the path. Every tiny but closer noise startled him. Meanwhile, Foggle-nogger smoked his pipe, rated his blue smoke rings on a scale of one to ten, and hummed an upbeat tune.

"Aren't you concerned about flying monkeys or something attacking us," Dennis asked, peering onto the sky.

"Flying monkeys?" chuckled Foggle-nogger.

"Or something."

"Heehee. Flying monkeys? Heehee, I've never heard of such a thing." Foggle-nogger blew a smoke ring and ranked it a seven point eight. "Where'd you get such an idea?"

"I saw it in a movie."

"A what? Heehee. What's a movie?"

"You know, a movie. Don't you know what a movie is?"

"No. Eight point six. What's a movie?"

"Well, it's a story shown in a series of moving pictures, so it looks like real people moving. You sit and watch the story."

"Huh?"

"You sit and watch pictures moving by so quickly that it looks like it's really happening right in front of you."

Foggle-nogger blew out another fluffy blue ring, "Oh, nine point five. But the story shown right in front of you is not really happening?"

"Nope."

"Then why watch it?"

"It's fun. Or scary. It's entertainment."

"But it's not real?"

"No, but it could be about something real."

"If it's not real, I don't see the point. Eight point nine."

"It's kind of like watching a book."

"Oh, I call that reading."

Dennis gave up trying to explain. His eyes scanned for potential dangers. Foggle-nogger resumed his humming. They stopped only to eat a few glorious strawberries they found growing along the path. They were as big as Dennis's fist and very juicy. As they ate their fill at the side of a creek, a polished green and black stone the size and shape of a big toe caught Dennis's eye. He picked it up.

"I sometimes collect things I find. If I was home, I'd keep this."

"So keep it," Foggle-nogger said. "It has a nice shine."

"No," Dennis shook his head and dropped the stone by the creek. "It's probably better not to weigh myself down with rocks in my pockets."

"Okay," Foggle-nogger agreed. But as Dennis rinsed his strawberry sticky fingers in the creek, Foggle-nogger stashed the stone in his satchel.

A little ways farther down the trail Foggle-nogger announced, "Oh, look. We have reached our destination."

"We have?"

"Look," Foggle-nogger pointed to a roughly constructed wooden sign nailed into a tree.

yO U A *RE* NO *WHER* E

"It says 'You are now here.' Heehee, I guess we are."

Dennis said, "That sign says 'Nowhere.' Looks like 'You are nowhere' to me."

"How can you be nowhere if you are somewhere? And somewhere we are, for we are, as the sign states, now here."

"I don't know," said Dennis.

Foggle-nogger took off his hat and rubbed his shiny bald spot. "Well, someone put that sign there, right?"

Dennis nodded.

"So someone had to be here in order to put that sign up, right?"

"Uh huh," Dennis agreed.

"And someone can't be here and nowhere at the same time," said Foggle-nogger, putting his hat back on. "So we are now here."

"Will you two shut-up!" roared a raspy voice.

Foggle-nogger grinned. "Harris? Heehee. Harris, is that you?"

A lumpy man lumbered out from the trees. He wore a wide-brimmed hat and his fingers constantly fidgeted and tapped on his thumbs. A bumpy toad sat on his shoulder. Wispy whiskers flowed from his chin and cheeks down to his bellybutton. His mustache jutted out in straight perches on each side of his face, upon which a family of gold and brown streaked finches perched and tweeted incessantly. "Who's there?" his raspy voice rasped.

"It is I! Foggle-nogger!" he said with outstretched arms. "How are you?"

"Mmm. Foggle-nog-gerrr," he growled the last syllable. "What do you want, Farshtinker?"

"All my friends call me Foggle-nogger."

"Clamant, who is this boy?"

"My name is Dennis. Is that your sign?"

"Mmrr. Yep. I hate that sign," he mumbled. It was difficult to hear him over the finches' tweeting.

Foggle-nogger said, "Dennis, this is Harris. Harris the Artist. Have you heard of him?" Dennis shook his head. "Oh. Of course not. Dennis is not from around here, Harris."

"Mmrr."

"Great to see you again. Hey, are we here or nowhere?"

Harris grumbled something entirely inappropriate.

Foggle-nogger continued, "Dennis is looking for a friend of his. Two friends, really. Have you had any visitors by?"

"I hate visitors," said Harris, picking up a stick and drawing in the dirt.

Dennis said, "Well, we won't stay. We're just passing through. But have you seen anyone who seemed out of place? Maybe a strange naked muddy boy bigger than me?

"Mmrr, a naked muddy boy?" Harris turned his back to have more of a dirt canvas to complete his picture. His toad crawled across his hat to the other shoulder. "No, I haven't seen any strange muddy naked boys. Nor do I want to." The finches twittered some chuckles.

Foggle-nogger also chuckled, "Of course you don't. Heehee."

"Saw a strange fully clothed and clean one once," Harris went on, "but I don't care to know where he ran off to. He didn't get the picture."

"What is this you are drawing?" asked Foggle-nogger.

Harris stood in the middle of an elaborate picture drawn in the dirt with his stick. He turned in a small circle, examined his creation, and made a couple of quick finishing touches with a poke or stroke of the stick. "I hate artists. I hate art. And I hate visitors," he said. Harris snapped his stick in two and trudged back the same way he had appeared. One of the gold and brown finches flew off ahead of him.

Foggle-nogger walked to the dirt drawing. "Oh Dennis, look at this. Is he not the most talented artist you've ever met?" Dennis looked at the realistic portrait of two men on horseback riding through the woods toward a narrow canyon. A witch hovered in the clouds, gazing down at them. Other than the footprints Harris left in the middle of it, it was an extraordinary and detailed drawing. "Oh well, we had better keep going."

"Wait," Dennis grabbed Foggle-nogger's arm. "Look! That's Mr. Dr. Rone!"

"Where?" Foggle-nogger asked. "Which?"

Dennis ran to the other side of the drawing to get a closer look at the men depicted on horseback. He pointed to the drawing. "Look! That one's Mr. Dr. Rone! Amazing!" said Dennis.

Foggle-nogger shuffled to Dennis's side. "I told you Harris is a phenomenal artist."

Dennis slapped his own head. "Don't you see? If he can draw a picture of him, he must have seen him! He saw him. He was here!"

"Hooray!" Foggle-nogger clapped his hands. "See, we were headed in the right direction the whole time! Whew, what a relief!"

"I wonder who that other guy is on the horse. They crossed this canyon here. Where is it?" asked Dennis.

"The Great Deep and Very Steep Gorge," Foggle-nogger whistled through his teeth and pointed. "It's just over that hill."

CHAPTER TWENTY-NINE:
Choosing Not To Believe

Several smaller trails branched off and conspired to confuse the travelers, but our friends used the hill as a guide. The path swerved around more times than a three-year old's scribble. They hiked over rocks and streams, by big purple flowers and small orange flowers and teeny-tiny red flowers, through tall trees and short trees, into both shadows and sunshine. They saw many harmless animals along the way, but no signs of Mr. Dr. Rone or the other guy on the horse.

About an hour later, in the midst of a green forest growing denser, Dennis wondered, "Do you think we're still headed the right way? I'm not so sure anymore."

Foggle-nogger said, "Listen to yourself. So full of doubts."

"It's just we've been walking for a while and I can't see the hill anymore through the trees."

"Trust me. This does not look at all familiar to me. So I can only presume I am about to see something or someone who is also completely unfamiliar to me."

"Huh?"

"Let me finish a thought, please," said Foggle-nogger. "And since neither this Bold Sebastian friend of yours, nor this Mr. Dr. Rone is familiar to me, I fully expect to see at least one of them very soon."

"I don't understand."

"You don't have to understand. Just believe. It is only logical."

As the two continued into the shadowy woods beneath the leaning and drooping trees, the temperature dropped. They could see their breath. The once-green forest became various shades of gray. Animals no longer scampered about.

"This is kind of spooky," Dennis whispered, noting how quiet it had become.

Foggle-nogger agreed. "I hope we do not run into any spirits. Seems to me this would be exactly the type of place they'd call home. And I have never seen one before so this is exactly the type of unfamiliar place I would see my first one. Do you think they will be friendly to us?"

"I don't believe in spirits," said Dennis.

"Oh, heehee, such nonsense."

"What do you mean? I've heard stories and seen some movies, but it doesn't make any sense to believe in them. At least not where I come from."

"The existence of spirits makes perfect sense," Foggle-nogger said. "To not believe is nonsense. Does everyone where you come from think like you do?"

"How can you believe in something you can't see, hear, smell, or touch?" Dennis asked.

"You forgot to include taste, but no matter," said Foggle-nogger. "In truth, I can and do quite easily believe in many things I cannot see, hear, smell, touch or taste."

Dennis challenged him to name one.

Foggle-nogger gave his beard a tug. "How about the wind? I'm quite certain there is a wind that sometimes blows fiercely, sometimes softly, and still other times it rests and does not blow at all. The wind is real even when it is not blowing."

"But that's not a good example," said Dennis. "I can see the wind."

"You see the leaves or kites or windmill blades moving *because* of the wind. But you do not see the wind. Nor do you taste it, smell it, or hear it."

"Okay," the boy conceded. "But I can feel it! Ha! I told you the wind was a bad example. I can touch the wind."

Foggle-nogger nodded his bearded head. "That is true. We can feel the wind. But perhaps the wind is still a good example because we can feel many things without touching them."

"Oh, really? What else can we feel without touching?"

"Love. Hate. Jealousy," winked Foggle-nogger. "Anger. Sadness."

"Okay," Dennis said. "I get your point."

Foggle-nogger started singing, "Embarrassment. Excitement."

"All right already. Okay, I understand."

"Worries. Pride."

"That's enough."

"Fear," he sang.

"Okay, I get it. I agree with you."

"So you believe in spirits now?"

"No," Dennis said. "I agree we can feel things without touching them."

"You do believe in anger, embarrassment, and worries, don't you?"

"Yes, but I told you," Dennis said, "those are different than spirits. They aren't the same."

"Of course spirits and worries are not the same. But everything is not the same as everything else," Foggle-nogger said. "The differences among things define what they are. At least now you understand things exist beyond what we experience with our senses. So if worries exist, why can't spirits?"

"Because they aren't real. You said you've never seen one, so how can you be so certain they exist?" asked Dennis.

Foggle-nogger replied, "How can you be so certain they don't?"

"I've never seen one."

"You make me dizzy." He straightened his bowtie. "You have never seen pride, jealousy, or the wind either, but you are equally certain they exist. It seems to me you are *choosing* not to believe in spirits. Choosing not to believe in something is so very, very different than professing with certainty the nonexistence of it. Don't confuse the two positions, for they are as different as wind and jealousy."

They trudged through the cold, dull woods for quite some time. But they never did see a spirit, which only solidified Foggle-nogger's belief in their existence. "Of course we didn't see one, Dennis. They're invisible! They are spirits, after all! Heehee."

CHAPTER THIRTY:
The Perfect Place for Gooblins to Hide

Finally, the trail led into a glade where the hill popped into view, casting a huge, long shadow. The path continued straight into a cave in the side of the hill. The two stopped at the cave's opening and listened as the breeze at their back echoed dully inside the dark cave.

"This can't be right," said Dennis. "Maybe there's another way around through the bushes or something. Or maybe we should climb over the hill."

"It must be right," Foggle-nogger said.

"Why do you say that?"

"Well, trim my ear hairs," said Foggle-nogger, "if the path goes through it, it must be right. I'd consider it wrong if the path stopped, but it doesn't. It keeps on." He pointed with his pipe into the mouth of the cave. Dennis and Foggle-nogger leaned into the dark opening. They smelled the cave's dampness. Foggle-nogger whistled through his nose. They enjoyed its brief echo.

Dennis said, "Look. There's some light back there." They could see a slight glow perhaps fifty steps into the cave. The light was steady; it did not flicker like a campfire would.

"This is the perfect place for gooblins to hide," said Foggle-nogger.

"You think they're in there?" asked Dennis.

"Oh, don't know about that," Foggle-nogger re-lit his pipe and whispered blue smoke rings over his head. "But it is the perfect hiding place for them. I mean if I were a gooblin, I'd hide myself in there. That's for certain."

The two held hands and tiptoed into the blackness. They proceeded toward the dim light. The air was warm and moist. Their palms grew slippery with perspiration.

Dennis whispered, "It sure is quiet in here."

"Yes it is," Foggle-nogger whispered back.

They kept on walking. Several steps on, Dennis whispered again, "The light doesn't seem to be getting any closer."

"No, it doesn't," Foggle-nogger whispered back. "Why are you whispering?"

"In case of gooblins," Dennis whispered.

"I don't think whispering will save us from gooblins," whispered Foggle-nogger.

Several steps later the glow still seemed no closer.

"Something's not right," whispered Dennis. "We should go back."

"Go back? Don't be a frimper," said the odd man, no longer whispering. "What will we do then? Sit outside until we determine to try again? We are already," he turned to look back, "at least halfway to the light. We should keep going."

"But we're not getting any closer," Dennis said, also no longer whispering.

"What do you mean, we're not getting closer?" Foggle-nogger argued. "Look behind us. We are getting farther away from the opening with every step."

Dennis looked back as they walked on. It was true. The light of the cave's opening was getting farther away, but at the same time the light ahead of them was not getting any closer. "We're going deeper, but we're not getting any closer."

"Don't be a glipglan, Dennis! That's impossible. How can we go deeper without getting closer to the end?"

Dennis jerked his partner's hand to a stop. "How? Look. It's the same size and brightness as when we started. If we were getting closer to it, wouldn't it be bigger or brighter?"

"Heehee, has it ever occurred to you that the light is moving? We need to speed up, not stop or slow down. Acceleration is the answer!"

The two hurried into the darkness with their free hands out in front trying to feel their way. Dennis told Foggle-nogger to slow down, but his plea was ignored. Foggle-nogger dragged Dennis faster and faster into the blackness. The slight glow remained in view, but instead of shining brighter or bigger, it, in fact, got smaller and dimmer. Dennis stumbled and fell. His sweaty hand slipped from Foggle-nogger's.

"Stop!" the boy shouted.

"Where are you, Dennis?" the odd man's voice echoed.

Twenty-nine minutes may not seem like a long time if you are playing a game or watching a TV show. Twenty-nine minutes is a short nap or lunch break. But trust me, twenty-nine minutes separated from your only friend blinded by darkness in a strange cave in a strange land is a very, very long time. Panic creased Dennis's face. His heart pounded. The echoes of their calls warped the distance between them, as the two searched for each other in complete blackness. They moped around in circles, their arms reaching in all directions.

Finally, twenty-eight minutes and forty-nine seconds into the nightmare, Foggle-nogger decided to calm his nerves by lighting himself a pipe. The match's flame beamed off the cave walls. And before the pipe could be lit, Dennis and Foggle-nogger found themselves standing but a few feet of each other. They hugged. The dropped match returned them to total darkness.

Dennis clutched his companion's arm. "Why didn't you light that match a long time ago?"

"I didn't want a pipe then."

"But we could have used the light!"

Foggle-nogger explained, "Pipe tobacco is getting so expensive. I've been trying to cut back."

"But we could have used the light!" Dennis repeated.

"Don't be a silly ubb, we may need matches later."

It was at this juncture both noticed they no longer had that glow in front of them. Or behind them.

"Foggle-nogger, we need a match right now. I've never needed a match as much in my life as I need one right now."

"Really?" said Foggle-nogger. "I once needed to relax very badly and I had my pipe and tobacco ready, but then I discovered I had no matches. Can you imagine? I was so sad! Heehee. I think that was when I needed a match most of all. Or maybe it was that time when—"

Dennis shook his friend's arm and said, "We need to know which direction to go." They both had gotten turned around and confused in their search for each other. "Please light another match now."

"Oh, okay." A flame shot up. In the moments the match burned, neither Dennis nor Foggle-nogger could tell which direction went forward and which backward. Both looked the same. Their footprints circled about and offered no clues. The match died into smoke.

"What now?" asked Dennis.

"We should run," Foggle-nogger whispered.

Dennis whispered back, "Why are you whispering?"

Foggle-nogger leaned to Dennis's ear and whispered more quietly, "I think something's back there. Behind you."

"What?" Dennis's whisper sounded shaky. "A gooblin?"

"Don't know. I've never seen a gooblin. We should run."

Dennis needed no more convincing. The two hurried in the opposite direction of whatever it was Foggle-nogger saw. Because they couldn't see as far as their elbows in front of them, they didn't really run as much as they quickly waddled off, holding hands with arms extended. They adjusted their course as necessary whenever they hit the cave's walls. Soon a tiny blue spot twinkled in the distance like a star. This time the blue got larger and brighter as they rushed toward it. It was the early evening's light shining into the cave! They sprinted out of the opening, alive and winded.

Foggle-nogger lit his pipe and propped his feet up. A blue smoke ring whizzed by Dennis's nose.

"What do you think it was?" asked Dennis.

Another smoke ring drifted into the sky. "Like I said, I've never seen a gooblin, but it sure makes sense to me if that's what it was. Of course, maybe it was just your flickering shadow. Or maybe it was a gooblin, truly. Didn't see a club, but…. What's wrong?"

Dennis shook his head, examining the surroundings. "This is where we started."

"What?"

"This is where we went into the cave."

Foggle-nogger looked around. "Are you sure?"

"That tree looks the same," Dennis pointed. "The cave opening looks the same. That rock above it, the bushes there on the side. Our footprints. We ran out the same way we went in."

"Hmm. Well I'll be a dimwhimmer, I think you're right! Heehee," laughed Foggle-nogger. "I guess we just have to go in again."

"What?"

"Come on, we'll try again."

"No, we won't," said Dennis. "I'm not going in there again. We will climb up this hill and look around to see if there's a path coming out anywhere on the other side. It's already getting dark, so we better hurry. Come on."

A smiling Foggle-nogger followed without muttering another syllable.

CHAPTER THIRTY-ONE:

It's Almost Magic!

The evening's first star shared its first twinkle as Dennis and Foggle-nogger reached the top of the hill above the cave. A flat meadow of tall grass spread out below them. The green grass looked silvery-gray in the twilight. Dennis saw what might have been a path leading out of the back of the hill, but it was getting too dark to really get a good look. They had no choice but to set up camp and sleep there. Foggle-nogger sprinkled his brown dust, lit a pipe, and wrote in his journal.

"What are you writing?"

"Oh, this? Hmm, I'll be happy to share it with you when I'm done. Until then, it's secret."

Dennis yawned. The rocky ground was hardly comfortable, but he was so tired he soon started snoring. He didn't stop until morning.

When Dennis awoke, Foggle-nogger was already awake and writing. It was as if he never went to sleep, but of course, he had. He hummed and whistled a tune as he scribbled in his journal. Before Dennis's squinting eyes adjusted to the sunshine, Foggle-nogger nearly shouted, "Well good morning, my boy!"

"Morning," he mumbled. Dennis sat up and stretched. His body ached from sleeping on the hard ground. He wanted his bed. He thought of his mother's "Good morning" and her smile. He hoped she wasn't worried about him. He hoped somehow Frank and Glenn had taken care of that.

Foggle-nogger shut his book and jumped up. "What a morning! Look at the sky! Heehee. It's going to be a great day!"

"Do you have to be so loud?" Dennis stood and stretched again. His face disappeared behind a massive yawn as he scratched his belly.

"My apologies. May I ask, why are you so grumpy?"

"I'm not grumpy, just tired. And I miss my home. Why are you so happy?"

Foggle-nogger closed one eye in thought. "What an odd question. Heehee, my goodness. Heehee. Why not be happy? We have beautiful weather. You snored all night long. What is there to be unhappy about?"

Dennis rolled his eyes and said, "Oh gee, let's see. I don't know where Mr. Dr. Rone is, remember?" Foggle-nogger nodded. "He's probably hurt somewhere and needs help. And King Urabus wants his Book back. I don't know where that is, either. And I can't go home until he gets it back. So I'm not happy because nothing good has happened to make me feel happy."

Foggle-nogger burst out laughing as if he had heard the funniest joke ever. He fell over holding his sides. "Heehee Ha ha Ha ha Ha Hee heee Ha Ha (snort) Hoo, Hee Ha!"

"Stop it. What's so funny?"

"Heehee Hee. Hmm," Foggle-nogger took a deep breath and wiped a laughter tear from his eye. "Sorry. I don't mean to be rude. But I've never heard of such a thing as not being happy unless something good has happened."

"You haven't?"

"No." Foggle-nogger flipped open his journal and jotted down a few words while tapping his pipe against a log. "Why be unhappy if nothing sad has happened? It is easier to be happy than to be unhappy."

Dennis wrinkled his eyebrows and chewed on his lip. "Not for me, it isn't. I can't be happy for no reason."

"Do you want to be happy?"

"Sure I do," Dennis said. "Everybody wants to be happier."

"I am not so sure I agree with you. Harris the artist is always grumpy. We all want good things to happen to us, but not everyone really wants to be happy. If they did, they would try harder to act like a happy person."

"That's easy for you to say," Dennis said. "You're always happy."

"Heehee Hee! I'm not always happy. Sometimes I'm only pretending. Faking it, heehee."

"How do you fake happiness?"

"Smile often. Be nice to others. Sing songs. Laugh. Dance. Do good deeds. Rejoice. Appreciate things."

Dennis didn't look convinced. "Those things will make me happy?"

"Don't be such a snassper, my boy. You'll be amazed. Heehee, if nothing else, those around you will think you are happy. And they will be happy you are happy. And if they are happier around you, you will be happier around them. Heehee ho, see how this works? You really will be happy and you won't have to fake it any longer. It's almost magic!"

Dennis decided to give pretend happiness a try during breakfast. With singing birds, the warm sun, and Foggle-nogger tripping backwards over his manuscript, Dennis soon forgot he was pretending. However, when he looked down the hill to see if another trail could be seen, confusion knocked him back a step.

"Hey, Foggle-nogger, look," Dennis pointed down to where they had seen the meadow the previous night. There was indeed a path leading away from the hill. "Something happened last night."

CHAPTER THIRTY-TWO:

Just Rocknocerus

"**L**ook!" Dennis pointed to a huge pile of stones as high as a two-story house. The rocks—some as big as cars, others the size of pumpkins—blocked the trail leading from the cave's back exit.

Foggle-nogger's blue eyes widened. "Whew, that's a lot of rocks!"

Dennis said, "Those rocks weren't there yesterday."

Foggle-nogger nodded in agreement before shaking his head and saying, "Well I'll be a dirty little toe jam sniffer. Imagine that."

"How do you think it happened?" Dennis asked.

Foggle-nogger adjusted his bowtie and twisted his back loose. He combed his beard with his fingers and said, "Way I see it, that could be due to a couple of things. Number one being we just plain missed this incredibly humongous mountain of rubble yesterday. After all, it was getting dark. Or number two, the incredibly humongous mountain of rubble wasn't there last night."

Dennis said, "It was getting dark, but it wasn't dark enough to miss that. But how could all those rocks, most bigger than me, just show up overnight?"

Foggle-nogger scrunched up his nose in thought. "Well, could be they were, umm, dropped here while we slept."

"Dropped here? You think they fell from the sky? We would've heard such an avalanche." Foggle-nogger shrugged his shoulders.

Dennis went on, "And wouldn't it take longer than one night to put all these rocks here? It's not possible, right?"

Foggle-nogger pointed a finger in the air, "Did I ever mention Rocknocerus to you?"

"Rocknocerus? No. What's a rocknocerus?"

"Not a rocknocerus, just Rocknocerus. A giant creature. Huge." Foggle-nogger spread out his arms. "I hear it leaves behind jumbo piles of rocks like this here jumbo pile of rocks."

"You really think Rocknocerus did this?"

"I can't claim to be a firm believer in Rocknocerus," Foggle-nogger shrugged, "but it is downright difficult at times to dispute evidence like that!"

"Why would the Rocknocerus grab up all these huge rocks and move them over here?"

"Not the rocknocerus, just Rocknocerus. And don't be ridiculous. He, err it, didn't grab up all these boulders and move them here. Heehee. To put it delicately, heehee, this is its potty pile."

"Potty pile?"

"Yes, heehee. I believe we are looking at Rocknocerus poopies. Or its eggs. Hard to tell. They both come out of the same end, you know."

"I mean this with all due respect, but that's insane."

"Insane?" Foggle-nogger lit his pipe.

"Yep," said Dennis. "Do you know how big, really big, Rocknocerus would have to be to leave behind this huge pile of… uh, rock poop?"

"Well, hmm, no I do not. There are a lot of things I do not know. And I know it. But not knowing something doesn't make me crazy. But I do know what it eats. Mountains and hills. That's how cliffs and canyons get made."

"And somehow this enormous creature that eats mountains somehow came by last night without being heard? It's not possible."

Foggle-nogger wiggled a finger in his ear and asked, "Why not? First off, Rocknocerus doesn't eat the whole mountain, for crying out loud. It just takes a few bites whenever it's hungry. It is supposed to be very nice and polite. And second off, the stars and moon and clouds

125

all passed us by last night and they are all bigger than Rocknocerus is supposed to be and we didn't hear them either. Besides, maybe it's invisible and therefore we could not have possibly seen him or it or her. And third off, why is something dismissed as impossible or insane because you personally cannot explain it? Seems downright arrogant if you ask me."

CHAPTER THIRTY-THREE:

A Surprise Visitor

To trek down the hill, over the incredibly humongous mountain of rubble, across the meadow, and into a grove of smooth white eucalyptus trees took all of the morning. Dennis and Foggle-nogger planted themselves on a fallen white log in the shade and shared a pile of nuts and berries. Dennis longed for a hotdog with ketchup. Or a slice of pizza. Foggle-nogger seemed very pleased with his meal, as if it was a grand feast. When he swallowed his last handful, Foggle-nogger cracked out a sharp belch in appreciation. Then he skipped off behind a tree to do what hikers sometimes must do behind trees.

Several sparrows fled a nearby bush at once, startling poor Dennis. Opposite of where Foggle-nogger had skipped off to, a tree branch snapped. Dennis swallowed. Dead leaves crunched. He picked up a rock and stood up from the log. Before he could turn to look, someone grabbed him from behind!

The grip squeezed his neck. He could not breathe. Things grew darker and darker.

Clunk!

The attacker collapsed unconscious.

Dennis rolled free and gasped for breath.

"I got him!" Foggle-nogger danced with his tree limb club. Dennis looked at the unconscious face and dropped his rock.

"Oh no. Foggle-nogger, that's Sebastian the Bold!"

"Heehee. Oops. Heehee. A surprise visitor! He looks different with clothes on."

Sebastian the Bold came to, blinked his eyes, and groaned. "Denny?"

"Dennis. It's Dennis."

Sebastian the Bold sat up, rubbed his yellowish blond-haired head, and stared at Foggle-nogger. "Who's your friend?" His words oozed out as if his tongue was too thick.

The bearded man apologized with a nervous chuckle.

"Oh, this is Foggle-nogger. Foggle-nogger, this is Sebastian the Bold."

"It's just Sebastian now," he said.

Dennis pulled just Sebastian to his feet and asked, "Where's Mr. Dr. Rone?"

"I couldn't find him. I looked everywhere. I only found some weird grumpy guy who mumbled cuss words, drew dirt pictures, and told me to go away."

"Harris!" yelled Foggle-nogger.

Dennis asked, "What was the picture?"

"I don't know. I didn't really look at it. Anyway, then I walked around for a couple more days. Got beaten up by some land pirates. That's when I decided to set up camp and keep myself safe. That's why I snuck up on you. I didn't know who you were. This place is freaky. And I couldn't find Rone anywhere."

"So you just stopped looking?" Foggle-nogger asked.

Sebastian's eyebrows scrunched into a glare. "I tried, okay. I don't have a clue where he is. He may be dead for all I know. Or he may have returned and left me behind."

"No," Dennis spoke up. "He's still in Croggerpooey somewhere. We came across the same artist."

"Harris!" Foggle-nogger yelled again.

Dennis said, "His picture showed us where to go. Past the ravine that's up a ways." He pointed in the direction.

"The Great Deep and Very Steep Gorge? It's pretty scary, Dennis," Sebastian said. "There's no bridge. The only way to get across is to go down into it. Who knows what's down there. I've heard noises."

"That's where we're headed," Dennis said. "Come with us. We'll find Mr. Dr. Rone together."

Sebastian looked down. "No thanks."

"What? I need your help."

"Well trim my ear hairs," said Foggle-nogger. "You're scared."

"Hey, listen you two. This place is weird. It isn't what I thought it'd be. I've been here longer than you, Dennis. I know things about this place you don't. Noises and pirates. Weird food. Strange people and animals. Just yesterday some two-headed monster chased me out of its cave!"

"Two-headed monster in a cave?" Dennis grinned at Foggle-nogger.

"Yep. I'm telling you it's scary here," he continued. "But Rick—"

"Horrible Rick?" Dennis interrupted. "He's the one who stole the King's Book of magic."

"Ah, I don't think he took the Book. He's not so bad. He found me a place to live. It backs up to the Great Deep and Very Steep Gorge so nobody can sneak up on me. And Rick also introduced me to a farmer. I've worked out a nice little deal where I do some work for this farmer and he gives me some good, somewhat regular food."

"But don't you want to go home someday? You can't just give up," Dennis said.

Sebastian shook his head. "You don't get it. I haven't given up. I've figured out how to survive. I feel bad about Rone and all, but I really did try. I'm the one who was abandoned here. And I've made the best of it. Now they've abandoned you here. Maybe Rick will help you, too."

"No. When I find Mr. Dr. Rone, I'll come back and take you home."

"Like I said, I'm okay here. The truth is that farmer...well, he has a daughter. She's really pretty and she likes me. A lot. And, well, they get married pretty young around here."

Foggle-nogger interrupted, "Married? Heehee."

"Yep," Sebastian blushed. "Why not?"

Dennis asked, "What's her name?"

"Molssie. Her name is Molssie," Sebastian glowed. "And she's worth all this."

"I don't know what to say," Dennis blinked. "Good luck."

"Good luck to you," Sebastian shook Dennis's hand without trying to hurt it. He did not shake hands with Foggle-nogger.

CHAPTER THIRTY-FOUR:
This Is It

Dennis and Foggle-nogger continued through the forest. Sunlight splashed through the tall, pleasant smelling eucalyptus trees. Bunnies dashed into shadows as the two walked by. Foggle-nogger hummed tunes as Dennis spoke about Sebastian. "I can't believe how much he's changed. He just gave up."

Foggle-nogger rolled his eyes, "You've already said that about ten times. He's a different boy. I get it."

Dennis went on, "But I don't understand. Why'd he give up looking for Mr. Dr. Rone so soon? Sebastian was so good at everything. It was all so easy for him."

"Precisely. Things got a little too difficult, and he wasn't used to trying hard," said Foggle-nogger, who resumed humming a happy tune.

"But he makes Horrible Rick sound like a normal, nice guy."

"You've already said that about ten times, too."

"Normal, nice guys do not kill people while trying to steal magic books."

Foggle-nogger patted Dennis on the back, "No, that does not sound anything to me like how a normal, nice person behaves."

Before they knew it, the trail veered left away from the trees. The two continued under the bright sun until the trail vanished abruptly at the top of a cliff. "Oh my greasy toes," whistled Foggle-nogger.

Dennis inched to the edge and leaned forward to peer down. The trail switch-backed its way down into the deep ravine and disappeared into a misty cloud. Some hundred yards or so in the distance another steep cliff rose out from the cloud. The Great Deep and Very Steep Gorge. Dennis squinted his eyes into a sharper focus and made out a series of trails switching back and forth up the opposite cliff's face.

"Zoonterst, that's a long ways down. Rocknocerus must have liked the taste of this one," said a wide-eyed Foggle-nogger. "Well I guess this is it, my friend."

"Yep. This is it." Dennis took his first steps down. "Let's go."

But Foggle-nogger remained there shaking his head. "No, no, no. Heehee. This is where I get off this little adventure of yours."

"What do you mean? Come on," Dennis reached up for his friend's arm.

Foggle-nogger kindly resisted. "Heehee. No, no, no. It's awfully deep. Deeper than I anticipated."

"I guess that's why it's called the Great Deep and Very Steep Gorge," said Dennis hopping back up to his friend. "What are you afraid of?"

"Well, heehee. I am like you, but upside down, heehee," replied Foggle-nogger with an embarrassed grin. "I'm afraid of depths."

Dennis blinked. "Afraid of depths? What? That's crazy."

Foggle-nogger nodded, "Not crazy, fearful. Depths. Extremely afraid of depths. You are afraid of heights. Well, I am afraid of depths. Do not mind the high things, heehee. Floating high in the air, high bridges, high trails, high trees, high chairs. Those I can handle. But not deep things. Deep things scare me. I get all loose in the knees and dizzy in the head and it gives me the collywobbles in the worst way."

"But you'll be on the ground the whole time," reasoned Dennis.

"Of course I will. But an awful lot of things will be above me. That's a long way down. It's too deep."

"Wait," Dennis's eyes widened. "You're really not coming with me?" He looked more disappointed than a tenth-grade geometry teacher correcting tests.

"No, heehee. Not going. But you will do just fine without me. Good luck finding Mr. Dr. Rone and the Book. Do good well. I will wait for you at Black Burp Swamp. Since that is where you came from, I suppose it is where you will leave from."

"But I don't know when that will be," Dennis said.

"Matters not in the least. Heehee. I will wait for you. I have waited before, I can wait again. I've got loads of writing to do. You're quite the inspiration."

The two shook hands, then hugged. Foggle-nogger dabbed his eyes with his sleeve. "Take this apple with you. You may get hungry. I look forward to hearing all about the rest of your adventure! Be careful now, my friend, and say hello to Mr. Dr. Rone for me, heehee!"

"I don't know if I'll ever find him."

"Believe the best and keep going, Dennis. Think good thoughts. Must believe the best!" And with that, Clamant Contubbnal Farshtinker the Fourth, known to his friends as Foggle-nogger, removed his hat and gave Dennis a deep bow. As he skipped off, the hairy-eared, bald man called back over his shoulder, "You make my feet warm!" Then he was gone.

Alone once again, Dennis blew out a deep sigh and began the trudge down the hard, rocky path into the Great Deep and Very Steep Gorge. Now was not a time for feeling sorry for himself. He had to believe he would soon find Mr. Dr. Rone.

The hike down the steep and treacherous, zigzagging trail was challenging. Dennis twisted his body sideways to keep his footing on the trail's narrow sharp turns. A small fall would hurt a lot; a big one would probably kill him. Some of the turns showed up more quickly than others, but again and again and again the trail turned back and sloped nearer to that gray cloud. Dennis felt like a human pendulum swaying back and forth as he descended deeper and deeper and deeper into the trench. Several times his footing slipped and sent rocks hurling off the steep ledge. Such a downhill hike over rocks and loose gravel takes a toll on a person's knees. And being a person, Dennis soon felt sharp pains with every step.

Finally, the misty cloud swallowed him up. Dennis welcomed the cool dampness. Because there were no places to sit and rest along the narrow rocky trail, when Dennis needed a break, he leaned against the cliff, shifting his weight back and forth, and allowed his legs to take turns being pain free. He enjoyed his apple, shook his legs, and continued downward. It got colder and grayer with every step as the sun gave up fighting against the fog. Back and forth, down farther and farther until at last Dennis penetrated the bottom of the cloudy mass.

Seeing the ground spread out below brought a much-needed smile. Several switchbacks later, he finally reached the flat terrain at the bottom of the Great Deep and Very Steep Gorge! He sat and massaged his aching knees until angry shouts rang out. The argument echoed louder and closer. About midway across the rocky ravine, Dennis spied two short, but thick, men yelling at each other.

Dwarfs.

CHAPTER THIRTY-FIVE:

Enzol Orffripp

One dwarf shoved the other, "Leave!"

"I did!" The other pushed back.

The two were stout and strong, about as wide as they were tall. Each wore thick layers of crudely trimmed brown animal skins for clothing and boots. Stocking caps flopped down their backs. One sported a reddish beard with gray streaks that reached his belly. His flat nose stretched into deep wrinkles about his eyes, which could hardly be seen through enormously bushy eyebrows. The other, though almost identical, had a smooth face. His beard lacked the gray whiskers and reached only past his neck.

"Believe you me, I don't want to hurt you!" The longer beard shook a fist.

"I do not fear you." The other jutted out his chin. "Believe you me!"

One kicked. Toes cracked against a shin. The other punched. Knuckles popped against a forehead. Both whooped in agony. One hopped about clutching his damaged foot; the other buckled over and rubbed his hand. They both growled ugly sounds. Dennis chuckled.

"You broke my toes," said the dwarf with the shorter beard.

"*I* broke *your* toes? *You* busted *my* hand!"

"You punched me!"

"You kicked me!"

The two dwarfs attacked again. One clenched a handful of the other's beard and swung him about in a circle, kneeing him about the thighs and groin. The other slapped at his attacker's belly and arms with one hand and twisted an ear with his other. Dennis laughed so hard he almost fell over. The two angry dwarfs stumbled about in circles spitting and hollering incredibly naughty curse words at each other until they fell in a heap and took a break to catch their breath.

"You must GO!" snarled the longer beard—now filled with twigs and leaves—to the shorter beard. "We are hermit dwarfs. Hermits! I don't want to hurt you."

The shorter beard threw a handful of dirt into the other's face. The longer beard spit and rubbed his eyes. They both armed themselves with thick tree branches and took turns clubbing each other's noggins until the blood flowed.

"Enough!" shouted Dennis.

The dazed and woozy dwarfs froze. They peered at Dennis for the first time with their mouths open and eyes glazed.

"Stop it. You're going to kill each other."

"If I must," said the shorter beard, still clutching his club.

"Hmmf, *you* kill *me*? That will never happen, believe you me," said the longer beard. "I made you joyfully, I can end you joyfully."

"Are you his father?" asked Dennis.

The longer beard nodded and a twig dropped from his messy whiskers. Stray hairs jutted this way and that from his thick, bushy eyebrows. Dennis wanted desperately to lick his thumb and press those unruly strays back into place. But, of course, he didn't dare.

Dennis looked at the other dwarf. "You're his son?"

The shorter beard nodded and wiped his bloody nose on his sleeve.

"Fathers and sons shouldn't fight," said Dennis.

The older one squinted one eye up toward Dennis. "Hold on there, trespasser. You have no right interfering with hermit family business. Who are you and what are you doing here?"

Dennis cleared his throat. "I wasn't trespassing. Just crossing the Great Deep and Very Steep Gorge. I'm headed that way." He pointed to the cliff on the other side. "To find my friend, Mr. Dr. Rone. You don't happen to know him, by any chance?"

The two shook their heads.

"I didn't think so. I'm Dennis."

"I hate dentists!" The older one picked up his bloodied club.

"Whoa, no, no wait," Dennis backed away with his hands up. "Not dentist. My name is Dennis."

"How long were you spying on us?" asked the older dwarf.

"I wasn't spying. I just didn't want you to kill each other."

"Why not?" asked the younger dwarf.

"Huh?" Dennis blinked.

"Seems to me," said the older dwarf, "watching two strong warriors pummel each other to the end would be quite entertaining."

"Yes," the younger dwarf said. "I do not understand. It was just getting good."

Dennis scratched his head. "Getting good?"

"Oh absolutely," said the older dwarf. "This mass of beaten meat was about to cease breathing."

"Me? It was your head I almost crushed like a rotten melon. Let us resume our battle!"

Dennis stepped between them. "Wait! Knock it off!"

"That is my intention!" The father raised his club again.

"Please! Hold on," Dennis said. "Fighting isn't going to fix anything. What're your names?"

"Bliffaron Alonus Orffripp," announced the older dwarf with his arms crossed proudly.

"I am Enzol Orffripp, first and only son of Bliffaron," the younger dwarf bowed.

"Mr. Orffripp, what are you fighting about?"

"It is time for him to leave. I live here," Bliffaron explained. "Respectable hermit dwarfs do not live so close together. Tradition dictates he move away upon his twelfth year. He turned twelve four days ago. Four days!"

"Wait a second," Dennis couldn't help himself. "You're only twelve?"

"Yes," Enzol said.

Dennis grinned, "That's quite a beard for a twelve year old." He ran his hand over his own baby-smooth cheek and thought of Sam's mustache.

But Enzol ignored the compliment and continued the argument. "Where should I go? Live among the grumpy trunk people or the soggy stream dwellers? Believe me, Father, it is not my great affection for your hairy backside or loud snoring keeping me close. There is nowhere else in the Gorge for me to go."

"Why don't you just leave this Gorge?" Dennis asked. "There are a lot of good places to live up there. You can come with me."

"Leave the Great Deep and Very Steep Gorge?" asked Enzol.

"Why not?" asked Dennis. "Would that be so bad?"

The three stared at each other until a clicking beetle interrupted the silence.

"So bad?" Bliffaron spoke up. "Listen here little boy, do not ask if it would be so bad. Ask if it would be any good!"

"Well, wouldn't it be good if you stopped fighting?" asked Dennis.

Bliffaron and Enzol looked at each other.

"Wouldn't it be good if you left each other alone?"

Bliffaron and Enzol nodded their bearded heads.

And, thought Dennis, *wouldn't it be good for me not to be alone?*

Enzol stared at his hurt toes. Bliffaron rubbed his sore knuckles.

"And who knows," Dennis added, "maybe Enzol will meet a girl. I hear they get married pretty young around here."

"Married?" Enzol's voice cracked.

The elder dwarf combed his stubby fingers through his long beard. Again the clicking beetle punctuated the silence. Dennis peered into Bliffaron's eyes, which wasn't easy with those unruly eyebrow hairs hanging down. Finally the elder dwarf whistled a long sigh. "The strange boy is right."

"He is?"

"I am?"

"Yes," Bliffaron said. "Go with him and search for a suitable home site. And a bride." Dennis thought he saw a white smile flash from within that reddish gray beard.

"A bride?" Enzol blushed.

"A nice squat woman with wide dwarf-bearing hips," Bliffaron said. "One who will do your thinking and keep you safe. And when all is accomplished, please come back for a visit. I will be thinking of you often."

"Yes Father. I will go with the dentist. And I will visit some-day with a family so you can teach your grandchildren how to fight. Farewell." Enzol hugged his father.

"Farewell," said Bliffaron. "Do not wait too long to visit."

With that, Enzol Orffripp packed a satchel full of dried fruit and nuts, some extra animal skins, and a lengthy knife. Together, he and Dennis crossed the Great Deep and Very Steep Gorge.

CHAPTER THIRTY-SIX:
But Let Me Ask You Something Else

The hike out was brutal. The steep trail reaching up and out mirrored the one going down and in. But this side had crudely carved uneven stairs covered with loose gravel and stones as big as Dennis's head. Unsure steps sent stones tumbling down to the ravine's floor. Some of the steps were rather high, and after ascending only a couple, Dennis's thigh muscles burned. But poor Enzol, who followed behind because the trail was so narrow, had to use his hands to hoist himself up to some of the higher steps. He grew increasingly grumpy as the trail switched back and forth towards the clouds. His short, stout body was built for power, not endurance.

"We can take a break," Dennis panted, "whenever you need one."

Enzol huffed and puffed, "A break? Dwarfs… need no breaks… believe you me."

"Well, I'm not a dwarf and I need a break. My legs hurt."

Enzol wiped his sweaty forehead with his sleeve. "Take a break… if you must. I will wait…for you…so we do not…get separated."

The breaks were filled with awkward silence. Dennis did not know what to say to a twelve-year old bearded hermit dwarf. Enzol remained silent, too. Mostly because he had terrible tooth problems and feared dentists.

Soon Enzol's hands bled from climbing over the rough rocky steps. That gave them something to talk about.

"I must be careful not to leave any blood on the trail. I do not want to attract hungry wolzelles."

"Wolzelles live around here?" asked Dennis.

"I believe so, yes. They roam all over."

"I've never seen one, have you?"

"No, of course not."

"Has your father ever seen one?"

"Of course not," said Enzol. "Stop asking such nonsense."

"I wonder if wolzelles are only a myth or something."

"A myth?"

"Yes. If you've never seen one, and your father's never seen one, how do you know they exist? Maybe they're a myth like Bigfoot or something."

"They are no myth, believe you me. I have seen the bones of men and animals stripped bare of meat. Myths do not kill. Wolzelles exist."

"Okay," Dennis said. "But why do you think no one's ever seen one?"

"Is it not clear that everyone who has ever seen a wolzelle, got eaten by it?"

Dennis nodded his head with widened eyes. And before they continued upward, Enzol asked, "What is Bigfoot?"

"Nothing," Dennis said. "A legend from far away. Forget about it."

Enzol said, "I will do that. But let me ask you something else. How did you, at such a young age, become a dentist?"

CHAPTER THIRTY-SEVEN:
Name and Cause or This One Bleeds!

Once above the Great Deep and Very Steep Gorge, walking on flat ground felt foreign for several steps. After the boys enjoyed a much deserved, but short rest, they carried on. The clearly marked trail snaked through the trees like a lost worm looking for love in a tub of linguine.

Enzol had never seen such surroundings. His head swiveled this way and that, taking in everything the late afternoon sun offered. He studied every detail: the wide-open blue sky, the trees' rough bark, the birds' chirps, the cooling breezes, the flowers' scents, the sun's warmth, the red and orange butterflies. It was a beautiful day. So beautiful, in fact, that despite their arduous climb, aching muscles, and the miserable uncertainty of where they were headed, both of them smiled as they strolled down the path.

Dennis asked, "Have you ever been out of the Gorge before?"

"Not often, and not far. There is a dwarf village a few days off, but I have never been there. This is wonderful. I have never seen such colors."

When Dennis noticed their shadows growing longer, he said, "Guess we should find a good place to sleep soon."

Enzol agreed and about a half hour later, they crawled under some low branches and made beds out of fallen, soft leaves. Both fell asleep easily. Dennis dreamed of cheeseburgers.

In the morning they each ate a handful of nuts and started down the trail, which rolled over and down several hills as it meandered through more of the same wooded landscape. The hills weren't too steep, but after the fourth or fifth one—combined with the near-constant five and a half days of hiking Dennis had done in the since he splashed down and ran away from the stinky swamp—Dennis's thighs and calves started to cramp up.

"I need a break. My legs are killing me. Aren't your legs sore?"

Enzol shook his head. But Dennis watched him lean against a tree and rub his thighs. Apparently hermit dwarfs didn't complain, and Dennis realized complaining wasn't as satisfying unless someone else joined in or agreed with you. When you are the only one complaining, it sounds like whining. Dennis vowed to keep his future complaints to himself.

After a few minutes, Dennis said, "Guess we should keep going."

"Are you sure we are heading in the right direction to find your friend?" asked Enzol.

"This is the only trail," said Dennis. "We must be."

The canopy of trees reached higher and provided more comforting shade. The mossy path twisted its way around thick trees. Bunnies hopped. Yellow and blue birds chirped and twirped. When a deer suddenly bounded across the trail, both boys jumped with a quick gasp.

They snickered at how easily they got startled.

And then someone tackled them!

The three tumbled off the path and into the leaves and dirt. The attacker pinned Dennis and Enzol down and covered their mouths. His eyes urged them to be quiet. With a jerk of his head, the stranger made it known someone or something approached from beyond the bend. Enzol's eyes lit up with excitement. The man freed their mouths and rose slowly into a crouch. He drew his sword. Dennis remained on his back, straining to see.

The sounds of horse hoofs and snorts seized their attention. The man pointed a commanding finger at both boys before disappearing behind some ferns. Enzol and Dennis knew to stay put. The approaching hoofs grew louder. They stopped and a horse whinnied.

Low whispers preceded several uneasy moments of deathly silence. Dennis struggled to breathe without disturbing the quiet.

CRACK! Birds shot up into the sky. Ugh! UMF! Dennis flipped himself around to see his assailant roll on top of another man who had been knocked off his horse. Enzol bounced on his knees, eager to enjoy a bloody brawl. Dennis's man stood tall, his boot heel pressing hard on the other's throat. Their tackler held the sharp point of his sword against the fallen man's chest.

"Name and cause or this one bleeds!" the man with a sword demanded. "Tell me! Name and cause!"

A calm voice from beyond Dennis's viewpoint replied, "He may very well bleed, but it will be you who will breathe no more. Know this: the two of us are not alone."

"Very well," their tackler continued, squeezing the man's gullet with his foot while increasing the blade's pressure on his chest. "Whatever you desire. First this one, and then you. For I am also not alone." Enzol pulled his dagger. Dennis looked about for a thick branch, a heavy rock, anything. He dared not move too much and crunch the dry leaves surrounding him, giving away his hiding place. He reached for a stone, which was heavier than he expected.

"I ask you one last time," the tackler threatened, pushing his shining sword into the man's ribcage with enough force to draw blood and make the man groan. "Your name and cause."

The hidden voice responded, "The elite members of Prince Zotch the Itchy's Royal Guardsmen bow to no outlaw's demands!"

"Show me the banner colored with Prince Zotch the Itchy's emblem, and I will release this man immediately!"

Dennis sat up, poised to hurl a rock. He dropped the stone as soon as he saw his protective assailant replace his sword in its scabbard. The other man winced as he rubbed his freed neck and patted the fist-sized stain of blood on his heaving chest.

"I heartily apologize to you both. I have known Prince Zotch the Itchy his entire life. While I disagree with his recent alliance, I still consider him a friend. I am a defender of King Urabus's throne. I am Sir Ambrose."

CHAPTER THIRTY-EIGHT:
Prince Zotch the Itchy

ennis's excitement hiccupped out of him. *My great-grandfather!*
The two Guardsmen glanced at each other.

"Sir Ambrose, you say?"

"Yes. Come on out, boys."

As Enzol and Dennis emerged from their hiding spots, brushing off the dead leaves and twigs clinging to their clothing, the Knight continued. "And gentlemen, may I introduce, umm, my squires."

"Your squires, you say?" snickered a mustachioed Royal Guardsman, now in plain view. "Nonsense. That's a dwarf. And the other is just a boy with no weapon."

"An old Knight traveling with a child and a dwarf?" laughed the other Guardsman. "Sounds like the beginning of a sad joke."

Sir Ambrose clutched the handle of his sword.

The Guardsman said, "Be calm, my good man. I have no quarrel with you."

"Then show respect," Sir Ambrose said. "For I presume it would be most embarrassing for you to explain to Prince Zotch…"

"Explain what?" A brightly adorned man on horseback, surrounded by a small entourage of Royal Guardsmen, rode into view.

"Prince Zotch the Itchy, it has been too long!" Sir Ambrose beamed as the other two Guardsmen bowed deeply.

The Prince assessed the situation while dismounting his horse. He scratched behind an ear and said, "Have my men been a bother?"

"Nothing worthy of drastic action," smiled the Knight as he and the Prince clasped hands in a hearty and affectionate greeting.

Sir Ambrose and Zotch the Itchy wandered off a few strides to speak semi-privately. Dennis and Enzol could make out only an occasional word of their discussion. The Prince never stopped scratching his pink, splotchy skin. Tiny scabs dotted his forearms from a rash rubbed raw. The Guardsmen gathered together in an opposite corner and also spoke in low tones, broken up every now and then with low sniggers and a snort or two.

Sir Ambrose waved Dennis and Enzol over and said, "Gentlemen, introduce yourselves to Prince Zotch the Itchy."

"I am Enzol Orffripp, first and only son of Bliffaron. It is an honor," the younger dwarf bowed.

Dennis stepped up and even though technically he was introducing himself to the Prince, he couldn't help looking at the legendary Knight when he said, "I'm Dennis Ponder."

Sir Ambrose looked as though he had been slapped across the face with a cold fish. The Knight blinked his wide eyes and stretched his neck before turning his attention back to the Prince.

"So tell me," Sir Ambrose asked. "What brings you so far from your castle?"

"I am supposed to be searching for you," said Prince Zotch the Itchy as he picked at a scab on his wrist. "My big brother wants you arrested for theft."

Sir Ambrose glanced over his shoulder at the Prince's men and said, "I merely stole back the Book, which is rightfully the King's."

"Relax, my good man. I have no intention of detaining you. My men will not harm you." Prince Zotch the Itchy focused on a persistent itch on his chest. "But you should know Horrible Rick has united the spirits, witches, and gooblins."

Sir Ambrose rubbed his forehead and asked, "What does he hope to accomplish?"

Prince Zotch the Itchy's cheeks turned red as he looked away.

"I apologize, my Prince, if I make you uncomfortable. But as I have been asked to rescue your younger brother, the good and ugly Prince Unfeeo, from the Caves in the Wall of Wards, allow me to ask if you know his cell number."

Prince Zotch the Itchy scratched his neck with more vigor. "No. Of the ninety thousand cells, I do not know in which one he lies. It would be nearly impossible to find him, and even more improbable to free him. As you know, no one has ever escaped from the Caves in Wall of Wards."

"And Roger Whee Rone. Do you know his whereabouts? Is he also imprisoned in the Caves?" Prince Zotch the Itchy looked at his feet and shook his head. Sir Ambrose detected dishonesty in his lack of eye contact. "Then we have no choice but to take up our cause with the Wiley Old Hag," the Knight said.

"Be careful," the Prince said. "We are not the only party out to arrest you. Take three of my horses and my map as well. Perhaps you can find a safer route off the path."

The two men shook hands with forced grins. Something in their smiles gave Dennis a chill.

CHAPTER THIRTY-NINE:
Who's This Wiley Old Hag?

Once the Prince and his Royal Guardsmen had galloped away, Enzol bowed on one knee before Sir Ambrose. He had never fathomed meeting the great Knight who had freed his people from the giant.

Dennis swallowed and said, "Grandpa?"

"It is an honor to make your acquaintance, young man."

"What?" asked Enzol.

"Yes!" beamed the old Knight.

Enzol's eyes whipped to Dennis and continued rolling up into his head. He swooned and fell face forward.

Sir Ambrose and Dennis's handshake evolved into a hug. The boy stared up at the Knight's face. With a neatly trimmed white beard and mustache, a head full of longish silver hair, and only a few wrinkles in the corners of his eyes, Sir Ambrose did not look old enough to be his great-grandfather. His shoulders spread broad and round. The sun reflected brightly off his thick, chain mail-covered chest, which sloped to a slim waist. Large hands rested at the end of muscular forearms. The Knight's wide smile burst into a hearty laugh, and he picked up Dennis as if he were weightless and hugged him again.

Enzol lifted himself into a crawling position. The revelation he had been traveling with Sir Ambrose's great-grandson—and the

Queen's great-nephew!—took its time settling into reality. He rattled his head twice to help it. *Wait till Father learns Sir Ambrose and the dentist boy are kin. And I, the first and only son of Bliffaron, am standing with the great Knight!*

Sir Ambrose recognized his own smile on Dennis's face.

"Why didn't you tell Prince Zotch the Itchy I'm your great-grandson?"

"You heard him, I am a wanted man. It is best to keep our blood connection to ourselves. No need to give anyone a reason to harm you simply for revenge against me."

"You mean Horrible Rick?"

Sir Ambrose nodded. "I do. He is an unstable murderer and masochist. We must avoid him."

"I do not like Horrible Rick," said Enzol.

"So tell me, what brings you two out to these untamed parts of the kingdom?"

"I am helping the boy find his friend, while I seek a bride," Enzol said.

Dennis spoke up, "We're looking for Mr. Dr. Rone, so we can get the Book back to the King and I can go home."

"I am on the same quest, and I would be honored to have you assist me," Sir Ambrose announced. "Indeed, I would love it!"

The Knight unfolded the Prince's map and Dennis discovered that although it lay flat, the map revealed the topography of the kingdom in three dimensions. The Great Deep and Very Steep Gorge appeared to dig into the map, while the hills seemed to rise from it. Dennis stared at the map. "Whoa, I can't really tell where we are."

"Lending us this map was extremely generous of Prince Zotch the Itchy," Sir Ambrose said. "It is a valuable guide of the whole kingdom and reveals more if you look at it from the right direction. If you cannot find your way, change your angle of perception. You cannot see what is above you while looking down. And you will never discover what is over there if you focus solely on what is here." He tilted the map and gave it a little shake. "We will save time if we cut from the winding trail here and make our way through this meadow and into the forest there. We are heading toward the Northern Down

149

Into. Right here we will be back on the path and proceed through these woods and around those boulders. And there lies the Wiley Old Hag's lair, up the steps carved into the mountainside."

Dennis asked, "Who's this Wiley Old Hag?"

"A witch," Sir Ambrose answered.

"I do not like witches," said Enzol.

I bet she's the witch in Harris's drawing, Dennis thought. "Is she dangerous? Why are we going to her lair?"

"Never allow danger to keep you from your purpose," Sir Ambrose winked. "I see no other way to get some answers. I fear the Hag returned Roger to Horrible Rick, who holds him in chains somewhere. I shudder to think what that whacko may do—perhaps has already done—to get his kicks at Roger's expense. So although the Wiley Old Hag hates unannounced visitors, we will go to her lair and find out if she knows where he is imprisoned."

Dennis began, "Do you think Mr. Dr. Rone is okay or…?"

"We can only hope and hurry. Roger Whee Rone's will is strong, but even the best can only hold on for so long. We should be off. Every moment we linger, is a moment my good friend may be suffering."

CHAPTER FORTY:

You Are Not Ready for War

reat-grandfather, great-grandson, and hermit dwarf mounted the horses and rode off the path. Once they cleared the forest, they trotted a bit faster across a desolate countryside full of dust, flat rocks and low brown plants.

"So this is your first time on a horse?" Sir Ambrose asked.

"A real one," Dennis answered.

"You are doing quite well. And you there, how goes it?"

Enzol, with his stubby and wide body, struggled to get the hang of riding such a large horse. He bounced clumsily in its over-sized saddle. "We don't... have hors... ses in... the Great... Deep... and Ver... y Steep... Gorge," Enzol stammered, clinging to the horse. "This is... quite a... challenge... for me. But... it is... much fast... er than... walking."

They went as fast as they could across the small desert without losing poor Enzol. Once the barren landscape finally dipped into a greener meadow, Sir Ambrose said, "Tell me, my boy, all about your time thus far in Croggerpooey?"

Dennis began with his splash landing into Black Burp Swamp, the giant snake, and the even bigger bird. He told about his funny new friend, Foggle-nogger, the intricate details of Harris's dirt drawing, and what a disappointment Sebastian had turned into.

"One never knows for certain how someone will handle adversity, even a promising Knight prospect. Tell me of your life back home."

Dennis put aside his embarrassment and described how he spent most of his time trying to avoid Bulldog. He told about Samir and Kimberly, and he shared all about Mrs. Goodwyn's belief in him and her sudden illness. Sir Ambrose listened attentively, riveted to every detail of the boy's life. Dennis mentioned Frank and Glenn, his struggles at the Academy, and how encouraging Mr. Dr. Rone had been.

But when Dennis said he missed having a dad around, Enzol interjected.

"Oh yes, someone to love and fight."

"No. We don't fight our dads back home. I don't want *my* dad back, but I'd like Mom to meet someone, you know? Make us both happier." Dennis's voice thickened with emotions as he talked about how hard his mother worked and how much he missed her. "I just have to find Mr. Dr. Rone and return the King's Book so I can go back home. Please help me, Grandpa."

"Grandpa. That is the loveliest thing I have ever heard." Sir Ambrose's eyes glistened with emotion. "I promise to do all I can. But first let us find a safe spot for the night. It will be dark soon."

They established a small camp by a cluster of taller trees and bushes. That night Enzol Orffripp snored as Dennis and his great-grandfather lay side by side gazing at the biggest stars Dennis had ever seen.

"Grandpa, would you really have killed the Prince's Guardsman for refusing to identify himself?"

"I trust it would not have come to that."

"How many men have you killed?"

"I prefer not to discuss it, Dennis."

"Why not?"

"If I described my deeds honestly, you would never see me with the same eyes again. My battle experiences would undoubtedly give you nightmares. And if I omitted the gruesome details, I would paint a false picture you may find romantic and enticing. In any event, on this journey I fear you may accrue your own stories to bury and keep hidden. But until then, hold on to your youth and innocence as long as possible."

"Today I almost threw a rock at that Guardsman," Dennis confessed.

"Oh, did you now? And what did you envision happening if it had hit him?"

Dennis hesitated, "I'm not sure."

"Or perhaps worse, what if you missed?"

"I don't know, but the point is I'm ready and old enough to go to war with you."

"War? Trust me, Dennis, you are not ready for war. Only a misguided child with a head full of fantasies wants to go to war. But, alas, sometimes it is our duty to fight. Of course, the trick is knowing when to fight and when to remain peaceful."

"Grandpa, how do you know?"

"When something is evil—not just wrong or bad—it must be stopped. And violence, unfortunately, is often the most effective way to stop it. If defeating evil is worth risking your loss of limbs or life, then act swiftly. Nothing is deadlier than a battle fought with hesitation and doubt. But if the cause is not noble and worthy, the foe not evil, then do not fight. Nothing is nobler than avoiding unnecessary violence."

"Is Horrible Rick evil?"

"I believe he is."

CHAPTER FORTY-ONE:
Step Forward and Fall

The next morning Sir Ambrose offered Dennis and Enzol a hearty breakfast of nuts and cherries and some bark that tasted like cinnamon. Between chews, he told of how he and Rone had succeeded in sneaking into Horrible Rick's castle and retrieving the King's Book without detection.

"Roger and I made it back to the forest's edge. Then the Wiley Old Hag paid us a visit. The next morning I awoke under a spell, unable to speak or move. By noon the paralysis lifted, and I discovered both Roger and the Book had vanished. I am afraid I wandered about confused for a couple of days before shaking myself completely free of the Hag's curse. Then providence brought us together. And now we must get moving."

The three mounted the horses and soon entered a thick wood of overgrown pepper trees and oaks. "Keep alert," Sir Ambrose warned. "This is an unfriendly forest."

"Should we look out for dragons?" asked Dennis.

Enzol snickered.

"I saw a movie once where a dragon attacked," Dennis explained.

Sir Ambrose said, "Dragons are extinct around here. Perhaps you should read more good old-fashioned books."

"Are you sure there are no dragons?" asked Dennis.

Enzol's snicker burst into a snort.

"I am certain," the Knight said. "I killed the last brood of Croggerpooian dragons myself." Enzol nodded because he knew. He remembered celebrating the dragons' demise for a month. "Waste no fear on dragons. Save it for real concerns."

"Like what?" Dennis asked.

Enzol's curious eyebrows arched up his forehead.

"Like Horrible Rick's thugs," answered Sir Ambrose. "Also, snatching swoopers, such as the giant bird you saw in Black Burp Swamp. Good thing it didn't see you or you would have been its lunch."

"I guess it was too busy eating that ginormous snake that was in the middle of swallowing an alligator or crocodile to notice me."

"There are no alligators or crocodiles in Croggerpooey, only bumpy allidiles," Sir Ambrose explained. "And the Black Burp Swamp is crawling with them."

"Allidiles, huh?" nodded Dennis. "Wow."

"Wow is right. Vicious eating machines," Sir Ambrose said. "But not as ferocious as wolzelles, which should be our biggest concern. Also worrisome are land pirates and gooblins."

Enzol shuddered and growled, "I hate gooblins."

Sir Ambrose nodded, "Best to avoid them."

The three rode slowly all day in a silent, single-file line through the trees, glancing this way and that at every chirp, croak, and acorn drop. Warm rays of sunlight shot down through the taller branches. Squirrels foraging for food bounded into bushes as the Knight, boy, and hermit dwarf passed. An orange butterfly the size of Dennis's hand glided by.

The forest abruptly cleared. They crossed a flat, brown, weedy patch and then a rolling, grassy field. They rode over a green hill and reached the Northern Down Into. Our travelers paused briefly only once at a creek for water. The urgency kept their hunger at bay. The man, the boy, and the dwarf proceeded through the Northern Down Into as the occasional trees once again jabbed into the sun setting on their left.

"Follow closely and be especially wary of Pits of No Pull."

"I saved Foggle-nogger from a Pit of No Pull."

The Knight beamed with pride.

Enzol asked, "How do you survive a Pit of No Pull?"

"If you find yourself going up," said Sir Ambrose, "and Dennis is not around to rescue you, just step forward and fall before you drift too high."

Morning came too soon. Both Enzol and Dennis hobbled about the camp rubbing their saddle-sore backsides. Their empty stomachs grumbled. Dennis craved stacks of butter-covered pancakes dripping with syrup. And hot scrambled eggs. And a big bowl of cereal. And bacon. Piles of crispy fried bacon. Dennis could eat it all. His stomach moaned again, begging for his imaginary breakfast.

"Eat, my boys." Sir Ambrose handed them each a large bowl-shaped leaf filled with slow moving, plump yellow caterpillars.

Dennis's face paled and twitched. "Uck, eat this?"

"Enjoy," Sir Ambrose plopped one into his mouth with a smile and a wink. "Try not to look at them or think about it. They live on those white-barked trees there. But leave the green ones alone; they do not taste right."

Enzol needed no encouraging. He gulped down his fill without hesitation. Dennis closed his eyes, wrinkled his nose, and threw a wriggly caterpillar into his mouth. Almost instantly his look of disgust disappeared. "Hey, these actually taste pretty good."

He tossed two more into his mouth as his great-grandfather chuckled.

The day got off to a quick start. After consulting the map once more, they mounted the horses and galloped at a decent clip through long grasses and occasional clusters of red flowers. Enzol jerked about desperately in the saddle and struggled to keep up, but he never once complained.

When they finally reached the well-worn trail cutting through the meadow, they veered slightly to the left and pushed the horses to run even faster. But before long, trees once again swallowed the narrowing path and slowed them down. A relieved smile flashed between Enzol's mustache and hairy chin. Dennis took the lead through the suddenly dense forest.

Creepy sounds and spooky shadows swallowed up the darker and colder scenery. Without speaking a word, all three agreed they should hurry and get through this forest as quickly as possible.

But they couldn't go fast enough.

CHAPTER FORTY-TWO:

Captain William One-eye and the Malodorous Land Pirates

Dennis's horse crashed onto its front legs, pitching him through the air. He skidded face first with enough force to erase an eyebrow. As the boy tumbled to a stop (with both eyebrows still in place, but the side of his face scraped red and raw), two awfully smelly men grabbed him. They smelled worse than a flatulent stray mutt with a belly full of pickled eggs.

Two other stinky guys, clenching knives in their teeth, swung on ropes across the path from opposite sides. One kicked Enzol off his horse. Several swarmed the hermit dwarf before he could unsheathe his dagger. At the same time, a score of other stinky men ran out of the forest shouting vile curse words and surrounded Sir Ambrose atop his horse. Before the good Knight could draw his sword, a gleam of steel against Dennis's neck stopped him.

A rough voice hissed, "Easy there, old man."

"We have no treasure," the Knight announced while slowly raising his empty hands.

Two dirty men yanked Sir Ambrose off his horse, forcing him to the ground. Another tore off the good Knight's belt and scabbard. Dennis tried to free himself from the sweaty men, whose breath stank worse than a vomit, onion, and anchovy smoothie. Enzol yelled some bad words at his captors.

The smelly gang's leader kicked the fallen Knight in the ribs and hissed, "Stay down, friend, or ye all die." His long face was grotesque, dominated by a black, empty eye socket.

Five or six men, who collectively reeked like dead animals wrapped in moldy cheese, searched the bags and saddles. Enzol saw them shake their heads in disappointment toward the leader, who wore thick gold hoops in both ears. Blue and black tattoos covered his neck and thin arms.

"Bring them two!" the leader commanded, his skinny arm waving a broadsword.

A pirate answered, "Aye aye."

The leader raised a hand and everyone froze. He pointed his broadsword at the one who had spoken. "How many eyes do ye see on me face?" he growled.

The young pirate's Adam's apple shook in his throat. He wet his pants and stuttered, "Wuh-one. J-just one eye, sir." He swallowed hard.

"Just one eye!" the Captain screamed. "Ever since me horrible archery accident!"

The smelly pirate holding Dennis's left arm whispered "Self-inflicted archery accident" to his stinky buddy holding Dennis's right arm. The two buccaneers struggled to suppress their giggles.

The leader's face wrinkled and flushed with rage. "Ye's all been told the proper response to me be one 'aye' and only one 'aye' because I'se only got the one eye! Understand?"

"I-I'm new. S-sorry."

"I asked if ye understand!"

"Yes sir. Aye-aye, I mean aye," the inexperienced pirate bit his quivering lip. "Oh dang."

Five quick strides and the Captain's broadsword slashed the new crewman's head clean off. He picked up the severed cranium, frozen with the classic 'Oh dang' expression, and punted the head beautifully over the trees.

"One aye!" he shouted to the rest of the crew, waving the bloody sword over his head.

"Aye!" they responded.

"Now, where was I?" hissed the leader, pulling Sir Ambrose's head up by the hair. "Oh yes, where ye be headed?"

"Beheaded," the smelly pirate holding Dennis whispered to his sniggering and stinking buddy.

"To the Wiley Old Hag," Sir Ambrose said, looking up at the Captain's bloodshot hazel eye. A fly buzzed out of the dead socket. Thin whiskers sprouting from the corners of his mouth hung beyond his chin.

"The Wiley Old Hag, eh? Tell her Captain William One-eye and the malodorous land pirates sends me regards."

Sir Ambrose said, "I will be pleased to relay your greeting."

"Ye'll do it without yer weapons." The pirates snatched away Enzol's knife and shook Dennis.

Sir Ambrose stood, one captor holding fast to each arm. "The boy carries no weapon."

"No?" doubted William One-eye. "How do he survive out here in the wild? I hear they be pirates about these woods." The whole lot burst out in laughter.

The Knight said, "I protect him."

"Seems ye don't do such a good job protectin' 'im."

"I cannot do much against so many," Sir Ambrose shrugged his shoulders. "But one at time…."

William One-eye grinned a most evil smile. The crowd murmured and began tapping their swords and knives in rhythm. "Let 'im go," ordered the Captain. He pulled a tiny pouch from his eye-hole and took out a pinch of tobacco from it that he shoved into his cheek. "Jorge!" he shouted while poking the pouch back inside.

A deep voice growled, "Aye, Captain." From among the band of pirates emerged a massive savage of a man. This tall fiend's upper arms hung thicker than most men's thighs, his hair pulled back in a long ponytail. He tossed his broad, shiny sword from one hand to another, cutting a terrifying image for Dennis. But Sir Ambrose did not flinch.

"Do I get my sword back?" the Knight asked.

"Sure," William One-eye tossed the sword at Sir Ambrose's feet. "Have a go with yer blade."

The instant Sir Ambrose picked up his weapon, Jorges rushed him, slicing his sword through the air. The good Knight skipped back and to the side to avoid the attack. Jorges paused long enough to take a deep breath, and then resumed his buzz saw assault with a war cry, "HEERYAH!!" Sir Ambrose jumped back again. The wild attacks continued and again and again Sir Ambrose retreated, scrambling on all fours at one point to escape death. Dennis looked on in terror, as his captors, still clutching his arms, laughed and cheered.

When Jorges paused once more to catch his breath, Sir Ambrose, also huffing for air and circling away from Jorges, challenged, "Is this the best you have, William One-eye? He hasn't even scratched me."

"Not yet!" answered William One-eye. "Go!"

"HEERAH!!" yelled Jorges. Sir Ambrose bounced in place as Jorges ran at him. The split second before Jorges reached striking distance with his swinging sword, Sir Ambrose threw dirt in Jorge's face, dropped to the ground and kicked his opponent's legs out from under him. With a mighty blow, the Knight lopped off the fiend's head. The cheering ceased as Jorge's shocked face rolled by. The limp body poured blood.

Dennis struggled unsuccessfully to keep his breakfast down.

Enzol glowed with admiration.

CHAPTER FORTY-THREE:
Eeber and Gragorri

William One-eye spit some tobacco juice and yelled, "Eeber!" The crowd roared as a shirtless man stepped forward. Tiny black flies circled about his head and shoulders. "This time," sneered the Captain, "no weapons." He motioned for a pirate to take Sir Ambrose's sword. The man approached the Knight with great caution, his hand extended. Sir Ambrose handed it over easily, staring at his new opponent the entire time. Eeber stood taller than Sir Ambrose. His evil eyes nothing more than deep brown dots. His muscles were long and well defined. He cracked his knuckles and swung his arms in large circles. Eeber nodded to the crowd and flashed a grin with as many gaps as teeth.

"Kill 'im!" shouted one pirate.

Another howled, "Destroy!"

A third screamed, "Tear da arms off 'im!"

As Eeber strutted into range, Sir Ambrose jabbed a stiff left into his nose and skipped to the side. Eeber chuckled and kept his hands at his sides. He stuck his chin out. Sir Ambrose tried a kick to Eeber's hip, but the pirate blocked the Knight's boot. Sir Ambrose shot two more lightning fast jabs into Eeber's face and swung a wide right that Eeber pulled back to avoid. Eeber swung and missed. The Knight clutched his man and drove a knee into his crotch.

The pirates collectively moaned, "Ooh!"

As Eeber bent over, Sir Ambrose rained a series of blows onto his head and gut. But Eeber took them well, and shoved his attacker off him. Sir Ambrose rolled on the ground, and Dennis saw him clench a small stone inside his fist. He bounced back up to his feet. Eeber landed a mighty blow to the side of the Knight's neck, causing him to stagger back.

"Hoorah!" the crowd cheered their man. The next punch glanced the Knight's ear, but then Eeber landed a crunching hammer fist to the top of Sir Ambrose's head. The Knight's knees wobbled and buckled.

A pirate yelled, "Get 'im!"

Eeber pounced on top of the fallen Knight. He squeezed and twisted the Knight's body into the dirt.

"Kill! Kill!" the chorus rang. Sir Ambrose gasped for air and shot three sharp elbows into Eeber's head. The last elbow loosening his hold just enough for Sir Ambrose to wriggle, kick, and punch his way free. The Knight used his right fist, hardened by the hidden stone, to bop Eeber first in the mouth and then on the nose. The punches clearly shook the pirate. A left hook into Eeber's gut drove the air out of him. Enzol shook with excitement and shouted encouragement. Sir Ambrose followed another hook to the side with a right uppercut to the jaw. Eeber staggered back. The Knight dropped the stone and kicked the dazed pirate between the legs. Eeber fell flat. Sir Ambrose circled behind the downed warrior and clamped his arms around the pirate's neck. As Eeber struggled to break free, Sir Ambrose jerked his neck hold tighter and tighter, and the pirate's scrunched face went from red to purple as his arms grabbed at air. The Knight squeezed Eeber's face from purple to blue as the curtain fell over those tiny eyes. The limp body sifted through Sir Ambrose's grip like the last grains of sands down an hourglass.

William One-eye yelled, "What is this?"

"Is that enough?" sighed Sir Ambrose.

"How's 'bout one more before we end this little party?"

"You are running short of men."

"Far from it," William One-eye pierced his lips and spit tobacco juice. "Gragorri! Come Gragorri!"

The crowd of pirates opened a pathway and a strong block of a man stood alone. His wide neck and jaw sloped upward to a disproportionately narrow and heavily tattooed bald head. His left arm ended in a stub at the wrist.

Sir Ambrose rolled his eyes. "This one's missing a hand. Is he really the best you have left?"

"'Tis true he have only the one fist," William One-eye grinned, "but he makes up for it with a mighty appetite." The pirate leader pointed at Sir Ambrose and yelled, "GRAGORRI! EAT! THAT! MAN!"

The cannibal stumbled forward a few steps. He wiped the drool from his chin with his dusky thick stub, leaving a dirty smear. His eyes blinked unevenly as he tried to grab a thought. "Him?" Gragorri asked in a slow, deep rumble pointing at Sir Ambrose.

William One-eye chuckled and spit on the ground. "Yes, Gragorri, ye big dumb beast. Do he not look tasty to ye? Make a meal of 'im and let's be off."

"Okey-dokey," Gragorri nodded and licked his teeth. The rest of the pirates laughed.

Sir Ambrose did not wait for the hungry simpleton to make the first move. Instead, he circled around by the trees and closed the gap between them. Gragorri smacked his lips. The stocky cannibal prodded forward with his thick arms reaching out. Gragorri's gut groaned and the pirates applauded with more laughter.

"The beast be hungry!" screeched one.

Yelled another, "Do 'im in, ya fat slob!

The smelly pirate squeezing Dennis's left arm whispered to the stinky one holding the right arm, "This shall be bloody gruesome." The other responded with a curled lip and a nod.

Enzol Orffripp looked on with intense interest.

The two combatants circled each other. Drool dripped from Gragorri's open mouth. He wiggled his fingers. Sir Ambrose lurched forward, but Gragorri slapped him away. With his one hand, Gragorri seized the Knight's neck and shook it. Sir Ambrose's eyes watered as his face scrunched bright red. He clutched desperately at Gragorri's grip. Veins bulged from Sir Ambrose's forehead. He began to turn blue. Gragorri whooped and the noxious crew cheered.

Dennis yelled, "No!"

But Sir Ambrose managed to squeeze a finger inside the death grip, allowing him to apply a most effective pinch-pull-bend-twist on Gragorri's middle finger.

The finger popped.

The cannibal yelped.

The grip loosened.

The putrid crew gasped.

Enzol and Dennis cheered.

Sir Ambrose escaped and applied a simple bend-jam on Gragorri's little finger.

Pop!

The malodorous crew cringed.

The man-eating pirate wailed and shook the two limp fingers. Tears filled the cannibal's eyes.

Enzol and Dennis cheered louder.

Then Sir Ambrose latched onto Gragorri's thick index finger and performed a perfect one-third jam immediately followed by a 270-degree full twist-pinch before finishing it off with an excruciating 155-degree pullback that dropped the cannibal to his knees.

The Knight took a deep breath and snapped the finger clean off!

The reeking land pirates covered their eyes.

Dennis flinched.

But Enzol did not blink.

Gragorri shook his throbbing hand, flinging a stream of blood all about. With an ear-piercing whelp, the cannibal's jaws snapped inches from the Knight's face. Sir Ambrose rolled back and crouched into a deep squat, ready to pounce. Gragorri bared his teeth and stomped forward. His jagged white chompers contrasted sharply with his dirty face. Sir Ambrose's eyes widened as the hungry pirate approached.

Still crouching, the Knight waited. When Gragorri took another step, Sir Ambrose launched himself to a tree limb and pulled himself up in one swift motion. As Gragorri turned and looked up,

Sir Ambrose, still hanging from the tree, wrapped his legs around the savage's neck and squeezed with all his might. Gragorri struggled to wriggle free. The bloodthirsty, stinky pirates screamed encouragement, but Gragorri could not breathe. His wriggling slowed, his shoulders slumped, and his knees collapsed. Sir Ambrose and Gragorri dropped in a heap. The Knight's legs still tightly gripping the one-handed pirate's throat until Gragorri's simple mind drifted into unconsciousness.

Dennis and Enzol whooped in joy as Sir Ambrose rose above his latest victim.

The other pirates' jaws hung open.

One stunned buccaneer applauded the Knight's fighting prowess, but another silenced him with an elbow jab to the ribs.

The Captain surveyed his crew. Their deliberate avoidance of eye contact and feigned attention to objects at their feet conveyed loudly and clearly to both William One-eye and the Knight: No more fighting today.

William One-eye, pulling at the ends of his mustache, broke the silence. "Both Eeber and Gragorri. Let us be on our way before this man kills ev'ry last one of ye cowardly polliwogs! Seize their horses!"

"But we need our horses!" Dennis said.

William One-eye shot Dennis a fiendish glare. "Be glad I be leaving ye with yer own legs still attached. Indeed, ye should rejoice I don't take me revenge on the three of ye with all me might. This old man may be able to defeat us one by one. But he never be survivin' an onslaught of us all at once. Not with all our swords, our appetite for pain. If I but mutter the word, all me men will torment ye three with such a bloody and slow evil it'll make yer nightmares blush like a little girl who caught herself a glimpse of something terribly naughty. No. Be glad, me boy. Be very glad all we be takin' is yer horses and not yer lives quite painfully. Let's get out now ye flea-ridden dogs. And ye three better pray we don't meet up again any time soon. For it won't be nice and pretty when we do. That is for certain."

And the malodorous pirates disappeared faster than they had attacked. Dennis ran to his great-grandfather to hug him.

"Are you hurt? You okay?"

"I am fine, Dennis. The battle is over. And William One-eye left behind our weapons. I'd rather be without a horse than without my sword. Enzol, take up your knife there."

Dennis hugged him once more with a laugh of relief. "That was awesome. Oh my gosh, totally awesome!"

"Now Dennis…"

"I can't believe you did all that!" Dennis now bounced around mimicking his great grandfather's combative movements. "You were fantastic! You're so great!" The boy leaped up and swung a fist through the air.

Sir Ambrose put his hands on Dennis's shoulders to calm him. "Winning a few fights does not make someone great."

"But you are a great fighter," said Enzol.

"What'd you do to his fingers?" asked Dennis. "Who taught you to fight like that?" He twisted his own finger and cracked a knuckle.

"Manny the Digit Manipulator of Painful Yelps taught me."

"How long did it take you to learn it? Can you teach me?"

"Me too," Enzol pleaded.

"Listen boys. It took minutes to learn, but hours to master. Come along now. And keep your eyes and ears open. More danger awaits."

CHAPTER FORTY-FOUR:
Laughing in a Wicked Way

Enzol welcomed the walk; he had had quite enough of flopping around in a saddle. After hiking for over an hour, they stopped at a babbling brook to drink in the dark shade of some tall, dense trees. The woods echoed with near constant noises—strange calls and high-pitched whistles. Dennis's wide eyes shot from tree to tree with every shriek, squawk, scream, and screech. A cold wind shuffled through the trees and blew chills up the backs of Dennis and Enzol.

"This is nothing like the Great Deep and Very Steep Gorge," the hermit dwarf said. "I do not like all the odd sounds."

Dennis admitted he too felt freaked out by the strange noises and "All the weird creatures and mean people and witches and stuff I don't know anything about."

Sir Ambrose chuckled and shook his head a bit. "Do not let your imaginations paralyze you. There are plenty of real life things around us to fear."

"Like what? More pirates?" Dennis scrunched up his nose. "They stunk so bad my eyes watered."

Enzol shuddered just recalling the stench.

"Oh yes," Sir Ambrose continued. "Their wreaking breath and armpits are enough to repel a speckled grangeprobnoscerus, which is why you never hear of a speckled grangeprobnoscerus attacking pirates. Instead, they run from the stinking thieves."

Dennis giggled even though he knew nothing of grangeprobnosceri.

Sir Ambrose grinned, "And their foot odor offends the sensibilities of garbage sorters, though it is an effective mosquito repellant. But I suspect they are long gone. We will, however, most likely encounter some ghosts."

Enzol muttered, "I do not like ghosts."

"Ghosts?" Dennis's voice cracked. "You mean spirits?" He knew Foggle-nogger was laughing somewhere.

"Yes, that's right."

Enzol grumbled, "I really do not like ghosts."

"Have you ever seen a ghost, Grandpa?"

"I most certainly have. But I must say ghosts are a bit overrated in the frightful department."

Enzol shook his head, "I still do not like ghosts."

Sir Ambrose went on, "They talk in spooky echoes, turn invisible, and do a few other neat tricks. But they seldom really harm you. Maybe an occasional bite or scratch. Rarely do they kill anyone."

Dennis's shoulders tensed. "Kill anyone?"

"Very seldom," said Sir Ambrose. "We may also come across some grumpy trunk people."

Enzol bragged, "I have battled grumpy trunk people many times. They are not so strong."

"Why are they grumpy?" Dennis wondered.

"Probably because they live in mossy tree trunks filled with mold and squishy bugs. Perhaps if they lived in the sunshine, they would be happier. But to each his own. Of course, we may also encounter witches."

"Witches?" Enzol asked. "I do not like witches."

Dennis asked, "Like the Wiley Old Hag?"

"She's the worst, but there are lots of witches," said Sir Ambrose. "Not all of them are old, and not all of them terribly bad. In fact, the young ones can be dangerously beautiful."

"I thought all witches were ugly," said Dennis.

Sir Ambrose clicked his tongue, searching for the right words. "Most are, Dennis. But not always at first glance. A young witch's first impression is one of such extreme beauty it disturbs the eyes."

Dennis blinked. "I don't get it."

"A truly attractive lady is not perfect," continued Sir Ambrose. "It is the odd twist of her lips when she smiles, or the slight bump on her nose, or her slightly uneven ears, or the snort in her laugh that makes her irresistible. However, witches enchant themselves so perfectly pretty, leaving out those tiny imperfections, that they end up ugly. Cannot help it, I suppose. You cannot expect them not to use their witchcraft. After all, they are witches."

Dennis said, "I'd use magic if I could."

Enzol Orffripp shook his head, "Magic always leads to trouble."

"And, of course, their cruelty makes them even more unattractive."

CAW-CAW CAW-AH-CAW!

Dennis jumped.

CAW-HAW HAW HAW HAW CAW!

"They are just birds," reassured Sir Ambrose. "Probably fighting over a worm or piece of fruit."

Dennis's eyes searched the high trees. He counted seven black birds.

CAW AH-HAW HAW HAW!

"They're not fighting over anything. Look!" Dennis pointed at the crows perched on a twisted tree limb bobbing side to side. "They're laughing in a wicked way."

CAW HAW-HAW-HAW AH! CAW-CAW AH HAW HAW! CAW!

"Maybe they are witches," whispered Enzol. He put his hand on his knife's handle.

CAW CAW! CAW-HAW-HAW HAW!

Dennis nodded, "They *are* witches! And they're looking at me."

Sir Ambrose's eyes narrowed as he scanned the surroundings. "Witches feel safer disguised as crows. Stop looking their way and keep walking."

HAW HAW HAW-AH HAW!

"I do not like witches," Enzol Orffripp said, pulling out his knife.

CAW CAW HAW-HAW! CAW-AH CAW HAW HAW!

"They're laughing at me." Dennis stopped walking and glared up at the birds.

"Ignore their taunts and jeers," Sir Ambrose said.

CAW-CAW HAW!

"I don't like getting laughed at."

"Nobody does. But my goodness, if being laughed at is the worst thing that ever happens to you, you will have lived a very charmed life."

The three made quick strides without glancing back. AH HAW HAW-CAW! AH HAW CAW! Ah Haw Haw Haw! Caw, haw haw haw. Caw caw haw... Finally, the wicked laughter faded into the distance.

"Why'd they do that, Grandpa?" asked Dennis.

"Because they can. It is what witches do. They were only amusing themselves. If they wanted to harm us, they would have."

Enzol shook his head, "Witches."

CHAPTER FORTY-FIVE:

We Forgot to Make It Cold

And the three trudged on and on through shaded forests and in and out of flowery meadows, snacking on various berries they passed along their way. Only so much conversation can revolve around observations such as 'Did you see that butterfly?' and 'Isn't this an interesting tree?' Dennis had regretted wishing aloud for a taco, because he had to spend the next several minutes explaining to Enzol what a taco was. So the three walked on quietly for some time. Enzol, being a dwarf, needed twice as many steps to keep up. Although his feet ached, he never complained. But he did secretly wish for another chance to ride a horse.

Sir Ambrose jerked Dennis to a stop. Enzol, lingering a few steps behind, also froze. The Knight pointed and whispered, "Do you see that?"

Enzol Orffripp pulled his dagger and looked to the left, then right.

Dennis's wide eyes scanned the forest's path. He shook his head no.

"Neither do I," the Knight continued, "but I should. Something should be there, but…."

"Wh-what?" Dennis's wrinkled his forehead. "What do you mean, something should be there?"

Sir Ambrose whispered, "A shadow. Look next to that tree there, at the leaves on the ground."

"There's a shadow, Grandpa," Dennis whispered back.

"Yes, but do you see one next to that tree there?"

"No," Enzol and Dennis said together.

Sir Ambrose studied the surroundings and explained, "The sun is shining on that tree at the same angle as that one. But there is no shadow."

"What does it mean?" Enzol asked.

Sir Ambrose whispered, "Ghosts neither cast shadows, nor allow shadows through."

"I do not like ghosts," Enzol's voice quivered as he raised his knife.

Dennis whispered quickly, "Do you mean there's a ghost standing right over there?"

"Don't be silly," Sir Ambrose shook his head. "Ghosts don't stand... they float."

"I do not like ghosts," Enzol repeated with an even shakier voice.

"Hello there!" the brave Knight called out towards the shadowless tree. "I hope we are not interrupting anything important."

Dennis and Enzol held their breath and listened.

Dead silence. Not even a breeze rustling the crisp leaves.

"Oh, stop pretending you are not there," the Knight said. "You are blocking that tree's shadow. I cannot see you just as plain as if you really were not there. If there are more of you ghosts about, I must say you are doing an excellent job remaining undetected. I cannot find any of you at all, unlike this ghost over here. No offense. I am quite certain all of you are quite scary. But my friends and I are in a hurry, you see, and we must be allowed to pass unmolested."

A deep, low moaning grew louder and louder.

Enzol jumped back.

Dennis stiffened.

"Now stop that!" yelled Sir Ambrose. "Stop it this instance!"

The terrible moans grew louder.

Dennis covered his ears.

Enzol Orffripp's eyes rolled backwards and he fainted.

A hot wind whipped up crisp leaves from the ground and hurled them at the travelers. But Sir Ambrose stepped forward and shouted through his hands, "I said stop! Stop! Let us pass or we shall tell the Wiley Old Hag about this!"

The moaning howl ceased in mid crescendo.

Leaves fell still.

A solo spooky voice echoed, "Wiley Old Hag?" A chorus of hollow, childlike ah's followed. "*The* Wiley Old Hag?"

"Yes," answered Sir Ambrose. "Her lair is our destination."

A dead silence befell the woods. Dennis looked to his great-grandfather who kept a steady gaze straight ahead.

Finally, the same slow, deep voice hissed, "Tell not the Wiley Old Hag about our attempts to haunt you. Go now."

"Thank you," the Knight called out.

As Sir Ambrose focused his attention to aiding poor Enzol, Dennis heard a high-pitched bodiless voice complain, "I knew he'd ruin it."

"Didn't mean to," hissed a whiney third ghost.

"We forgot to make it cold," groaned another. "That usually works."

"Cold is good," wheezed still another. "But I find a howling wind helpful in setting the mood."

"Decent first effort," boomed the first voice. "All of us were once new at haunting. Let them pass in peace. This time."

Dennis jiggled his head. The phrase 'This time' replayed in his ears. Sir Ambrose patted Enzol's face and shook his shoulders until he regained his senses. There was no time for embarrassment on the hermit dwarf's part. The three mortals quickened their pace once again and soon the shadowless tree was but a speck in the distance.

CHAPTER FORTY-SIX:
Wolzelles!

"**K**eep alert, boys," Sir Ambrose said. "The birds have quieted and chipmunks are hiding. Something is amiss."

Enzol wondered, "More ghosts, you think?"

"No, ghosts are the least of our problems now. I am concerned about wolzelles."

"Grandpa, have you ever seen a wolzelle?"

"Yes. In fact, I defeated a small pack once. Terrible, wild canines. Very fast and gracefully vicious. Excellent at hiding and surprising their prey. They attack out of dead silence. If we come across a pack, climb a tall tree as fast as you can or the wolzelles will tear our limbs off and eat us."

"Eat us!"

"Everything but the bones."

"How did you defeat them?" Enzol asked.

"Two overweight men somehow had made it up a tree. Their screams for help alerted me to their plight. The wolzelles were much more interested in the two plump men sitting on sagging tree branches than they were in someone as lean as me."

"Did you kill the whole pack?" asked Dennis.

"I did not have to, thankfully. But I killed and injured enough to scare away the rest. If they attack us, I will do my best to ward them off while you two run to safety or climb a tree. You have no hope without a sharp weapon."

"I will stab them with my knife in one hand and poke them with a sharp stick with the other," said Enzol, picking up a fallen tree branch.

"No," said Sir Ambrose, "a stick will not do. Wolzelles will bite right through it." Enzol tossed it aside and picked up a heavier, gnarled branch. The Knight gave the map a shake and examined it. "The road to the Wiley Old Hag's lair soon bends to the south. These boulders up ahead are not on the map. Rocknocerus, that good fellow, must have done his thing."

Dennis shook his head with a smile, thinking of Foggle-nogger. The funny little man was right again.

The Knight continued, "This is good for us. Wolzelles prefer flat ground to rocks. We will climb over these boulders. It will take longer, but it is safer."

With every step leading to the boulders, Dennis tried not to panic about wolzelles. Or the Wiley Old Hag. Or Horrible Rick and all the other terrible creatures. But he failed. He feared each of them. Finally, he asked, "Grandpa, how am I supposed to survive Croggerpooey and get back home?"

Sir Ambrose continued walking as he spoke, "There are many bad things here. Those you can outthink, you will outthink. Those you can outmuscle, you will outmuscle. Against some, you may need to do both. And for others, you must rely on something else."

"What is that something else?" asked Dennis.

Enzol also looked up for an answer.

Sir Ambrose chuckled, "I don't know, but I am sure you will think of something."

Dennis, Enzol, and Sir Ambrose climbed their way up and over the rocky terrain. The poor dwarf, fearful of falling too far behind, worked hard to keep up. At the peak they could see a hill across a short field. A steep stairway carved into the hill led to a guarded gate in a wall surrounding the Wiley Old Hag's lair. They were very close. The three began their jagged descent. Again, Enzol's height deficiency made it difficult for him to stay close. Sir Ambrose and Dennis reached the bottom together.

Two steps later, a deep, thick growl froze them.

Wolzelles!

Dennis ran to a tree. A wolzelle nipped his heel before Dennis shinnied up out of reach.

Enzol, still on the rocks and armed with both his knife and club, ducked behind a large rock. He was too wide to squeeze between the stones, but it did not matter. The wolzelles focused on the Knight.

Sir Ambrose began swinging his sword all about him, slicing as the beasts surrounded him and snapped at his arms and legs. The Knight cleaved off a wolzelle's leg. Another lost its snout and whimpered away out of sight. Dennis watched a wolzelle bite his great-grandfather's arm. The Knight stabbed it through the ribs, used his boot to free his sword, and slashed another as it bit into his kneecap. He knocked one on its head with the hilt of his weapon, and stabbed another in the shoulder, causing it to yelp and limp off. The last three beasts darted away. Sir Ambrose dropped his bloody sword. He had survived the wolzelles once again.

Dennis jumped down from the tree and ran to hug his great-grandfather. When Enzol emerged from his hiding place in the rocks, he saw blood covered much of Sir Ambrose's left arm and leg.

CHAPTER FORTY-SEVEN:
Take My Satchel and Sword

The gallant Knight hobbled over to lean against a rock and told Dennis to fetch his satchel. Dennis listened as his great-grandfather told him what to take from his bag to clean the wounds. The leg bite was particularly nasty.

"I will need to rest this leg," he told Dennis after it had been bandaged. "You two go and seek an audience with the Wiley Old Hag. I will be here when you return."

"I can't go without you," objected Dennis. "We can't leave you alone."

"I cannot climb those steps, and time is not a luxury our friend Roger Whee Rone can afford."

"I'll stay here with you. Enzol can go."

"I am not going," the hermit dwarf folded his arms.

The Knight said, "Dennis, this is your task. It is why you were sent here."

"But I don't want to. I can't."

"Yes you can. And you will," said Sir Ambrose. "I am not asking; I am telling you. You have to go speak to the witch."

"But what about the guard at the gate?" asked Dennis.

"The guard will listen to reason. Convince him you are not a threat, and he should let you pass. Explain to him the peace of mind that comes with doing the right thing."

"But the witch…"

"She has no cause to harm you. We need to know where Roger is being held. Be strong and respectful. Respect earns respect. She may try to trick you and change the subject, but do not let her. In the end, she will either help us, or she will not. You can do this, Dennis."

"No, I can't."

Sir Ambrose placed a firm hand on Dennis's shoulder. "Yes you can. Sometimes heroes have to do the unpleasant. Put your fears aside. Take care of business. Keep your chin up and shoulders back. Look her in the eyes and find out what where Rone and the Book are."

"Do I have to?"

"Yes. I will wait for you here. Now stop debating and go."

Dennis told Enzol, "You should stay here and take care of him. I'll be right back. I hope."

Sir Ambrose smiled as Dennis turned to go. "Keep our family ties secret. She's not too fond of me. And do not call her the Wiley Old Hag. Address her as Lady Skulldigger. That is her given name."

"Okay, thanks."

"Oh, and Dennis," added the Knight, "better take my satchel and sword."

PART THREE

CHAPTER FORTY-EIGHT:
A Piece of What?

E ndless uneven stone steps led up to the gate. It wasn't as bad as the hike out of The Great Deep and Very Steep Gorge, but the sword was heavy, and Dennis's heel, bloodied from the wolzelle's bite, stung with each step. But he climbed and trudged and panted and stepped and climbed and sweated and crawled and dragged and stepped and pulled his way up higher and higher to the Wiley Old Hag's guarded front gate. Finally at the top of the crude stairs, Dennis took a couple of deep breaths, unsheathed his sword, and approached the gate.

A heavy man in a fancy but dirty uniform leaned against the stone wall by the entrance. He looked as though it had been a while since he last showered, and dark circles drooped under each eye. Before noticing Dennis, he let loose a tremendous belch.

"What do you want?" the man asked before picking at his teeth with his dirty thumbnail.

"I am here to see Lady Skulldigger," Dennis announced.

"Who? There's no Lady School Digger here. You're lost," the man shook his head and shooed the boy away. "This castle belongs to the Wiley Old Hag."

Dennis tried again. "I wish to see the Wiley Old Hag."

"Oh really," the fat man grinned with an interested cocked eyebrow. "And who are you?"

"I'm Dennis."

The man scratched his rough chin and flicked something from his fingernail. "I don't like dentists."

"I'm not a dentist. My name is Dennis."

"Well, Dennis," he snipped, "our lady, the Hag, is none too fond of visitors. What's your business with her, if you don't mind me asking?"

"I do mind," Dennis stood tall with his chin up and shoulders back and did his best to sound important. "My business is with the Wiley Old Hag alone. Step aside and let me pass."

"Your business may be with her alone, but my business is to *keep* her alone. She does not like unexpected and unannounced guests. Turns them into fuzzy little ferret-men."

Dennis thought of Frank and Glenn and swallowed hard. "Well, if you announce me, I won't really be unexpected, will I?"

"If I announce you, I will be disturbing the Wiley Old Hag. Do you know what happened to the last guard who disturbed the Wiley Old Hag? Do you?"

"No, I don't."

"Neither do I. No one ever saw him or heard from him again. He disappeared. The Hag summoned a chambermaid to mop up a puddle. I suspect *he* was that puddle. Do you honestly want that to happen to me?"

"But I need to ask her something. It won't take long. If you won't announce me, then I... I'll just have to introduce myself." Holding his great-grandfather's sword gave him courage.

The fat guard wiped his mouth with his sleeve while staring at Dennis. He put up one chubby finger as if to say, "Wait here a moment." The guard opened the heavy gate only enough for him to squeeze through. It slammed closed behind him and he bolted it shut from the inside. Dennis fidgeted for several minutes, trying to figure out how to get in. Finally, the guard returned and spoke to Dennis through a small barred opening in the gate.

"The Wiley Old Hag does not know you. She does not want to know you. She does not like dentists. So go away."

"But I can't go away. I must speak with her. Today. Now."

"No," the guard mocked. "Shoo. Go away. Today. Now."

Dennis retrieved a silver coin from the satchel. "Hey, look."

"What's that? A coin flip?" the man said. "Heads you go away, tails you leave."

"No, I don't do coin flips anymore. If you let me in, you can have this."

The man glanced over his shoulder to ensure their privacy. He leaned in close to the bars separating himself and Dennis. "For two coins, I'll unhitch the lock and look away."

Dennis winced at the guard's foul breath. "I only have one. But open the gate and it's yours."

"What else do you have inside your bag, hmm? Jewelry? Precious stones? Snacks? Naughty pictures?"

"What?" Dennis pulled away, wishing he had some toothpaste to offer. "I don't have any of those, but I can, however, promise you peace of mind."

The guard cocked his ear forward. "A piece of what? Gold?"

Dennis spoke up. "No. Peace of mind. You know, for doing the right thing? Come on, a man's life is at stake. A very important man. You will be playing a vital role in his rescue. Please let me in."

"Peace of mind, huh? It would be nice, you know, to breathe easier and relax. Get a good night's sleep and all that. Plus a silver coin," the heavy man smiled.

"Plus a silver coin."

"And your sword?"

"What?" Dennis asked. "No. I can't give you this sword. It belongs to my great-grandfather."

"It's a nice one. I sure would like to have it," the heavy guard licked his lips. "That would provide a little more peace of mind, if you know what I mean."

"You can't have it."

"Then you can't pass."

"Do you want this coin or not?"

"Oh, I want it. Definitely. But this sword…it looks familiar. Let me see it." Dennis held it up for easy viewing. "Yes, I know this sword. You say it belongs to your great-grandfather. If that is true, you are related to a courageous man. Sir Ambrose the Knight saved my life once with that very sword! Are you really his great-grandson?"

"Yes I am," Dennis smiled and nodded. "He saved your life?"

"He rescued me and my brother from an angry pack of flea-bitten wolzelles. They chased us up a tree. Your great-grandfather did not even know us, but he still fought for our lives. My brother and I offered to pay him for saving us, but he just laughed and shook our hands. He told me to pass along his good deed someday to another deserving soul."

"Maybe I am that soul," offered Dennis.

"Perhaps you are. Is your great-grandfather well?"

"He just got injured in another wolzelle attack. But he'll be okay."

"Good," the guard smiled. "Good. My brother and I are still indebted to him."

"Will you let me through the gate then?"

"Let me hold the sword for a second before you come in."

"You'll give it right back?"

"Do I live to fight back?" the guard cupped a hand to his ear.

"I said," Dennis repeated slowly and loudly, "will you give it right back?"

"Yes, I will. I promise." The guard reached his chubby hands through the barred opening. Dennis could almost hear the ooh's and awe's filling the guard's thoughts.

After handing the sword back to Dennis, the guard opened the gate.

CHAPTER FORTY-NINE:

Lady Skulldigger

Once inside the castle, Dennis walked down a long, dim corridor toward a faint light glowing from a slightly ajar door. *I can do this, I can do this*, he thought over and over. But he wasn't convinced. Dennis pushed the massive wooden door and poked in his head. It smelled like dusty spices—like a stale peppermint stick coated with stray hairs and fuzzy lint balls. Several flickering candles brightened the room. A figure sat at a table facing the back wall shelves labeled *Potent Potions, Remedial Remedies, Cunning Cures, and Icky Intoxicating Persuaders.* They were filled with differently shaped, colorful bottles and jars.

Dennis took a deep breath, cleared his throat, and said, "Excuse me, my lady."

The figure rose and turned. Her black cape hung loosely to the floor.

"My lady?" The Wiley Old Hag's orange eyes glowed out of her wrinkled, gray face. "Nice touch. How did you get in here?"

"I snuck in. I was wondering about Mr. Dr. Rone."

"That criminal and nuisance!" she hissed. "What is your connection to Rone?"

Dennis recalled his great-grandfather's advice and remained focused. "He is my teacher and I need to ask a favor."

The Wiley Old Hag's wicked cackle jiggled her black shawl. Dennis shuddered. "A favor? For Rone? I don't do favors, honey." She moved towards the boy. "They never get repaid."

Dennis swallowed hard and offered, "I'll repay it. I'll owe you one."

"What could a little boy like *you* possibly do for *me*?" She leaned into him with a sneer, exposing her crooked and rotten teeth. "Did not your teacher ever tell you how dangerous it is to bargain with a witch?"

"I've been told not all witches are bad."

The Wiley Old Hag paused. "Well I am. And as you are about to discover, I do not tolerate bothers. A pink twitching nose and some fur might teach you a lesson." She raised her arms and spread her crooked fingers.

"Lady Skulldigger, wait!"

"What did you call me?" The witch dropped her arms.

"Lady Skulldigger. That is your name, isn't it?"

"Yes." Her widened eyes smoothed a wrinkle or two out of her gray face. "But nobody calls me that anymore."

"I can't go home until I find Mr. Dr. Rone, and you are the only one who can help."

She reached out and touched Dennis's hair. "Your teacher stole from Horrible Rick. Then he and that Knight called me a liar and accused me of plotting against the King. So I hexed your dreadful teacher and his goody-good pal. Horrible Rick's men captured Rone. I know not how the Knight escaped. Rone rots in the Caves in the Wall of Wards where the snatching swoopers perch and wait to pluck a free meal."

That's where the good and ugly Unfeeo is imprisoned, Dennis recalled. "Will you help me free Mr. Dr. Rone? Please. I really miss my home."

"Rone is not mine to free. Horrible Rick minds the Caves. But perhaps...." Lady Skulldigger stepped away and strolled to her desk. "Come and sit with me, young man."

Dennis did his best to hide his trembling knees as he sat facing her *Icky Intoxicating Persuaders*. He read the faded labels on her peculiar bottles and jars:

Toe-jammed Tinged Torn-off Toenails	**Floating Frogs**	Belly Button Lint
Earwax	Bat's Eyelids	Snake Sheddings Bear Flatulence
Morning Eye Crusties	Callous Scrapings	Blister Juice
	Blackhead Pellets with Pimple Pus	

She sprinkled some earwax and callous scrapings into a ceramic pitcher. She then tilted the pitcher and trickled an inky liquid into a shallow bowl. The witch bent close to the bowl and blew a long breath over it. Dennis couldn't help but breathe it in. Somehow its smell reminded him of Mrs. Goodwyn's house.

"I wish to know you better. Stare into this bowl."

Dennis swallowed and did as he was told.

"Do not look away from it. Good. Do not be afraid." The witch touched Dennis's hair again and then also stared into the liquid. Even as he fought the urge to relax, Dennis's tense shoulders dropped.

"You are a son, I see. Tell me, Dennis, are you a good son?"

"I think so," he answered, very aware he had not told her his name.

"You are a terrible son," she continued with a soothing voice. "That is why your father abandoned you."

"He didn't leave because of me. He doesn't even know me." Dennis knew he should be upset, but he could not feel anger. Nor could he look away from the bowl. "I'm a good son. Ask my mom."

"A good son would be home taking care of his mother."

"I love my mom."

"You abandoned her, just as your father did."

"No."

"You are no better than he is."

Dennis's body and words remained at ease even as his mind raced. "My father did mean things and hurt my mom."

"Have you never hurt her?"

"Not like he did," Dennis became aware of the witch's cold hand on his cheek. "My father's a liar and he cheated...."

The witch leaned close and hissed in his ear, "You are a liar." And, like a shuffling deck of cards, every little lie and fib Dennis ever muttered flashed in the liquid.

"You are a cheater." And a series of pictures revealing each time he ever cheated on a school assignment, a test, or game reflected from the liquid. Some of these incidents he did not even recall, but each dishonest act poked sharply into Dennis's ribs. He could not look away. He could not blink. Her knotted finger tapped the bowl's oily surface, and the images disappeared.

"Oh," she cooed. "You share the same blood as Sir Ambrose and Queen Lisseve." A chill tugged his shoulder blades back. "Oh, that's very interesting. Ah, how intriguing. Perhaps you can help.... Yes. You came to Croggerpooey pretending to be a Knight."

"I'm not pretending," Dennis mumbled. He felt dizzy.

The Wiley Old Hag tapped the bowl again, bared her rotting teeth, and taunted, "Ah, beaten and bloodied by a girl." This felt like a punch to the gut. "And you know Mrs. Goodwyn. Suffering from a broken heart. Poor Rosie. My dear sister."

"Sister?" His surprise came through the muted tone of his voice.

"Yes! You disappointed her so. Your failure here will kill her."

Dennis's mind pushed against an unseen force. It was like those dreams when you can only run in slow motion because your legs are too heavy.

Then, as if Mrs. Goodwyn were right there talking to him, he heard her say: *You are destined for greatness. You have the potential to do great things. Great things. You are Knight material. You can do this. You are Sir Ambrose's great-grandson. I've done all I can to help you along. You're ready. This is your shot at greatness.*

He blinked and looked up at the witch, away from the bowl. The tiniest of grins graced his lips.

"You are wrong, Lady Skulldigger. I will succeed. With or without your help."

The old hag bolted upright, knocking her chair over backwards, and swiped the bowl off the desk. It shattered on the floor. Its contents sizzled and evaporated. The witch rubbed her face with her crooked fingers. It struck Dennis how fragile and pitiful she appeared.

He put a hand on her caped shoulder. It felt much bonier than he expected. And weaker. "Lady Skulldigger, please tell me where Mr. Dr. Rone is in the Caves in Wall of Wards."

The witch, examining her empty hands, said, "First, you must convince that vindictive selfish brat, Horrible Rick, to leave me alone. Then I will help free your teacher."

"I don't think I can do that without Mr. Dr. Rone. Help me first."

"Then you will free me from Horrible Rick?"

"I promise."

They looked at each other's eyes. Dennis sensed a smile coming upon her face, but it never quite cracked the surface. She brushed her hand against his hair again and removed a grapefruit-sized crystal ball from her drawer. She took a deep breath and exhaled rather slowly while staring into the orb.

"615-749Q," Lady Skulldigger said. "His cell in the Caves: 615-749Q." Dennis repeated the number several times in his head. "But locating Rone is the easy part. Nobody escapes from the Caves in the Wall of Wards. Nobody."

"Are there any tricks or spells you can give me?"

"No, but I can make your journey easier." She whistled through her teeth and clicked her tongue. Several battle-worn cats crept into the room from behind draperies and under furniture. Each carried a tiny pouch in its teeth. One after another, they hopped up onto the table and dropped their pouches. One larger tabby cat nudged a jar from the Cunning Cures shelf over to its master. Lady Skulldigger rubbed her hands and chuckled. A few wrinkles disappeared. "Let me see that bloody foot of yours."

CHAPTER FIFTY:
That Very Sad Day

The fat guard waited for Dennis at the gate. His fat brother waited with him. They offered the boy a loaf of bread as a thank you gift for Sir Ambrose. The second brother giggled as his chubby hands held the sword used to spare his life. Finally, Dennis bid the men farewell and skipped down the hard steps, his injured heel no longer an issue. He was eager to rejoin his great-grandfather and Enzol and share what had happened with Lady Skulldigger.

The good Knight leaned next to Enzol, clearly favoring the injured leg. Dennis shared the bread and explained from whom it had come. He rubbed a yellow paste on Sir Ambrose's wounds. It was the same paste Lady Skulldigger had prepared and applied to Dennis's heel. The pain all but disappeared from the Knight's injuries. The three studied the map and located the massive mountain into which centuries ago the Caves in the Wall of Wards had been carved. Getting there wouldn't be easy, but the three continued their adventure with renewed zeal. They looked forward to finding Mr. Dr. Rone. Although, none had a clue how to get him out.

The road narrowed to a trail that disappeared into a forest of thin black, leafless trees. It continued beyond through a wide meadow littered with flowering bushes and piles of large, smooth boulders. Birds chirped. Colorful flowers dotted the green, knee-high grass. Bees buzzed from flower to flower. The Caves in the Wall of Wards could be seen in the far distance, its magnitude starting to be appreciated.

Dennis passed several bushes bearing clumps of familiar pink and yellow berries speckled with blue flecks. He thought of Fogglenogger, for these were the same poisonous berries his friend had fed him. Dennis could not help but laugh at the memory. He hoped his friend was safe and avoiding deep places.

About a fourth of the way across the meadow, Sir Ambrose huddled up the boys. "Be vigilant," he whispered. "Stay alert. Keep your eyes and ears open. It is awfully quiet."

Dennis hadn't noticed, but indeed the birds had stopped chirping. The bees had disappeared, too. The three walked on, looking around, searching for any signs of a wolzelle pack. They saw none. But Enzol and Dennis had learned there would be no forewarning; when wolzelles are close enough to be detected, it is too late. The path bent in between enormous boulders.

Sir Ambrose heard it first.

A long growl.

Enzol heard it next and promptly fainted.

The moment Dennis heard it his instincts commanded him to run. So he did.

He and Sir Ambrose sprinted through the wildflowers and scampered up the boulders. The snarling wolzelles, flashing their sharp teeth, surrounded the rocks. The beasts scaled the smooth rocks, closing in on the two. Hot breath stung the back of Dennis's neck. He turned. Jaws snapped at his face, just shy of the tip of his nose.

"No!" Sir Ambrose yelled.

Dennis screamed as a second snap clamped onto his forearm. Sir Ambrose sliced off the wolzelle's head in a single slash. The dead jaw let go the arm. Dennis wedged himself into a crevice in the boulders. It was barely wide enough for him to squeeze into. The wolzelles twisted their heads and necks, trying to push into the gap. But its narrowness kept the snapping jaws at bay. The growling animals sprayed spittle on Dennis's face as he pressed himself back. The frustrated beasts abandoned him and ran out of view. But the clamor of barking and snapping, yelping and growling grew louder.

Dennis kept himself wedged between the stones a long time. He saw some of the beasts run off. But he could hear snorts and growls and grotesque chewing noises. After all the disturbing sounds stopped and he was confident all the wolzelles had run off, Dennis gathered the courage to pull himself out.

Enzol lay facedown.

Dennis started toward his friend but stopped.

Sir Ambrose lay in a deep puddle of blood. His majestic sword still clutched in a dead hand. All the flesh and muscle not covered with chain mail had been devoured, exposing bone.

Hard sobs jolted Dennis dizzy.

He passed out.

When Dennis came to, Enzol Orffripp's teary face looked down upon him. Dennis blinked. "You're alive."

"Yes," Enzol wiped his eyes, "but…"

"I know," Dennis swallowed.

As Enzol buried Sir Ambrose's body on that very sad day, Dennis walked about in slow motion with his great-grandfather's sword clutched to his breast. The two did not speak as they stared at the grave.

They did not speak the rest of the day or night as they continued onward toward the imposing Caves in the Wall of Wards, making it to the edge of the Gray Twisted Forest.

In the morning, Enzol put down the map. "The dwarf village is due west. Not hermits, but perhaps I will find my bride there. I am afraid I must go now."

Dennis gave a slight nod.

Enzol Orffripp brushed some dirt off Dennis's shoulder. Then he wrapped his strong, but stubby arms around Dennis and said, "Thank you for being my friend. Good luck."

CHAPTER FIFTY-ONE:
In A Most Terrible Way

Dennis ate the last of the bread and strode away from the Caves in the Wall of Wards. He retraced the exact steps Enzol and he had made the day before. He walked briskly and without pausing until he reached where his great-grandfather lay buried. Dennis yanked a handful flowers out of the dirt and placed them upon the grave. He ventured out again to collect pink and yellow berries speckled with blue flecks. Dennis sat aside the mound of dirt, quietly weeping with two handfuls of poisonous berries. Several times a hand touched his lips, but he couldn't bring himself to take the final step.

A memory crept from his brain.

He and Mrs. Goodwyn were playing checkers. He had only a few pieces still in play. *I quit*, he recalled himself saying.

But Mrs. Goodwyn didn't let him give up. *You will never accomplish anything if you give up when things get difficult.*

But I can't win, he remembered himself saying. *You're too good for me.*

Then Mrs. Goodwyn lifted his pouty face with a gentle hand and a smile. *Victory when you expect to lose is the sweetest. But I will not let you win. Keep trying. Giving up can be habit forming.*

Dennis stood and threw down the berries.

And froze.

Growling wolzelles surrounded him, baring their teeth in a most terrible way. Thick drool oozed from their mouths.

The sword lay out of reach by the grave. This was it. Dennis dropped to his knees and surrendered. He closed his eyes. The wild dogs snorted and closed in. They tugged at his clothes. Sniffing noses poked his neck and arms. Dennis remained still. The growling stopped.

The wolzelles ran away.

CHAPTER FIFTY-TWO:
At Ease

Dennis looked to the sky, blew out a loud breath, rubbed his face, and laughed. It was the kind the laugh that sneaks out as a single short burst at first, as if the body spit out a happy thought, but then continues unabated. He couldn't stop giggling. Dennis laughed the way the great inventors must have when their experiments finally worked. Like Edison at his light bulb's first steady glow, or Orville Wright as he soared in flight.

Dennis had discovered how to defeat the wolzelles! He now knew why the unconscious and defenseless Enzol had survived unscathed. Wolzelles only attack those showing fear or fighting back! The fainted hermit dwarf neither ran nor fought. This time Dennis had not run. He winked at the grave and ground the poisonous berries into the dirt. Still laughing softly to himself, Dennis started back toward the Caves in the Wall of Wards.

Not too far beyond the point where Enzol had departed, Dennis entered a thick forest of big gray pines twisting up like warped corkscrews into the sky. Blueberries and shrubs exploding with dark nuts grew in the gray forest. Odd apple trees, thin from growing in the shade, offered tiny fruit. Blue-flowered vines tangled themselves between bushes and trees and swallowed the path. Dennis used the sword to hack his way through the thick growth of the Twisted Gray Forest toward the towering Caves in the Wall of Wards.

For the first time in a very, very long time—perhaps for the first time ever—Dennis felt at ease.

CHAPTER FIFTY-THREE:
The Hiss of a River

The Twisted Gray Forest did its best to keep Dennis away from the Caves in the Wall of Wards. The forest's density, lack of a smooth path, and hanging vines slowed Dennis. But his sword, though not made for the task, proved to be an exceptional machete. He hacked his way through the overgrown plants and clinging vines, stubbing toes, turning ankles, and tripping over tree roots and half-buried rocks along the way. But Dennis did not give up. Sunlight flashed through the twisted treetops, reminding Dennis of the annoying strobe lights at school dances or neighborhood Halloween haunted houses. He expected to hear exotic animal calls and whistles like the ones heard in all the jungle movies he had ever seen. But, other than the thrashing of vines and snapping of low-hanging branches, the only noises Dennis heard were his own footsteps and heavy breathing.

That is until the hiss of a river arose from somewhere in the distance.

The hissing began as a whisper, but grew louder as Dennis plodded on until the roar of the unseen river reached deafening levels. He worried about crossing such a fierce current. As he trudged on, the river's thundering roll pounded Dennis's thoughts. Then, as if stepping through a heavy stage curtain, the thick gray pine forest opened.

Dennis lifted his exhausted head. He blinked several times and stood with his mouth open at the bank of a stormy black river, but not one of charging water. This sickening current consisted of millions and millions of slithering serpents racing over and around each other.

Dennis consulted the map seeking some way to cross the River of Snakes. The map offered no solutions. Up river to Dennis's right, the forest extended to the very edge, prohibiting any easy passage. One misstep or stumble and he would fall into the rapids. To the left, the River of Snakes tumbled more violently downstream. Writhing thick serpents sporadically flopped above the fray. However, downstream the river narrowed and presented Dennis a glimmer of hope.

Our young hero made his way downriver, keeping as far from the snaky edge as possible. He decided to make a bridge by chopping down a tree tall enough to fall across the narrow, but rough serpent current. Now, while swords are generally good for piercing and slashing (and clearing vines), they are not made for chopping wood. But Dennis had to make do. He chopped at the base of a twisted gray pine growing near the river. The soft bark and pulp chipped away. Again and again, Dennis slashed into the thick trunk. Needles fell from its branches. His face shined with sweat. The tree leaned a little tiny—and encouraging—bit. The echoing rumble of hissing snakes drowned out each grunting chop. Finally, the twisted pine tree snapped to a sharp angle. Dennis dropped his sword and pushed with all his might against the cracking trunk, doing his best to direct its fall across the disgusting river. After a few more whacks and shoves, the tree fell and slammed over the current of angry snakes.

Dennis took a deep breath and hopped onto his makeshift bridge. It swayed and jiggled against the serpents. After a couple of unsteady steps, he could see the warped pine tree did not fully reach across the river. Dennis hopped back to the bank and watched as the thicker end of the fallen tree rose into the air. Within minutes the river engulfed the entire tree.

He found a taller tree to chop down. Unfortunately, it was also thicker. Dennis knew it would take a long time and a lot of energy to get this tree to fall in place over the River of Snakes. He also knew if he was to make it across the river before snakes covered the fallen tree, he would have to move fast once it fell.

Dennis whacked the sword against the wider, twisted trunk again and again. His hands stung with every chop. The hissing thundered. Dennis worked and chopped and whacked and sweated until the tree finally started to lean. More silvery-gray needles drifted down and stuck to Dennis's sweaty head and arms. He gasped for breath and concentrated his sword's chops so the tree would fall at the most advantageous angle. The tree leaned more, but refused to topple. Dennis pushed a shoulder into the trunk. It did not fall. He hacked again and again at the underside of the trunk. It did not fall. The stubborn pine leaned across the hissing rapids at a low angle, but would not topple.

Dennis crawled up the tilting tree, hoping his weight would snap the twisted gray trunk. Or, if it didn't fall, perhaps he could get close enough to jump to the other side.

The first few feet were easy. Because the tree did not rest upon millions and millions of unhappy snakes, it did not sway from side to side; it only bobbed a bit up and down underneath Dennis's weight. He crawled farther up the tree, winding around the twisting cork-screw trunk. He foolishly looked down about halfway across. He was a good twenty or twenty-five feet high. The wriggling and thrashing snakes did not seem to notice him. It was all they could do to survive their own onslaught.

Through the unending blare of hissing, Dennis continued hand and over hand up the tree and across the river. The trunk grew thinner with each crawling step. He had to climb around branches covered with silvery pine needles. The twisted trunk jerked down several inches, freezing the boy in his place. He caught his breath and inched himself forward. Dennis swung a leg around a branch and reached higher to steady himself. He tugged his body farther.

The tree gave way.

The trunk crashed to a halt and slid sideways above the furious reptiles. Dennis hugged the tree, his cheek pressed against the bark. He tried swinging his legs over the trunk, but something pulled at them like an anchor.

Snakes! Snakes slithered up his legs! Their hisses drowned out Dennis's scream. He shook off two or three. But several others wrestled each other up his legs. They quickly reached his waist. His new pair of thick, wriggling black pants weighed him down and made it much harder for Dennis to hold on. He clenched his teeth.

His grip slipped.

Dennis plunged onto a raging sea of writhing, muscular, legless bodies and flicking tongues.

The mighty serpentine current flushed Dennis downstream. Most of the snakes slithered off him and rejoined the downstream rush. He rolled and bobbed at an incredible speed above the serpents. Flailing his arms and legs, Dennis rolled and jerked and twisted and twitched his way along the surface toward the opposite shore. Safety was so close, but the riptide of snakes pulled him from shore. Several times Dennis's outstretched hands grabbed the riverbank's dirt, leaving long claw marks in the mud, before he managed to drag himself out of the river.

Dennis threw clear, slapped off, and kicked away every last slithery snake off his body. He fell under the trees on his back. It took a long time for him to catch his breath.

CHAPTER FIFTY-FOUR:
The Caves in the Wall of Wards

more of the Twisted Gray Forest lay between the River of Snakes and the Caves in the Wall of Wards. Dennis persisted and hiked through the thick gray pines, clinging vines, and uneven ground. After tramping and tromping an hour or so around a peanut-shaped lake, the twisted pine trees thinned. Dennis found himself gazing up at a steep cliff. It was like somehow a whole mountain had been sliced in half.

The Caves in the Wall of Wards.

Innumerable neat rows and columns of teeny square caves pockmarked the cliff. The cells began about thirty feet up and continued higher and higher. Clouds hid the top of the Wall of Wards. Snatching swoopers circled in and out of those clouds, patrolling the captives. Their enormous shadows darkened and chilled the forest below them. The prisoners huddled in the back of their shallow cells, hiding from the gigantic birds.

From his safe spot just inside the forest's edge, Dennis watched a snatching swooper swoop down, pluck a prisoner from his cell, and swallow him whole. Dennis heard the inmate's smothered shrieks fade as he slid down the bird's massive gullet.

Staring up at the Caves in the Wall of Wards, Dennis scratched his head and tried to think of a way to find jail number 615-749Q without getting eaten. If he somehow figured that out, he would still need to come up with a way to get Mr. Dr. Rone out safely. Dennis scratched his head again and shut his eyes to concentrate. This was tougher than any Sudoku puzzle he ever tried at Mrs. Goodwyn's. *What would they do in the movies? Dress in camouflage and scale the rocky wall? No, the snatching swoopers would get me. Build a really big catapult? Out of what, and how? A huge trampoline? Nope.* He wondered how Horrible Rick got the prisoners up there in the first place. *I would have to fly to get a close look into the cells. And I can't fly. Maybe I could capture and train a snatching swooper.* But he knew that wouldn't work. He had seen too many movies. A prisoner's death wail jarred Dennis.

If I can hear them, maybe they'll hear me. From a good hiding place, I'll yell until Mr. Dr. Rone yells back. Then at least I'll know where he is.

A snatching swooper's shadow engulfed the forest's edge. An enormous squawk echoed through the air. Dennis jumped back under the trees and watched the snatching swooper alight against the Wall. It wore a huge saddle! Three men stepped off the giant bird's back. One had his hands and feet bound. The other two untied the bindings and shoved the prisoner into the cave's shadows and climbed back atop the snatching swooper. The huge bird flew back the same way it had come.

Dennis smiled.

That's it. I'll somehow hitch a ride on a snatching swooper. I'll just sneak onto its back and fly close enough to the Caves in the Wall of Wards to find Mr. Dr. Rone. He started to jog off in the same direction the snatching swooper flew.

But several steps into the forest, Dennis crossed into a squishy patch of grass between two tall twisty gray pine trees. He stepped with his right foot, but it did not come back down. Neither did his left. Dennis drifted up. And up.

CHAPTER FIFTY-FIVE:
That Was Not Mr. Dr. Rone

A Pit of No Pull! Dennis remembered what his great-grandfather told him and took a step forward onto nothing. He fell several feet and landed with both a thud and a solution. The plan hit him like a surprise water balloon attack on a hot summer day.

Dennis gathered fallen pine needles and blue vine flowers the rest of the day. There was no shortage of them throughout the forest floor. Back and forth he worked, raking up armfuls of pine needles and flower petals and dumping them in a heap in front of the Pit of No Pull. Back and forth, collecting and dumping, he worked until he had amassed quite a mound that he patted into a thick mattress. The pile ended up wider than two big beds, and as high as Dennis could reach. He hoped it was good enough.

The plan seemed simple enough: 1.) Step onto the Pit of No Pull, 2.) Float higher and higher between the tall gray trees while calling Mr. Dr. Rone's name and looking for a cell marked 615-749Q, and 3.) Step out of the Pit's range and fall to a soft landing on his pile of pine needles before he floated too high. 4.) Repeat this floating / yelling / falling routine over and over as many times as necessary until he found Mr. Dr. Rone's exact location in the Wall of Wards. Of course, he'd still have to keep an eye out for hungry snatching swoopers. Dennis hoped their enormous wingspans prevented them from flying between the twisted trees.

Dennis stood next to the Pit of No Pull. He raised his foot several times, only to put it back down. His fear of heights paralyzed him. He closed his eyes. *Come on, come on. I can do this.* He thought of Mrs. Goodwyn. He remembered his great-grandfather defeating the smelly land pirates. He thought of Sebastian. Not the Sebastian the Bold he knew from the Academy, but the Sebastian the quitter in Croggerpooey. Dennis opened his eyes, exhaled, and jumped onto the Pit of No Pull.

Up he went.

The stiff silvery needles of the gray trees' lower branches swiped his face and arms as he rose. And as he rose he hollered with all his lungs' might, "Mis-ter! Doc-tor! Rone! Where! Are! You?!" Nobody answered. The cell numbers once carved into the cliff were now weathered and difficult to read. Dennis stepped out of the Pit's range and dropped to his soft pile of gray needles and faded blue flower petals.

Dennis tried again. "Rone! Rone!" Still no reply. He cut short his next attempt because of a low gliding snatching swooper. With every try, Dennis found it easier to take that first step and float a little higher. But no one ever yelled back. He needed a way to stay up longer.

He found a fallen tree limb about twice as long as he was tall and carried it between the trees to the Pit of No Pull. He rose slower due to the added weight. As he approached the treetops, Dennis stopped his ascent by wedging the limb under branches extending from either side. "Mis-ter! Doc-tor! Rone! It's Den! Nis!" he yelled over and over until his throat grew sore. He listened for an answer. "Rone! I Know You're In There! It's Dennis! Mis-ter! Doc-tor! Rone!"

Finally a scratchy voice called back, "Here, boy! Over here!" Dennis looked up and to his left. He squinted to focus on a disgustingly ugly man waving his arms. That was not Mr. Dr. Rone.

"There!" the ghastly prisoner pointed to the cave next to him. "He's in there!"

Dennis examined the faint number scratched into the stone beneath the indicated cave. *That could be 615-749Q.* But the shallow cave looked empty. "I don't see him!"

The grotesque man called out. "He's...!"

But quicker than the inmate could say 'there,' a swooping snatching swooper snatched Dennis.

CHAPTER FIFTY-SIX:
But the Worst Part Is...

Dennis bounced about the dark and slimy mouth of the snatching swooper still clutching to his tree limb. It stunk like ten thousand large rotting fish. The giant bird couldn't swallow; Dennis's tree limb prevented it. So the snatching swooper hocked and twitched and opened its beak. In mid-flight, it spit Dennis free.

"WHOOOAH!!"

He fell faster than an angry seven-footer's slam-dunk. Foggle-nogger's words echoed inside his head, *The falling part is fun. It's the landing part....* Dennis splashed into a lake like an anchor dropped from a helicopter. Thoughts of bumpy allidiles helped get him to the shore quickly. Dennis checked his unbroken and non-digested body and chuckled at his good fortune.

Can't wait to tell Foggle-nogger about that.

Not only had he survived a snatching swooper, but he had also found Mr. Dr. Rone! Dennis shook himself as dry as possible and started back. Walking alone has a way of helping people think. And before Dennis made it back to his pine needle mattress, he knew how he'd rescue Mr. Dr. Rone.

Dennis filled his satchel with nuts, apples, and blueberries. He stripped several long vines of their blue flowers, braided them together, and tied one end of them around the hilt of Sir Ambrose's sword. He hopped onto the Pit of No Pull and floated up, counting up and over, homing in on his destination. The boy flung the sword into Rone's cell and gave the vines a sharp tug. The sword caught itself on the cave's rough ledge. Dennis, seeing no snatching swoopers, gripped the vine, stepped out of the Pit's range, and swung towards the Caves in the Wall of Wards.

He crashed into cell number 615-749R, startling the deranged naked man imprisoned inside. The toothless prisoner jumped up and down and greeted Dennis with grinning gibberish. Dennis smiled and gave him some blueberries, which he gummed down with a grateful giggle. As Dennis offered the insane man another handful, a snatching swooper plucked him. The prisoner disappeared in a flash.

When the sky cleared of snatching swoopers, Dennis started up his vine to Rone's cave. Gripping the vine and walking up the Wall while pulling with his arms took all the strength Dennis could muster. And he dared not look down. The ugly man watched from the shadows of his cave, yelling encouragement. A snatching swooper's shriek provided Dennis with enough adrenaline to pull himself up and into the cell. As he did so, a chunk of the ledge crumbled loose and fell, smashing into dust on the ground below.

Mr. Dr. Rone sat with his arms around his knees, rocking slightly. His shirt was torn and he looked thin. He seemed to have more gray speckled in his hair. His bruised and lumpy face needed a shave. The boy's presence did not shake the man's stupor.

"It's me... Dennis. I'm here to rescue you. Don't you remember me?"

Mr. Dr. Rone's eyes remained fixed on the distance. Thick welts covered his teacher's bare shoulders.

"Were you whipped?" Dennis handed him an apple. Mr. Dr. Rone stared at it before taking a bite. Then he took another. Dennis stood against the back of the cave, staring at the broken man who had been so helpful and kind. Rone needed to be much stronger before they could try their escape.

"Thank you."

Dennis grinned. "You're welcome."

"How are you?" asked Mr. Dr. Rone, taking another bite.

Dennis laughed. "I'm better now. How are you?"

"Did you bring water?"

"No. I'm sorry. I have blueberries."

"Blueberries would be delightful." A snatching swooper's shriek and passing shadow reminded Dennis to keep away from the edge. Mr. Dr. Rone devoured the blueberries, some nuts, and another apple. He even ate the core.

"Where is the Book? Frank and Glenn told me to return it."

"Oh, Dennis," Mr. Dr. Rone looked up with wet eyes. "Sir Ambrose and I stole it back from Horrible Rick. Then the Wiley Old Hag cast a spell on us. Sir Ambrose wandered off muttering nonsense, while I sat drooling over my toes. Horrible Rick's men seized me. They took the King's Book. But the worst part is…."

"What?"

"While his men tortured me, Horrible Rick forced… I'm afraid I might have revealed things about the Book. Important things in it, including traveling between our worlds. If he deciphers that coded spell…."

"So that's why the Book is so special," said Dennis. "What else is in it?"

Mr. Dr. Rone stared at his feet. "Wisdom, history. Lots of answers, excellent questions, the portal location, many secrets, and spells. All written in different codes, different alphabets. Animal spells on page fifty-seven, insect spells page eighty-one. Protection from poison, page sixty-six. Bending time, page 112. Or is it 102? Everything we need is in the Book. How to travel between worlds, page forty."

Dennis tried to reassure his mentor, "We'll just have to steal it back."

"That will be quite a feat."

"We can do it. We'll use your magic?"

Mr. Dr. Rone explained, "King Urabus granted me the knowledge and ability to use magic only when it helps someone else. It's limited. I can't use magic for my benefit. Nor can I use it against another. We can't rely on magic."

"Maybe Lady Skulldigger will help us."

"That crone?"

"Yep. Why didn't you tell me she's Mrs. Goodwyn's sister?"

"She stopped being a sister and started being a witch a long time back. Didn't you hear me? She's the reason I was captured and tortured. Why would the Wiley Old Hag help us?"

"I don't know." Dennis gave his mentor more nuts. "Eat these and get stronger. We have to get the Book back before Horrible Rick figures it out, or I won't ever get home. And the witch said if I failed here, Mrs. Goodwyn will die. Is that true?"

"It may be, but I wouldn't trust anything the witch says. To be safe, let's not fail."

"We can do it."

"I admire your optimism," Mr. Dr. Rone managed another smile. "Thank you for believing."

"I think I can get us out of here."

Dennis applied the witch's yellow paste to Mr. Dr. Rone's back and face and told about how he had used the Pit of No Pull.

"Brilliant, my boy. Very clever. I can't wait to hear your escape plan. Once we're free, we'll find Sir Ambrose and get the King's Book. What's the matter?"

Dennis shook his head, put on his best poker face, and tried to hide the heartache.

"Nothing," he bluffed. "I've already found Sir Ambrose. Or, he found me."

"Great! Why didn't you tell me? Where is he? We're bound to succeed now!"

"When we get out of here, I'll take you to him. He's waiting for us… it's a long story. Part of the plan." Then Dennis changed the subject, which is always a good strategy when you aren't being fully honest. "I need to ask something. Frank and Glenn said the other Knight prospects couldn't come here for all kinds of strange reasons. Were they telling me the truth?"

"I am certain whatever Frank and Glenn said about your fellow Knight prospects was true. However," Mr. Dr. Rone winked, "*how* it all became true, well, that's another story."

"So why me? Why wasn't I unavailable?" Dennis put air quotes around unavailable.

210

"Because you're Dennis Ponder, Sir Ambrose's great-grandson. I doubt any of them could have accomplished what you've done."

"What have I done?"

"You found me. Now, tell me how we're getting out of here."

CHAPTER FIFTY-SEVEN:
Another Good Done Well

Dennis shared his escape plan. They decided to give it a go in the morning after a good night's sleep. Mr. Dr. Rone was not convinced it would work, but he was willing to try anything.

In the morning, true to the old saying about the early bird getting the worm, Mr. Dr. Rone and Dennis watched—with their backs against the shadowed back wall—as snatching swooper after snatching swooper searched for easy breakfasts in the Caves in the Wall of Wards. With a wink and nod, both Dennis and Mr. Dr. Rone locked arms and held onto each other and the sword with all their might. They exhaled and stepped into the sunlight of their cell.

It didn't take long.

A snatching swooper nabbed them. They bounced up and down and sideways inside the beast's beak. Dennis used the sword to prevent getting swallowed, poking the snatching swooper's tongue and jabbing its beak. They were supposed to get spit out. But when the beak shot upwards, Dennis and Mr. Dr. Rone toppled over and slid down its stinky tight gullet. They plopped into its stomach.

It smelled worse than a baby's three-day old diaper. Yucky chunks of fish, dead prisoner bits, and who-knows-what-else sizzled in digestive juices. Tingling slime covered Rone and Dennis from head to toe. It was all Mr. Dr. Rone could do to keep from throwing up. Dennis, however, failed to exercise such control.

"Dennis! It's digesting us! Use the sword! Cut us out of here!"

Dennis stabbed the sword down between his feet, barely piercing the stomach's lining. Mr. Dr. Rone helped Dennis raise the weapon again. Together they plunged it deep into the lining. Blood flooded the stomach. The snatching swooper squawked. They rammed a third slash. Daylight shined through!

Dennis dropped to his knees for a peek. "We're too high!" Dennis yelled. "We'll die!"

The flying beast let loose another deafening screech and went into a dive. Rone and Dennis somersaulted forward through the bloody digesting muck. Then they tumbled backwards as, like the end of a rollercoaster ride, the bird jerked to a stop. They swayed gently as if on a boat. Water rushed through the laceration.

"We're on a lake!" shouted Mr. Dr. Rone. "Use the sword!"

As Dennis raised the weapon above his head, the snatching swooper took flight again. Dennis wobbled off balance. It was like trying to stand in a bouncy house while the bigger kids jumped.

Mr. Dr. Rone steadied the boy and one last slice allowed them enough room to jump out. They splashed down seconds before the snatching swooper plunged into the lake. It did not happen exactly as planned (things rarely do), but they had survived.

"Watch out for allidiles!" Dennis called out while treading water.

"Don't worry about them," said Mr. Dr. Rone. "I'm sure that huge bird tastes better than us."

The swim through the lake rinsed off the bird belly's blood, slime, and stink. Once they made it to shore, Dennis found the path he had cut through the Twisted Gray Forest. As they hiked back towards the River of Snakes, Dennis told his teacher all about his adventures and trials in Croggerpooey. With wide eyes and quick words, Dennis shared how he had splashed naked into Black Burp Swamp and how an enormous snake saved his life before a snatching swooper ate it. He told about Foggle-nogger's playfulness and funny way of thinking. He explained how he had rescued Foggle-nogger from the Pit of No Pull, and their misadventure in the cave. Dennis reported how Harris, the anti-social artist, had drawn a picture showing where to go. He told how Sebastian had given up and fallen in love with Molssie. He recounted hiking into the Great Deep and Very Steep Gorge, Enzol's vicious fight with his father, and the hermit dwarf's search for a bride. Dennis recalled meeting Prince Zotch the Itchy, and gave a blow-by-blow account of Sir Ambrose's unforgettable battles with the stinky land pirates.

"And where's my good friend now?" asked Mr. Dr. Rone. "Is he far off?"

Dennis never had to break such sad news before. He started and stopped a few times before finally finding the words. Mr. Dr. Rone took a knee, stunned and speechless. It is always strange for a child to console a grieving adult; it's not supposed to happen that way. But Dennis put his arm around Mr. Dr. Rone and together they cried. Another good done well.

CHAPTER FIFTY-EIGHT:
Something Bad

Once they had regained their composure, they continued hiking. Tangled vines drooped over both sides of the hacked path. Several minutes later, Mr. Dr. Rone asked, "So where exactly are we headed?"

Dennis explained they needed to return to Lady Skulldigger's castle because he promised to get rid of Horrible Rick for her if she helped him find Mr. Dr. Rone. And now they needed more of her help.

The man shook his head. "Something's not right. Witches cannot be trusted. The Wiley Old Hag is tricking us. I wish you had never made a deal with her."

Dennis reminded him, "I never could have found you without her. And who else can help us get the Book back from Horrible Rick?"

Mr. Dr. Rone had no reply.

"And a promise is a promise," said Dennis.

The hissing of the River of Snakes grew louder and louder until nothing else could be heard. When they reached the river's edge, Dennis pointed to the tree he had felled in order to cross. The end closest to them lay submerged beneath the squiggling serpent surface, but the wider end at the opposite side remained exposed. They chopped down a tree tall enough to complete the bridge and crawled across the logs without any serpentine trouble whatsoever.

The two continued through the Twisted Gray Forest. The distance reduced the mighty roar of the River of Snakes to a mere whistling hiss. Finally, the two could enjoy a conversation without shouting to be heard.

Dennis asked, "How are you doing? You feeling okay?"

"I'm still a little weak, but my back's all better, thanks to the witch's paste. I'll be good as new soon enough," Mr. Dr. Rone smiled. "I wish I had a pizza."

"Me, too!"

Despite the smile, Mr. Dr. Rone's eyes showed self-doubt and disappointment. Losing the Book clearly troubled him. He was at a loss for how to get it back. For all he knew, Horrible Rick had already cracked the codes.

The forest cleared to a meadow, and the boy and his teacher reached the mound of dirt under which lay the great and good Sir Ambrose. Rone paid his respects in silence for quite some time. When he finished, they proceeded down the trail into the woods, more determined than ever.

Most of the trees were bare. A sudden breeze brushed Dennis's hair to the wrong side of his head. A silence slammed them as if someone had pulled the plug and everything stopped. No rustling leaves. No chirping birds. No buzzing insects. Uneasy feelings filled the air—like a nagging doubt that you did the wrong homework. Or you only just now found out that big, important test you really need to ace is not tomorrow, but today. Right now.

Something bad waited to happen.

Both of them felt it.

And both of them expected that unknown doom to strike very soon.

CHAPTER FIFTY-NINE:
What in the Name of King Urabus?

As the two weaved among the skeletal black trees, a couple of crows alighted on a branch. More crows hopped along the trail. Mr. Dr. Rone noted how the black birds stared at Dennis. The boy kicked a rock in their direction, scattering the crows into the air. They circled above before perching down trail, facing the two travelers. Ten to fifteen others crows arrived and fanned out in a semicircle on the ground, somewhat surrounding the two. Mr. Dr. Rone and Dennis stopped in their tracks. The murder of crows flapped their shiny black wings. Their yellow eyes glowered at them.

"This isn't good," said Mr. Dr. Rone.

AH HAW HAW-CAW! AH HAW CAW! Ah Haw Haw Haw! Caw, haw haw. CAW CAW HAW!

Dennis closed his eyes and thought of his great-grandfather's bravery.

AH HAW-CAW! AH CAW HAW CAW! Caw Haw! HAW HAW! Caw, Haw. CAW CAW HAW!

"Stop, witches!" Dennis yelled. "Get out of here!"

The entire murder flew off as one without a single 'caw' or 'haw' more. It was like when a little kid hides behind a door, planning to jump out and scare his sister. But the sister announces 'I see you' before entering the room, and the jokester sulks off in disappointment. Mr. Dr. Rone laughed at the crows' lack of conviction. Hearing him laughing once again made Dennis smile.

"That was a little too easy," said Mr. Dr. Rone. "I suspect we'll see them again."

"Probably," agreed Dennis.

The trail wound its way around more leafless trees and large boulders. It did not always look familiar to Dennis, but occasionally they passed a certain tree with gnarled limbs or an odd rock formation that he remembered. As the two hiked around a sharp bend in the path, they came upon an awful surprise.

Grrr-rrrrrrrr! Grarr! Grrrr! Wolzelles circled, snorted and barked.

Mr. Dr. Rone turned to run.

"No!" Dennis seized Rone's arm with both hands, jerking him back. "Don't move! Trust me. Stay still."

Grarr-rrrr! Grrr! Rawf! Gruh! Grrr!

"Stay still? Don't be foolish," Mr. Dr. Rone's voice quivered with fear. "These are not crows."

The pack crept in. Their deep growls rumbled between bared fangs. White foam filled the corners of their mouths.

Dennis gripped Mr. Dr. Rone's wrist as three of the rabid beasts snapped at the air, inches from Dennis and Mr. Dr. Rone.

The man's knees rattled.

"Go away," Dennis commanded. "Go on!"

The wolzelles looked at each other with the most confused little doggy faces. They stopped growling and barking and snorting and drooling. They put away their fangs. One of them whimpered. Another trotted off with its tail between its legs, which apparently seemed like a good idea to the rest of them. As the pack ran off, some glanced back at the two humans, wondering what went wrong.

"What in the name of King Urabus? How did you do that? Was that one of the Wiley Old Hag's spells?"

Dennis explained wolzelles never bite unless you attack them or run away. Mr. Dr. Rone beamed a wide smile at the boy, "Do you realize, Dennis, what a tremendous discovery this is? How many lives this will save?" Another good done well.

As the sun set, Dennis and Mr. Dr. Rone found a suitable place to sleep just off the trail and surrounded by some dense shrubbery. After clearing some rocks and chasing away a couple of small gray spiders, they settled down for a much-needed night's sleep.

Mr. Dr. Rone wasted no time, dozing off in the middle of a conversation. Although exhausted, it took Dennis several moments to calm his mind. It had been quite a day. They were close to Lady Skulldigger's castle. He missed home and hoped this adventure was coming to a close. He wondered what his mom was doing. He imagined her doing laundry, but hoped she was relaxing in front of the television or reading a magazine. Temporarily ignoring the uncertainty of whether he would ever return home, Dennis wondered, *How am I ever going to tell her about all this?* After counting shooting stars for a time, he fell asleep flat on his back.

The sleep was unnaturally deep, which was precisely the problem.

CHAPTER SIXTY:
The Silky Grave

What seemed like minutes later, the early morning sun yellowed the insides of Dennis's eyelids. He knew Mr. Dr. Rone was still asleep by the sound of his steady snoring. Dennis felt warm and snug, as if wrapped tightly in a thick sleeping bag. But Dennis did not have a sleeping bag.

Something tickled his cheek. He tried to scratch it away, but couldn't. His arms were pinned to his sides.

Opening his eyes, Dennis discovered himself cocooned in a thick white blanket of spider webs. Hundreds, or maybe thousands, of tiny gray spiders skittered and scattered across the web. Only his head and neck remained exposed. "Mr. Dr. Rone!" he shrieked. "Help me!"

There was no answer.

Dennis tried to rock himself back and forth, hoping to roll away from the spiders, but he wouldn't budge. The white silk held him fast. More spiders scampered across his face. Dennis felt web sticking to his chin and cheeks. He shook his head from side to side. Though his hands remained pinned against his sides, the fingers on his left hand could move a bit. Dennis scratched and poked at the silky grave until his hand tore through.

This seemed to upset the spiders quite a bit. They scurried faster and faster, working to repair the damage and encase Dennis's

220

neck and head. It's tough to win a race against an army of spiders. But Dennis did just that. He tugged and tore and stretched the hole bigger and bigger until it grew wide enough for him to wriggle free. He slapped at the little stragglers still crawling on his arms and neck, and grabbed the sword.

Mr. Dr. Rone lay fully encased, except for the top of his head. Dennis sliced at the cocoon, careful not to cut too deeply and stab his teacher. Soon Mr. Dr. Rone rolled out of his webbed tomb. He jumped and jiggled several tiny gray spiders off his body. The tiny gray spiders retreated as one large group. They looked like a dingy cotton blanket rolling away in the wind.

"Well, good morning." Mr. Dr. Rone chuckled and shook his head, trying to make sense of what had just occurred.

"Good morning," Dennis laughed.

They decided to skip breakfast and leave right away in case the spiders returned. The two practically skipped down the trail, sweeping off the last remaining invisible, but tickling strands of web.

Dennis asked, "Has that ever happened to you before?"

"No," Mr. Dr. Rone shook his head. "I've never even heard of such a bizarre thing happening before. Feels like Horrible Rick has decoded some of the Book. Wonder what's next."

CHAPTER SIXTY-ONE:
I Hate Horrible Rick

When they arrived at Lady Skulldigger's castle gate, the fat guard, despite a mouth stuffed with food, welcomed Dennis. "Fmennis! Foog do fee foo again. Fow are foo?" He put down his plate of food, wiped his sleeve across his mouth, and unlocked the gate. He twisted his neck with a big swallow and said, "So sorry to hear about your great-grandfather. He was such an honorable man." Bad news always spreads faster than the good. The great-grandson forced a smile.

Mr. Dr. Rone decided to wait for Dennis with the guard. "She and I didn't exactly part on friendly terms the last time we crossed paths. And Dennis, don't make any more promises. Remember, she is, above all else, a witch."

Dennis walked down the castle's dim hallway to the massive door outside the Wiley Old Hag's—or Lady Skulldigger's—sitting room.

The boy took a deep breath and opened the wooden door enough to poke his head inside. "Lady Skulldigger?"

"Well, well, well," she cooed. "How about that? You made it. Sit." She asked how Dennis had managed to rescue Rone from the Caves in the Wall of Wards. Dennis explained crossing the River of Snakes, harnessing the Pit of No Pull, and escaping in the belly of a swooping snatcher. The witch appeared genuinely impressed. Then she asked Dennis how, now that Rone was free, he planned to convince Horrible Rick to leave her alone.

"Umm, I don't know yet. I need your help with something else first."

Under a cocked eyebrow, her eyes narrowed. "I already helped you. Now you must help me. You promised."

Dennis nodded, "I'll keep my promise. But I need to get back King Urabus's Book before I can do anything else."

Lady Skulldigger rose from her chair. "Everyone who asks me for a favor, comes back wanting another." She paced around the room, picking up a jar of floating frogs. "Some want revenge. Others grovel for better health or riches." She replaced the jar of frogs, and examined a six-legged lizard skeleton on her shelf. "Some want help rescuing a teacher. But after I give them what they want, they want more. They get greedy. Like you."

"Me?" said Dennis. "I'm not greedy."

"Greedy and deceitful!" shouted the witch. "You lied to me!" Her head hung low and she continued in a low voice, "You cheated me. I hate Horrible Rick. He enjoys reminding me of who I once was, and what I have become. Laughing at me. I need to be rid of him once and for all."

"Why don't you get rid of him with your magic?"

Lady Skulldigger leaned close to Dennis's ear and whispered, "He knows terrible things about me. If anything happens to him, his henchmen will reveal those secrets. They will be known throughout Croggerpooey. I cannot allow that to happen."

"He's blackmailing you. Are your secrets really that bad?"

The witch hung her head. "My sickest evil, my greatest regret."

"So help us get the Book, and we'll help you get rid of Horrible Rick. You'll get what you want."

CHAPTER SIXTY-TWO:
Quite an Interesting Proposal

Lady Skulldigger slouched and clutched her head with her bony fingers. Her shoulders shook. Dennis suspected she was crying. Finally she looked up and whispered, "What I want is a different existence. A new life. Free from the weight of terrible secrets. Free from people's suspicions."

Dennis looked at his feet and blinked. He rolled his tongue around inside his mouth in concentration. "Maybe you could come back to my world with me."

"Such nonsense!"

"Wait, maybe you can," he said. "No more Horrible Rick. You'd have a fresh start. Nobody knows you. They won't be suspicious at all. Think about it. I even know where you can live."

Lady Skulldigger eyes sparkled. "That is quite an interesting proposal."

"But Mr. Dr. Rone and I need to get the Book back from Horrible Rick first. Can you tell me where it is?"

Lady Skulldigger retrieved a jar from her Potent Potions shelf and took it to her desk. She sprinkled a foul, crunchy powder over a map laid out flat on her desk. An additional pinch from whatever was inside a cat's pouch and Poof! Delicate billows of smoke rose from the parchment, which she inhaled. She closed her eyes and rolled her head. "I see Horrible Rick. In his Eastern Up castle. He is agitated. He blames the good and ugly Unfeeo for Rone's escape."

"Can you see the Book?"

"It is well guarded. He has been studying its pages." Her head stopped rolling in mid-tilt. "Dennis, what can Horrible Rick learn from the Book?"

"I dunno," he shrugged with his best poker bluff. "I was told to return it to King Urabus, that's all. So I can go home. Can you see it?"

Lady Skulldigger closed her eyes and sniffed at the air. "It lays upon a table. In his study. On the second floor of the southern wing. Opened to page forty."

"I gotta go now. Thank you, Lady Skulldigger," he started for the door.

"Wait!" she seized his arm. After rummaging through a drawer, she pulled out two masks. "Take these. Wear them to get into his castle."

He thanked her and again turned to leave.

Lady Skulldigger again grabbed his arm with surprising strength. "If you succeed in retrieving the Book, you will take me back to your world?"

The boy's mind skipped over all careful consideration. He blurted, "Sure!"

And the deal was sealed.

CHAPTER SIXTY-THREE:
Sweet Victory At Last!

As with most major decisions made too quickly, Dennis immediately felt uneasy. Maybe it was the sudden glint in her eye. Maybe it was Mr. Dr. Rone's advice to avoid promising the witch anything more. Whatever the reason, before he reached the sitting room's door, Dennis wished he could take it back. He decided not to tell Mr. Dr. Rone.

"Well, how did it go?" asked his teacher.

"Good," Dennis said. "Lady Skulldigger told me where the Book is. She wants to help us."

"She wants to help us? What is in it for her?"

"Maybe she just wants to do something nice."

Mr. Dr. Rone burst out laughing. He could not help himself. But after seeing Dennis's frowning face, Mr. Dr. Rone asked, "Since when does a witch want to do something nice? No, be very careful here, my good boy. The Wiley Old Hag is up to something. We welcome her help, but we must be on our toes."

Dennis nodded and said, "She doesn't like being called that. Her name is Lady Skulldigger."

A sad grin slipped onto Mr. Dr. Rone's face.

Dennis and Mr. Dr. Rone hiked over jagged rocks and around gurgling mud puddles on the unpleasant journey to Horrible Rick's castle in the Eastern Up territory. To avoid complaining, they pretended to ignore their growling stomachs, the black clouds forming overhead, and the various moans echoing from behind deep shadows. They crawled over fallen logs and through drooping willow trees. They pulled themselves up steep hills only to slide and tumble down the other sides.

Finally they could see the castle. The lowered drawbridge beckoned. Dennis removed the masks from his sack. "We're supposed to wear these. They're from Lady Skulldigger." Mr. Dr. Rone looked at the floppy mask of a droopy, expressionless face. Dennis put his on and looked like a movie character preparing to rob a bank.

Mr. Dr. Rone said, "There's no telling what Horrible Rick will do to us if we get caught. You understand? Once we retrieve the Book, let's get out of there as quickly as possible."

The two approached the lowered drawbridge. Sentries posted at the entrance let them pass without question. Mr. Dr. Rone and Dennis nodded at each other. Soldiers and laborers inside the fortress walls paid them no attention. Dennis resisted the urge to needle Mr. Dr. Rone for being wrong about Lady Skulldigger. *People can change, even witches*, he thought.

They made their way to the second floor of the southern wing. One door was ajar and candlelight flickered from within. They peeked inside. Shelves of leather-bound books lined the walls. Dennis and Mr. Dr. Rone saw no one, but still dared not make any noise. They took in the grandeur of flowing red draperies, a thick burgundy rug, and a great leather chair pushed against a table littered with a ruler, a magnifying glass, quills, ink wells, and several sheets of parchment paper filled with line after line of crossed out terms and misspelled words.

And there, just as Lady Skulldigger had said, lay the Book opened to page forty.

Mr. Dr. Rone clutched it to his chest. Dennis jumped in the air as an athlete does after scoring a winning basket or touchdown. Ah, sweet victory at last! They turned to leave.

A tall man in a black cape filled the doorway. He started laughing.

CHAPTER SIXTY-FOUR:

Hey, Remember Me?

Horrible Rick strutted into the study. Seven muscled men with swords followed.

"Well done, Hag," he looked beyond the two visitors. From behind the silky red draperies, the Wiley Old Hag showed herself.

"You?" sighed Dennis. "I trusted you. I believed you."

The witch's eyes avoided Dennis.

"Save your breath," Mr. Dr. Rone advised, wiping the mask off his face. "She's a witch. It's what they do."

Horrible Rick rubbed his hands together with excitement. "Well, well, well, well. Mister Doctor Roger Whee Rone, how very nice to see you again. Won't you introduce your young friend?"

"Something tells me you already know his name."

"Yes, I do. I know a lot of things, don't I Hag?" He stuck out his tongue at the witch. "But you know what I don't know. At least not yet. I don't know the code to that precious Book. Perhaps you will reconsider helping me with that?"

"Never," said Rone.

"Then I guess the kid will, whether he wants to or not."

"He doesn't know anything about the Book's secrets."

"I am not so sure. Hey boys, seize them."

The henchmen dragged them into the torch-lit corridors of the dungeon. Four men disappeared with Mr. Dr. Rone to the left. The other three took Dennis to the right. One shackled a heavy ball and chain to Dennis's ankle, while another cuffed a thin wrist to a chain anchored in the floor. Then they left.

Dennis closed his eyes. *Mom. I want to see Mom again.*

A quiet "psst" caught his attention.

It came from a shackled prisoner across from Dennis. "Hey, remember me?"

"It's too dark," Dennis whispered. "I can't see you."

He leaned into the dim torchlight. "From the Caves in the Wall of Wards."

Dennis flinched at the extreme repulsiveness of the man's face.

The prisoner grew excited. "I knew it was you. Was that Rone with you, the one you rescued?"

"Yes. My name is Dennis."

"I am the good and ugly Unfeeo."

"Nice to meet you, Prince."

"Oh, you know who I am?"

Through a whispered conversation, Dennis and the good and ugly Unfeeo became well acquainted with each other. Dennis learned of Unfeeo's affection for his father, King Urabus, and his disappointment in his older brothers, especially Horrible Rick. The good and ugly Unfeeo cried when told the bad news about Sir Ambrose. Dennis also told about his difficulties training for Knighthood and his adventures in Croggerpooey. And Unfeeo learned all about Dennis's battles with Bulldog and his kind neighbor, Mrs. Goodwyn.

"You do not mean Rosie Goodwyn, do you?" asked the good and ugly Unfeeo. "She cared for me in Castle Neede."

Then it happened.

Loud footsteps preceded the presence of three large shadows.

CHAPTER SIXTY-FIVE:
Maximum Pain

Two guards pulled Dennis to his feet. Horrible Rick stepped so close Dennis could see his reflection in the man's dark eyes.

"Do you know who I am?" he asked with a smile.

Dennis nodded.

"Oh good. What's my name?"

Dennis swallowed before answering. "Rick."

"Almost. It's Horrible Rick. Do you know why?"

"Umm, I heard you stick your thumbnails into apples."

"Oh really? Someone told you? Yes… I haven't done that in quite a while. But it is a horrible thing to do, isn't it?"

Dennis nodded.

"I'm a horrible person. Or at least I try to be. I've worked so hard at it, you know, doing horrible things."

"Like murder?" Dennis didn't mean to say it out loud.

"Murder? I've never murdered anyone," he rolled his eyes. "At least not yet."

"Mr. Dr. Rone told me you killed Fred Goodwyn."

"Oh my. Oh my my my," he laughed. "Poor Roger thinks *I* did *that*? For all these years? I almost feel sorry for him. Wow, no, I did not kill Fred. I was not alone that day. But anyway, where was I? Oh yes, tell me what you know about the King's Book."

"I don't really know anything about it."

"Don't do that. No, no, don't refuse to help me. I'm not in the mood for games." Horrible Rick whispered in his ear, "You know, Den-nis, I can make you important. Throughout Croggerpooey, everyone will know your name. Den-nis. Just tell me the code. Tell me what the spells will do."

"I've never read the Book. Until today, I'd never even seen it."

Horrible Rick tilted his head back and forth with each word, "Tell… Me… The… Secrets."

"I don't know any…."

The good and ugly Unfeeo spoke up, "He can't tell you what he doesn't know."

Horrible Rick squatted and screamed into the good and ugly Unfeeo's ear, "Oh do shut up, rude little brother! No one is talking to you!" He stood up and calmly said, "This could get painful. You know, my guards—especially these two guys here—are *really* mean people. Tell me and they will only hurt you a little. Keep quiet and they will hurt you a lot."

"Please, I…I really don't—"

"Stop! I don't believe you. I need those secrets. I will get those secrets. Understand?"

Dennis nodded.

"But you won't tell me, will you?"

"I don't—"

"Know!" Horrible Rick interjected again. "I don't know, I don't know, I don't know. Okay. Hey guys," he called to his guards, "why don't we go get that torture chamber all set up and ready to go. The boy has decided he doesn't want to be important. He doesn't want to hurt just a little. He's opting for maximum pain."

The good and ugly Unfeeo said, "He's only a kid, Rick, don't."

"The name's Horrible Rick!" he kicked the seated Prince in the face. "And no one is talking to you, my dear little brother. Boys, set up the torture chamber for two."

Horrible Rick and his guards left.

231

Even in the dim light, Dennis could see one of Unfeeo's eyes was already swelling into a purple ball.

Moments later, an unexpected visitor entered the dungeon.

"There you are, my boy," said the Wiley Old Hag.

CHAPTER SIXTY-SIX:
Making Amends

"**L**ook, child. Look what I have for you." The witch placed his satchel, a key, and his sword on the ground. "Free yourself and go!"

Dennis stumbled over his thoughts. "What are you up to?"

"Setting you free," Lady Skulldigger grinned. "Look!" She opened the satchel and revealed the Book. "Take it and go!"

Dennis raised the sword. "I don't trust you!"

Lady Skulldigger bowed her head and said, "I know. I made a terrible error and do not deserve your trust. Nor could I blame you for striking me down. But I am trying to help. I am making amends." Lady Skulldigger picked up the key and unlocked his chains.

"Do you have anything that will heal his eye?" Dennis asked, pointing to the good and ugly Unfeeo.

Lady Skulldigger nodded and withdrew a handful of purple dust from underneath her shawl. She blew it onto the Prince, as Dennis unlocked more chains. The swollen and bruised eye shrank back to its ugly norm.

"Where's Mr. Dr. Rone? You have to get all of us out of here."

Together they tiptoed down the corridor over several snoring guards and found Mr. Dr. Rone.

"I don't know why you're doing this," Mr. Dr. Rone said to the witch after being unchained, "but thank you."

"What do we do now?" Dennis asked. "How do we get out of the castle?"

Mr. Dr. Rone grinned. "The snatching swoopers Horrible Rick keeps to transport prisoners sleep in the castle's courtyard. Maybe one will be kind enough to swallow us and fly away."

"Or we can jump into its saddle and fly it to the swamp," Dennis said.

The good and ugly Unfeeo asked, "Why do you wish to go to the swamp?"

"That's where we will give King Urabus his Book," said Mr. Dr. Rone. Then I will escort Dennis home."

Lady Skulldigger said, "Take the stairs at the end of this hall down to the courtyard. Go now! Run before the slumber spell wears off. I will meet you at Black Burp Swamp."

"What?" Mr. Dr. Rone's eyes bugged out. "There's no reason for you to go to the swamp. You've done enough."

"Tell him, Dennis," Lady Skulldigger said. "Tell him what you promised."

Mr. Dr. Rone looked at Dennis, who was looking down at his feet.

"I promised I would take her back to my neighborhood."

Mr. Dr. Rone's eyes bugged out again, "What? Why?"

"She helped us. More than once. I promised."

"I need to see my sister," she said.

"We'll discuss it later," Mr. Dr. Rone said, clutching the Book. "Let's go."

The sun had just started to spray the cloudless dawn sky pink. Five or six snatching swoopers sprawled across the courtyard, sleeping with their beaks tucked under a wing.

"Find one with a saddle," Dennis whispered to his companions. "And stay close together." Dennis drew his sword and locked arms with the others. "If it wakes up before we can get on its saddle, we'll need it to swallow all of us."

"Those two by the wall have saddles," Mr. Dr. Rone noted.

They crept past the first snatching swooper. It did not have a saddle. Neither did the second. As the good and ugly Unfeeo passed the third saddleless snatching swooper, it opened an eye.

Before they knew it, the snatching swooper gobbled them up. All three slipped down its gullet and rolled into its mostly empty stomach. The stench nearly suffocated them. Having been inside a giant bird before did not make the odor any less disgusting. Unfeeo's ugly face turned green. He gagged back the impulse to vomit. They tumbled into the sticky walls on unsteady legs. The swaying and their popping ears convinced them the snatching swooper had taken flight. "Do you think it's going to Black Burp Swamp?" yelled Dennis.

Mr. Dr. Rone shrugged. "Who knows? We can only hope. It could be going to the Caves in the Wall of Wards for all we know."

Dennis hadn't thought about that. They could end up anywhere.

Just then the bird's stomach rolled and groaned. "I could be mistaken," the good and ugly Unfeeo shouted, "but I believe this bird is still hungry!"

"They eat prisoners at the Caves," said Mr. Dr. Rone.

"They also eat giant snakes and allidiles at the swamp," said Dennis.

The three bounced about the snatching swooper's belly for quite some time. If the guts didn't stink so horrendously, the ride could have been fun. They took care not to stew too long in one spot and allow the digestive juices to sizzle on them. Mr. Dr. Rone did all he could to protect the Book and keep it dry. Finally the bird-beast landed in a thud, tossing all three like dice.

Mr. Dr. Rone and Dennis realized right away the absence of a steady sway meant the snatching swooper did not land on water.

"Cut us out of here," Mr. Dr. Rone said. "Hurry, before it takes flight again."

Dennis raised his sword above his head, thrust its point into the pink floor, and slit the gut open. The snatching swooper shrieked and flopped on its side. The good and ugly Unfeeo, Mr. Dr. Rone, and Dennis stumbled through the bloody laceration and ran. The fresh air shocked their noses and throats. They stopped under a tree, sticky and stinky.

The Book was safe.

Mr. Dr. Rone surveyed the unfamiliar landscape and asked Dennis to check Prince Zotch the Itchy's map. They needed to get their bearings and figure out which way to go. Trees dotted the field, and only a nearby stream and a small hill might be significant enough to be on the map. After a quick bath in the stream, they decided to hike up that hill to get a better look around.

But before they ventured on, Mr. Dr. Rone opened the Book and carefully read page fifty-seven. He held a hand over his head and, while still reading the page, trilled and clicked until a dove alighted on his finger. The man held the dove to his lips and whispered the words from the page. He kissed the bird and released it. The dove cooed away, flying above the trees and out of sight.

"There," Mr. Dr. Rone smiled. "Our messenger is off to Castle Neede."

"Messenger?" asked Dennis.

"Yes," Mr. Dr. Rone said. "How else will King Urabus know to meet us at Black Burp Swamp?"

The good and ugly Unfeeo beamed, "That's amazing!"

The hike up the hill was not too difficult. But as they reached the top, a familiar stench overpowered them. They flinched as though someone had thrown sand in their faces.

CHAPTER SIXTY-SEVEN:
A Familiar Face

"Don't be tryin' nothin' foolish now." Captain William One-eye and his band of malodorous land pirates surrounded them, their cutlasses and knives drawn. "Well, well, well, looksee who we have here. Nice to see ye again, young one. Ah, nowadays ye be carrying a weapon. Nice sword. Where be yer so-called protector, the good Knight?"

Dennis leered back.

"Keep an eye out for the Knight!"

"Aye!" they answered in chorus. William One-eye thought he heard an extra 'aye' from one of the group. The men shrugged and looked at each other, all feigning innocence.

One jokester elbowed his pirate buddy and snickered, "Keep an eye out. Get it?" His buddy stifled a laugh as the Captain returned his attention to Dennis.

William One-eye said, "Tell me where—"

"I am Prince Unfeeo the good and ugly," he interrupted, "Son of King Urabus!"

"Good to make yer 'quaintance," William One-eye bowed. "Ye are good and ugly, to be sure. I heard ye be in prison. I'll be bettin' Horrible Rick would pay for yer return." The Captain smashed a knee into Unfeeo's groin. The pirates laughed.

The Captain pointed at Mr. Dr. Rone. "What's that ye be hug-gin' to yer chest?"

"It's a book. I don't suppose you like reading?"

But before William One-eye could respond, his attention shot to the left. A band of sixty or seventy dwarfs thundered up the hill waving knives, axes, clubs, and spears.

"Don't just stand there, ye idiots!" shouted Captain William One-eye. "Attack!"

The dwarfs and malodorous pirates stabbed, chopped, and clobbered each other. They tackled, punched, and kicked. The good and ugly Unfeeo and Mr. Dr. Rone joined the fray. Confidence surged through Dennis's veins. He grabbed William One-eye and pushed his sword against the pirate's skinny belly. "Don't move," he warned.

"Looks like ye's got me," winced William One-eye, slowly rais-ing his noodle-thin arms. But quick as a blink—or in the Captain's case, quick as a wink—he yanked Dennis over his shoulder, flipping the boy onto his back. "Or maybe I's got ye. Don't move yerself."

Dennis glared up at William One-eye's single eye and sneered with delicious defiance, "Aye-Aye."

The Captain raised his broadsword with a vicious grunt.

Dennis winced as warm drops splashed his face.

He opened his eyes.

A bloody knife jutted out from William One-eye's chest. The pirate swayed. The blade twisted and disappeared into his chest. Blood gurgled from William One-eye's mouth as he crumbled face-down into the dirt.

A familiar face smiled down at Dennis, his beard close enough to tickle the boy's nose.

"Enzol!" Dennis yelled. "Oh man, am I glad to see you!"

The band of dwarfs outnumbered the pirates and proved them-selves the better fighters. One by one, the still able-bodied outlaws skipped off into the woods, hurdling their fallen, pungent comrades.

Mr. Dr. Rone and the good and ugly Unfeeo greeted the dwarfs with cheers of gratitude and hearty handshakes.

Dennis wiped off William One-eye's blood. "Thanks," he smiled and brushed some dirt off Enzol's clothes. "Thanks for saving my life. But how did you...?"

"We were hunting," explained Enzol. "I suspected something was wrong when I saw a grangeprobnoscerus running away. Then we heard the pirates' laughter. And we caught a whiff. I recognized that awful stink! The dwarfs know I am a friend of Sir Ambrose's great-grandson. The noble Knight saved many of their grandparents from the giant. They were eager to come to your aid and protect your friends from the smelly savages."

Dennis wished he could visit with Enzol longer, but time did not allow. Prince Unfeeo, Mr. Dr. Rone, and Dennis said their goodbyes to the dwarfs and continued on their way. They soon found themselves winding through a lush part of the forest. The trail unrolled like a dizzy letter S trying to make all the wrong words plural. Small, furry critters scampered under bushes. Birds flitted and chirped all about. A deer ran off. The good and ugly Unfeeo skipped along, lost in the thoughts inside his good but ugly head. Mr. Dr. Rone, still clutching the Book to his chest, focused on the pretty flowers framing their path. Dennis pictured Foggle-nogger writing as he waited by the Black Burp Swamp.

But, alas, their lack of focus resulted in more trouble.

CHAPTER SIXTY-EIGHT:
Warlock!

Prince Zotch the Itchy and his angry-looking Royal Guardsmen dismounted. A second wave of Royal Guardsmen with even meaner faces rode up. Dennis, Mr. Dr. Rone, and the good and ugly Unfeeo found themselves surrounded by at least thirty men. Making a run for it was out of the question.

"Hello, brother," Zotch the Itchy said. He scratched at a scab on his elbow. "Horrible Rick sends his best regards to all of you. Where is the Wiley Old Hag?"

"She isn't with us," Mr. Dr. Rone said.

"We know she helped you escape."

"That's a witch for you," Mr. Dr. Rone said. "Just can't trust them nowadays, can you?"

"Silence!" yelled Zotch the Itchy, scratching his shoulder. "I will contend with her later. I must return you three to Horrible Rick."

The good and ugly Unfeeo started, "But brother—"

"No," Zotch the Itchy interrupted him. "Horrible Rick made it very clear. If I do not return with you, I will be the one tortured. Seize them!"

The Prince's men bound Mr. Dr. Rone's hands and tethered him to a horse's saddle. They did the same to the good and ugly Unfeeo. But before they tied up Dennis, he called out, "Prince Zotch the Itchy, what if I help you escape Horrible Rick's torture?"

Mr. Dr. Rone shook his head.

The scratching Prince walked to Dennis's side. "And how do you suppose a boy like you can help me?"

"Well, what if I take you somewhere far away? You know, give you a fresh start."

Mr. Dr. Rone looked down and sighed.

"What are you, some kind of warlock?" the Prince laughed. "Crafting a magic spell for a fresh start in a new kingdom? Grant me a new life as a salamander or an eagle? Stop mocking me."

"No, if you want me to, I can give you a chance," Dennis said. "Untie them and send away your men. Let me help. My great-grandfather, Sir Ambrose, he really liked you."

Prince Zotch the Itchy stared at Dennis. "You are his great-grandson?"

Dennis nodded.

The Prince looked about and shook his head. "I am too ashamed to return to Castle Neede. You cannot help me."

"I really can," Dennis tried again.

The Prince's forehead wrinkled in thought. His eyes smiled and he let out a snicker. "Gentlemen," he called to the soldiers. "Be careful of this one. We have a warlock in our midst." The men laughed. And as they did, Dennis happened to look up. Something shiny directly overhead caught his attention. Something reflected the sunshine. Prince Zotch the Itchy continued, "Perhaps we should release him before he turns us all into six-legged lizards!" More laughter roared from the men.

Amidst the merriment, Prince Zotch the Itchy caught the look on Dennis's face and followed his gaze as people do when they notice someone staring at something. And just as the Prince tilted his head upward, a rather heavy coin plunked him on the forehead. It knocked him out cold.

The Guardsmen's laughter ceased in mid-guffaw. They went pale and looked at each other with the oddest expressions. They no longer looked so mean.

One whispered, "Warlock."

241

Another wasn't so quiet or calm. He pointed a trembling finger at Dennis and shouted, "Warlock! Warlock!"

Each and every Guardsman hopped on a horse, and fled quicker than a slurped-in noodle.

Dennis untied his companions and picked up the shiny coin that had fallen from the sky. It had a familiar L-shaped scratch across its heads side.

"Ah, Foggle-nogger," chuckled Dennis.

He used a dirty twig to scratch out a note on a flat piece of white bark.

DEAR PRINCE,
HOPE YOUR HEAD FEELS BETTER SOON.
I AM NOT A WARLOCK.
HERE'S YOUR MAP.
THANKS,
DENNIS

Next to the unconscious Prince, Dennis placed the note on top of the map, using a rock as a paperweight. For the map was, as you recall, rightfully Prince Zotch the Itchy's property. The boy hoped the Prince would not harbor any bad feelings.

Mr. Dr. Rone put a hand on Dennis's shoulder. "You can't keep offering everyone a free pass into your world. The Wiley Old Hag and Prince Zotch the Itchy aren't stray pets in need of a home. And she's a witch who cannot be trusted."

"I'm only trying to help."

"You must consider the possible unintended consequences of your choices," warned Mr. Dr. Rone.

"But she told me she wants a new start."

"A witch will say anything to get what she wants."

"But Lady Skulldigger doesn't want to be a witch anymore. She wants to be good."

"Dennis, listen to yourself."

The boy looked into Mr. Dr. Rone's eyes. "I promised."

The man sighed. "Promises must not be broken, which is precisely why they should be made only after careful consideration. Even if the Wiley Old Hag is being absolutely honest, bringing her to your neighborhood carries a huge risk. We're talking dire repercussions. Your responsibility doesn't end once you fulfill this promise. She'll have to be watched very closely, which is a big job for someone not yet a teenager."

The three walked on toward the swamp. The good and ugly Unfeeo whistled back at the birds in the trees. Dennis carried Foggle-nogger's silver coin in his hand as his mind drifted like a released helium balloon. Thoughts of Samir and his mustache and loud voice came first. Then he recalled Kimberly bravely waving her violin case over her head. Bulldog popped into his mind, but Dennis wasn't afraid; she was nothing compared to wolzelles and ghosts, or pirates and spiders. He imagined sharing pizza with his mom. So lost in thought was Dennis, that he failed to notice the sparrows had stopped chirping.

Dennis also failed to notice how some of the trees' shadows did not fall where they should have.

CHAPTER SIXTY-NINE:
Howling Mists

A howling wind chilled our travelers. Deep moans echoed through the trees. Dennis stashed the good luck coin and showed the sword.

An unseen force knocked Mr. Dr. Rone backwards onto the seat of his pants.

Dennis recalled what Sir Ambrose had said to the spirits and hollered, "Stop it right now!"

Spooky laughter echoed around them. Another unseen force slammed the good and ugly Unfeeo against a tree.

Dennis tried again, "Stop or I'll tell the Wiley Oh—!"

An invisible punch to the gut doubled him over. Dennis fought to get his wind back. The good and ugly Unfeeo bounced off another tree.

Mr. Dr. Rone regained his footing. "We mean you no harm!" he shouted into the wind. "Let us pass!"

"Wah whoa!" The good and ugly Unfeeo swung around and around through the air.

Mr. Dr. Rone staggered back. Something had smacked him in the face.

Howling mists raced by. One after another after another slapped past Dennis, whipping his head from side to side, stinging his face with icy blows. He dropped his weapon and wrapped his arms around his head.

"Enough!" a woman's voice screamed. "Enough!"

The winds ceased. The good and ugly Unfeeo's body flopped to the ground and rolled to a stop. The howling mists abandoned Dennis. But the air remained cold. Very cold. Dennis could see his breath.

The woman's voice shrieked, "Be gone from this place, pathetic spirits! Be gone now or suffer my wrath!"

Little breezes shot by and tiny ah's could be heard. The temperature rose to a comfortable level. Mr. Dr. Rone rubbed his stinging face. Enjoying his dizziness, the good and ugly Unfeeo remained on his back, watching the trees—now all rightfully casting shadows— whirl by.

Lady Skulldigger emerged with arms raised and poised to zap, searching for lingering ghosts.

The good and ugly Unfeeo steadied himself on shaky legs. He smiled a woozy smile and shook his woozy (and ugly) head. Mr. Dr. Rone and Dennis thanked Lady Skulldigger. As soon as Unfeeo was able, they continued on their way. Black Burp Swamp was not far off.

CHAPTER SEVENTY:
A Dark Shadow

"I waited for you!" Foggle-nogger cried tears of joy at the sight of Dennis. "Just as I promised! My little long while was beginning to turn into a big long while. But here you are! Now I don't have to wait anymore. Want to play a game?" Mr. Dr. Rone enjoyed a good laugh at the odd little man's exuberance and how he fumbled with his pipe. The good and ugly Unfeeo and Lady Skulldigger looked around, moving their eyebrows and feeling a little out of place.

"I don't know when King Urabus's men will arrive," said Mr. Dr. Rone. "To be safe, maybe I should send you back before they get here. You've fulfilled your mission."

"That'd be great," Dennis smiled as visions of his mom, pizza, cheeseburgers, Samir, and Kimberly whirled through his mind.

"Oh zoikos," said Foggle-nogger, "but my eyes have not even dried up yet, and I haven't shared my writings with you yet, and I have been waiting and hoping and worrying and thinking about you for the longest little while."

"I thought of you a lot, too" Dennis said to his hairy-eared friend. "Okay, show me what you wrote." Foggle-nogger fetched his journal.

Mr. Dr. Rone said, "I don't feel good about sitting around and waiting. It's dangerous." He hid the Book behind a log and brushed some fallen leaves over it.

"Let me see what he wrote and then I'll go," Dennis answered. That now familiar disappointed look crossed Rone's face. He scanned the horizon. The good and ugly Unfeeo and Lady Skulldigger gathered around Rone. Her fidgety hands betrayed her eagerness to cross over. As Foggle-nogger shoved his manuscript into Dennis's hands, a dark shadow swept past.

Everyone looked up. A squealing snatching swooper soared over them and landed at the edge of Black Burp Swamp. Horrible Rick's black cape fluttered behind him as he slid off the giant bird's back. It was a dramatic entrance worthy of a standing ovation (if it wasn't so scary).

Our friends had but a second to react.

Foggle-nogger rolled himself under some bushes.

Lady Skulldigger crouched low.

Mr. Dr. Rone and Dennis stood frozen. The boy still held Foggle-nogger's book.

"Oh Roger," Horrible Rick said. "I recently heard the most dreadful rumor that I simply must dispel: I did not kill your bestest buddy Fred."

"Then who did?" asked Mr. Dr. Rone.

"Ask that witchy mass of frightened hagness. She knows."

But Horrible Rick didn't give him the chance. He cracked a great whip across Rone's chest, dropping him in agony. "That's for stealing from me and causing me all this inconvenience!" He raised the whip again.

"Stop it!" the good and ugly Unfeeo stepped forward.

Horrible Rick whistled for his snatching swooper. It hopped with extended wings.

The good and ugly Unfeeo said, "I have had quite enough of this. When father—"

"Fool!" Horrible Rick shouted. He seized Unfeeo by the shoulders and flung him toward the giant bird. Faster than a finger snap, the beak shut over Unfeeo. The bird raised its head, and swallowed.

"No!" cried Mr. Dr. Rone.

Horrible Rick fixed his gaze on Dennis. "Guess I am a murderer after all."

The boy dropped Foggle-nogger's book and ran.

CHAPTER SEVENTY-ONE:
It Started With a Tickle

Dennis barely reached the open field before Horrible Rick, riding the snatching swooper, caught up to him. The bird's huge talon pinned Dennis against the grass and Horrible Rick tied him up.

"There will be no escape this time, you little troublemaker." Horrible Rick tied Dennis up, threw him onto the bird, and flew back to the edge of Black Burp Swamp.

"Stand back!" Horrible Rick ordered. He cracked the whip once more across Mr. Dr. Rone's back and called Lady Skulldigger some terrible names before grabbing the book Dennis had dropped. Horrible Rick hopped into saddle and flew away with Dennis.

Mr. Dr. Rone, Lady Skulldigger, and Foggle-nogger—who had rolled himself out from the bushes—shrank in the distance below.

At the Eastern Up castle, Horrible Rick dragged Dennis into his chambers. Needless to say, Horrible Rick was not pleased to discover the book he had nabbed was full of Foggle-nogger's writings instead of coded magic spells. His hands trembled with rage and Dennis could see the sides of his jaw bulge with tension. Horrible Rick turned his angry eyes on Dennis and cracked a wicked grin.

"This is all your fault. Oh my goodness, how can a measly child do this to me? I don't think you are going to enjoy what happens next." He flicked Dennis's nose with each added word, "Not…one… bit. But I will! What's my name?"

"Horrible Rick," answered Dennis.

"That's right! You remembered. Hey, let me ask you. I've been thinking of changing it to Horrick. Condensed, you know? Horrible. Hor-Rick, get it? Horrick! Do you think it sounds scarier, more horrible?"

Dennis did not answer.

"Well, you can tell me what you think later. Right now, we have things to do. Hey, guys!"

Horrible Rick's men strapped Dennis to a rough wooden slab. The torture commenced. It started with a tickle. Yes, a tickle. Horrible Rick poked his wiggling fingers into Dennis's armpits and rib cage. It was the last thing Dennis expected and being caught so off guard, he giggled. He squirmed and giggled some more. But the tickling grew rougher. Dennis stopped giggling and tried wriggling, but the straps were fastened tightly. Splinters plunged into his back.

"Stop!" yelled Dennis.

But the tickling quickened. Dennis writhed in anguish.

Horrible Rick paused. "Which sounds scarier? Horrible Rick or Horrick?"

Dennis was too busy trying to catch his breath to answer.

"Okay, you can tell me later." He snapped his fingers and pointed to Dennis's feet. "He's all yours, boys." The men pulled off Dennis's shoes and attacked his feet with feathers. The more Dennis squirmed, the more splinters he suffered.

The torture progressed to nipple twisties, earlobe busters, and paper cuts. They splashed lemon juice on his paper cuts. Next came bent-back fingernails and noogies. It dragged on and on. Nonstop for hours. When the torturers needed a break, a second-string of ruffians rushed. Towel snaps and wet willies. Open-mouthed stinky, moist belches in his face.

Then it really got ugly.

One of the attackers blew a handful of blue dust into Dennis's eyes. It stung and blinded him. Then the sadistic underlings pushed, pulled, shook, and shoved Dennis like a hapless human pinball in the middle of a scumbucket scrum. After what seemed like hours, they tossed the boy into a cell like a soggy load of laundry.

Every inch hurt. His head throbbed, ribs ached, and eyes stung. He was beyond exhausted. But every time Dennis nodded off to sleep, the guards doused him with a bucket of ice water. This happened again and again before finally the abuse ceased.

Dennis couldn't know how long he slept before a hooded man scooped him up and carried him through unlit corridors and up several flights of stairs. Dennis's damaged eyes could not make out the man's face. When he felt the cold night air on his skin, Dennis knew they were outside. The man carried him to the edge of the tower and stepped onto the ledge. It had to be a long way down.

A snatching swooper's squeal shattered the night's silence. The man squeezed Dennis in his arms, and leaped off the tower.

As they fell, Dennis thought, *So this is how it ends.*

But the fall ended too soon.

And too gently.

CHAPTER SEVENTY-TWO:
Drowning in Shame

They did not smash onto the hard ground.

They were not squished into a gross puddle of bloody guts.

Instead they landed on a snatching swooper.

And off they flew into the night.

When the snatching swooper landed, the man placed Dennis on soft grass. He heard a familiar voice say, "Well done."

Lady Skulldigger chanted odd phrases and sprinkled Dennis's body with various powders and herbs. Her voice warped and slowed. She rubbed an ointment over his eyes. His body tingled and twitched and grew numb.

Free of pain, Dennis slept.

When he opened his eyes, sunshine streaked the eastern horizon. Several heads stared down at Dennis. He blinked them into focus and recognized Lady Skulldigger and Foggle-nogger. Mr. Dr. Rone smiled at him. Dennis sat up with some help.

"How do you feel, young one?" asked Lady Skulldigger.

Dennis blinked again. "Fine," he whispered. He cleared his throat and looked around. He sat near the edge of the swamp. A smile stretched across his face. "I feel fine. I'm okay!" Mr. Dr. Rone helped Dennis stand before Foggle-nogger knocked him down with a clumsy hug. "What happened?"

Mr. Dr. Rone pointed behind Dennis and said, "Ask him."

"Good morning, warlock," Prince Zotch the Itchy smiled. "I hope I have atoned for my past actions."

"You sure have," Dennis said with Foggle-nogger's arms still wrapped around him.

Mr. Dr. Rone clapped his hands, "Well, Dennis, ready to go home?"

"Yes! Prince Zotch the Itchy, are you coming with us?"

Mr. Dr. Rone rolled his eyes.

"No," Prince Zotch the Itchy answered. "I will not run from this. I will apologize to my father and do what I can to make everything right. I will avenge my baby brother's death." The Prince handed Dennis the book Horrible Rick had mistakenly stolen.

Dennis gave it to Foggle-nogger. "I'm sorry I didn't get the chance to read any of it."

Foggle-nogger pushed it back to Dennis. "It's for you. Take it. It's all about us! You! Your story here."

Dennis smiled, "Thank you, Foggle-nogger Farshtinker."

"You are welcome," the big-eared bald man bowed. "But you must keep going with it. Finish your story. Do good well. I think it will be quite adventurous. And one more thing." He dug into his pocket. "Here, I kept this for you." He handed over the smooth and shiny green and black stone Dennis had so long ago admired. "I know you wanted it. I hope it brings you joy."

"Thanks again, Foggle-nogger," Dennis put the stone in his pocket. The two friends hugged again.

Mr. Dr. Rone rubbed Dennis's head and told him, "You have accomplished a great deal, my boy. I'm not sure how you did it all."

"I believed," he beamed. "In you and in me."

"I owe you my life," Mr. Dr. Rone said.

"So do I," Lady Skulldigger added with a slightly whiter smile. Quite a few of the deep creases in her face were now not as severe.

"You healed me," Dennis thanked her.

"I cannot imagine a better final act of magic in Croggerpooey," she said. "You kept your promise. In your world, I will be rid of Horrible Rick."

"Hold on," said Mr. Dr. Rone. "I can't let you leave with Dennis without approval from King Urabus. And you need to explain what Horrible Rick meant when he said you know who killed Fred?"

Lady Skulldigger's eyes welled up. She swallowed hard and said with a soft voice, "Please believe it was an accident, and I have been drowning in shame and regret ever since. I am solely responsible. I killed my sister's husband."

CHAPTER SEVENTY-THREE:
King Urabus

"**Y**ou murderess," hissed Rone.

"I cannot expect your forgiveness, but I am so sorry." The witch walked away.

"Lady Skulldigger, wait!" Dennis said.

"Let her go," said Mr. Dr. Rone.

"But I promised her."

"It was not your promise to make. The King will decide her fate."

"But she helped us a lot. I couldn't have saved you without her."

They watched her sulk into the woods. Mr. Dr. Rone put an arm around the boy. "You would have found another way. You did this, not her. You did good very well. A lot of good."

"So am I a Knight now?" asked Dennis.

"That's up to the King, but I think you still have so much to learn."

"Does that mean more training at the Academy?"

"I hope so."

"Will I have to come back here someday?"

"Perhaps."

"I'm not sure I'd like to."

"It may not be up to you," winked Mr. Dr. Rone.

"I just really want to go home."

But before Mr. Dr. Rone could open the Book to the spell that would send Dennis out of Croggerpooey, a great bustle arose from down trail. Foggle-nogger again rolled himself under some bushes. Dennis raised his sword. But Mr. Dr. Rone placed a calm hand on Dennis's arm. He was smiling. Several white steeds muscled their way into view. The neatly groomed men stepped down from the horses. A large company of soldiers marched in as a horn announced the presence of someone important.

A man approached. A formal white beard bordered his squared jaw. Purple silk accented his white shirt and his black leather boots glistened in the sun. He did not stand tallest among his entourage, but he stood straighter. He was not as muscular as Sir Ambrose, but something genuine about the man inspired awe. Something about the mighty gentleman captivated everyone. His eyes gleaned with the wisdom of understanding and consideration.

Dennis bowed at the feet of King Lewis Urabus.

"I came to thank you all," the King said. "Word of your courageous acts reached all the way to Castle Neede. Good done very well, indeed. I will not forget your bravery, especially you, Dennis Ponder. Please rise."

As Dennis tried his best to make himself look taller than he was, a low whine grumbled from Mr. Dr. Rone's stomach. Dennis realized how hungry he was, and how soon he would be eating cheeseburgers, burritos, and ice cream. Another low tummy growl caught everyone's attention. Dennis glanced at Mr. Dr. Rone.

"Sounds like you're hungry," the man said.

Dennis shook his head, "That wasn't me."

A third low murmur grew into a loud crash. The King's men pointed toward the horizon. Several V-formations of screaming snatching swoopers darkened the sky, dropping boulders like bombs.

A call to arms blared from a horn.

CHAPTER SEVENTY-FOUR:
Something Wonderful

King Urabus shouted commands. The archers scrambled into position and readied their bows. Prince Zotch the Itchy unsheathed his sword and took his place among the King's soldiers.

Two men escorted the King toward the relative safety of the trees. King Urabus stopped and turned. He directed his men to protect Dennis. His Highness shouted a few more commands before another boulder smashed into the ground, narrowly missing the King.

Crouching between tall trees, Dennis watched the archers down a snatching swooper. The bleeding bird splashed into the Black Burp Swamp, kicking up an allidile feeding frenzy. Mr. Dr. Rone was spotted under a tree with the Book open in his lap, flipping the pages and searching for helpful spells.

Snatching swooper shrieks filled the air as more boulder bombs exploded.

BAM!BOOM!

CRASH!

THUD! WHISH!

The attack lasted only a minute or so, but it seemed like half an hour to Dennis. When the boulders stopped falling, many men lay injured or lifeless. Fortunately, all our travelers and King Urabus survived unscathed.

The King jogged into the clearing, warned of a second attack, and issued more commands. Some of the men tended to the injured. One soldier on horseback rode off in a flash. Dennis hoped he was dispatched to retrieve more troops. He observed the King extend his hand up to the trees and a dove alight on his finger. The King held the bird close to his mouth and released it into the air. Off it flew.

A lieutenant barked, "Focus on the northern hills. Don't fear an attack from the south; our position against the swamp is secure!" This seemed logical and comforting to Dennis until he peeked back at the Black Burp Swamp and noticed hundreds of hungry bumpy allidiles swimming toward shore.

"Look out!" cried Dennis.

Mr. Dr. Rone ran to the water's edge and read aloud from the Book. Pointing at the gurgling water, he shouted a series of rhyming syllables, repeating the same spell over and over. The allidiles glided faster and faster towards Mr. Dr. Rone. He threw a handful of dirt into the swamp.

Then something wonderful happened.

Snakes!

Enormous serpents rose from the stinky muck, coiling their bodies and striking at allidiles. The snakes—too many to count—attacked and wrapped their thick bodies around the bumpy allidiles, who fought back best they could with their jaws, claws, and tails. But the snakes constricted the bumpy bodies until the tails stopped flailing and the jaws ceased snapping. The snakes swallowed them whole.

Soon there were no more allidiles to be found—some undoubtedly escaped to the bottom of the murky waters. The fattened snakes slithered away deep into the swamp's shadows.

Mr. Dr. Rone skipped back to his safe spot with a 'Take that!' smile as King Urabus and his soldiers applauded. Dennis, Fogglenogger, and Prince Zotch the Itchy joined in the cheers.

But the celebration was brief.

CHAPTER SEVENTY-FIVE:
A Thumping Rumble

An icy wind blasted the Black Burp Swamp. Foggle-nogger rolled back into the bushes. Dennis wondered if it was part of Mr. Dr. Rone's spell. One glance at the man's worried face answered that question, and Dennis dove back into the trees.

Ghosts whipped about in blurring waves, slapping and scratching the soldier's faces. The men waved their arms in vain, as if swatting at invisible bees. Ghosts dragged some soldiers into the clearing and tossed them about. Swords slashed. Archers shot. But the ghosts, immune to swords and arrows, howled in delight.

A discordant chorus of CAW HAW-HAW-HAW AH! joined the howls.

A murder of crows circled above, turning the sky black.

CAW! AH HAW! CAW-CAW! AH HAW HAW! CAW!

They swooped to the ground and transformed into a horde of witches. They surveyed the army flailing at ghosts and cackled with delight.

The witches unleashed an enchanted arsenal. A barrage of silver ice spears and orange fireballs zipped through the air. The archers shot back between ghostly slaps, but an unseen black magic force deflected their arrows wide. A soldier staggered from the bushes, impaled by an ice spear. Another, hit by a fireball, burst into flames. The witches' cackling boomed louder and louder.

More ice spears found their marks. More fireballs ignited their targets. More ghosts slapped and scratched the overwhelmed soldiers. Defeat seemed imminent.

Then an abrupt sonic boom jolted the battleground. The ghosts vanished. An uncomfortable calm draped over the scene. The awestruck soldiers looked about for the cause of the powerful interruption. A scream pierced the silence. Dennis poked his head out and saw a witch collapse on fire. Another witch staggered about engulfed in flames. Three or four crows flew away, at least one with singed wings.

A few silent moments later, the witches' cackling started anew as another round of silver and orange blurs shot toward a solitary figure tromping into war.

Lady Skulldigger!

She dodged the ice spears and fireballs and zapped blue flames from her fingertips. Her targets disintegrated in a poof of smoldering black feathers.

And just like that, this battle ended.

"You came back!" yelled Dennis.

"Well done, my lady!" praised Prince Zotch the Itchy. Lady Skulldigger's chest and shoulders heaved as she caught her breath. She struggled to walk. Two soldiers helped her to the relative safety of the bushes. They got there just in time.

A pack of wolzelles crept into view! The fur on their backs spiked with excitement.

The lieutenant readied his men. Swords were drawn and bows were stretched.

"No! Wait!" shrieked Dennis. "Don't!"

The lieutenant looked as if he had swallowed a bitter insect. "Get back, child! They will destroy us. No one survives a wolzelle attack."

"I have!" Dennis grabbed the officer's arm. "Listen, stay still. Don't run or fight and they won't attack."

The snarling pack prowled forward.

"It's true," called Mr. Dr. Rone. "I've seen it. I survived."

The lieutenant wiped his sweaty forehead and glanced at the King. "Sire, what shall I do?"

The growls amplified.

King Urabus asked, "Dennis, are you certain?"

"Yes sir. I swear."

"No need for that," said the King. "Lower your weapons, men. But stand your ground."

The pack filled the clearing. Foam oozed from their mouths. Sniffing and growling, the wolzelles stalked the men. One soldier made an uneasy noise, like a nervous squeak. Another shook as he fought the urge to run. One circled the lieutenant and nudged his leg.

Dennis approached the biggest wolzelle. Its fangs were as long as a man's fingers. Dennis spoke in an even tone, "Go on, get out of here." A smaller one ran off. Then another slinked off with its tail between its legs. Then another. But most stayed put, awaiting their pack leader's silent order.

The top dog put away its sharp teeth, sat, and stared at Dennis. Its cocked head looked neither mean nor happy.

Sweat now poured from the lieutenant's brow. He held his breath.

"Go on," Dennis said calmly. The leader of the pack tapped Dennis with its nose and turned away. He looked back at the brave boy and retreated. The rest followed.

The lieutenant resumed breathing. The relieved soldiers congratulated each other for remaining still. King Urabus was the first to shake Dennis's hand. Foggle-nogger's hug almost knocked the boy down.

"Allidiles, ghosts, and wolzelles?" Dennis asked. "This can't all be a coincidence."

"No way," Mr. Dr. Rone shook his head. "Horrible Rick must have decoded some of the Book's spells."

"Yes," agreed King Urabus. "I'm afraid this is just the beginning."

As if on cue, a thumping rumble rolled down the hills and through the swamp. It sounded like all the Ernest Q. Klibzowski Middle School students tapping their desks in a mock drumroll while stomping their feet. Foggle-nogger disappeared into the brush again. Everyone else turned to look.

A gray sheet slowly spread down the distant hillsides. It looked like paint spilling over the countryside.

CHAPTER SEVENTY-SIX:
A Giant Giant

The soldiers exchanged confused shrugs. Mr. Dr. Rone squinted into the distance. One of the officers handed the King a spyglass.

"Spiders!"

Billions and billions of tiny marching spider legs. The mass of spiders flowed like a wave over the hill. Everyone would soon be stuck in suffocated webs or bitten to death. The swordsmen picked up their weapons. Some soldiers armed themselves with stones to smash spiders.

"Steady, men!" called King Urabus.

A man pointed up and yelled, "Look!"

A new flock of V-formation snatching swoopers appeared over the horizon, carrying another round of boulders. The archers readied their bows.

"Steady, men!" called King Urabus.

Another man yelled, "There!"

A helmeted platoon of Horrible Rick's bicycle-riding mercenaries pedaled from the forest across the meadow. They whooped like an undisciplined band of outlaws and waved daggers, chains, and battle-axes above their heads. They outnumbered what remained of King Urabus's men by at least two to one.

"Steady!" called King Urabus. "Patience!"

"Patience?" asked Prince Zotch the Itchy. "Father, how? We are seconds away from a three-pronged attack."

The King scanned the incoming troubles with a surprisingly unworried face. "Do not doubt me."

The gray avalanche of spiders rumbled closer.

More giant birds darkened the sky.

The whooping mercenaries raced closer.

The Prince looked to Mr. Dr. Rone. The man only shrugged.

Snatching swooper shrieks filled the air. "Take cover underneath the trees, men," commanded King Urabus. "Spread yourselves out best you can."

BOOM! THUD! CRASH!

Boulder bombs dropped all around them. Dennis closed his eyes and cowered in his hiding place.

BAM! BOOM! BOOM! THUD!

The snatching swooper shrieks changed into higher pitched wails. The bombing ceased. Softer sounding, squishier explosions began.

Splat! PFFOO! Squish! PLOP!

Men started cheering and Dennis opened his eyes.

He blinked several times to make sure what he saw was really there.

The word 'giant' does not adequately describe the creature dominating the meadow between the swamp and the hills.

It was a giant giant. An enormously huge giant giant.

Foggle-nogger jumped up and down and giggled. "Rocknocerus! Look at that, Dennis! Rocknocerus!"

The massive creature's round face rested on its chest. It had human-like hands but its legs folded under like a lizard standing upright. This giant giant plucked snatching swoopers out of the air. It crushed them in its massive fists and tossed them aside.

SPLAT! Squish! PFFOO! PFFOO! Plop! Splat! PFFOO!

Dennis just stared. He couldn't close his mouth or eyes.

If a snatching swooper soared out of reach, Rocknocerus scooped up a refrigerator-sized boulder and hurled it at the snatching swooper. It aim was deadly accurate. And it never ran out of ammunition; whenever Rocknocerus needed a boulder to throw, it dipped into a squat and piles of rocks appeared between its feet.

More snatching swoopers plunged to the ground.

PFFOO! SPLAT!

When the giant giant took a step, Dennis braced himself for an earthquake. But somehow the Rocknocerus's light steps caused no tremors. Given its enormous girth, Dennis couldn't understand it. Perhaps its crouching lizard legs absorbed the impact.

A lone, snatching swooper turned in flight and escaped with its rider. With the rest of snatching swoopers taken care of, Rocknocerus turned its attention to stomping on the gray sea of spiders cascading toward the swamp. The spiders soon covered Rocknocerus's feet and ankles. Colossal hands brushed off millions of spiders with each casual swipe.

With Rocknocerus occupied with the spiders, the soldiers readied for the mercenaries pedaling their way.

CHAPTER SEVENTY-SEVEN:
Stay Here

King Urabus searched the distant hills and forest through the spyglass. A wide smile showed his relief.

"What is it, your Highness?" Mr. Dr. Rone asked.

"The dove delivered my messages in time. The Weasel Men are running to our aid. They will use slingshots to attack the bicyclists from the east."

King Urabus handed the spyglass to Mr. Dr. Rone and pointed to the trail that led to Castle Neede. An endless procession of royal soldiers marched their way.

The lieutenant spoke up, "The Second Battalion will attack from the west. Horrible Rick's army will not survive the day."

"Do not be overconfident," warned King Urabus.

Horrible Rick's mercenaries caught on to their predicament and huddled to devise a strategy. Dennis sensed dissent among the ranks when one muscled soldier of fortune shoved another off his bicycle, knocking his helmet off. The helmetless mercenary's yellowish blond hair shined in the sun. Dennis squinted to see if that could possibly be whom he suspected. But a fight broke out among them and the crowd engulfed the two. When the fracas broke up, everyone wore a helmet again. It was impossible to tell them apart. After some yelling and pointing, the mercenaries turned and rode their bicycles toward the Weasel Men. Horrible Rick's soldiers understood taking on one threat at a time improved their chances of victory.

The King yelled, "Mobilize men! We must help our tiny friends!" The royal archers and swordsmen raced in formation toward the meadow. Prince Zotch the Itchy joined the ranks behind the lieutenant.

"Give me your sword," Mr. Dr. Rone said. "Stay here with Foggle-nogger and Lady— "

"No," interrupted Dennis. "I'm going, too."

"No you are not," the King looked down from atop his horse. "Stay here."

"But—" A sharp elbow and a stern look from Mr. Dr. Rone communicated how improper it was to argue with the King. Dennis looked down and handed over his sword. He recalled Sir Ambrose saying, *Trust me, Dennis, you are not ready for war.*

Foggle-nogger put his arm around Dennis and pointed toward the mass of dead spiders. Rocknocerus was gone. Nobody had heard it leave.

The Weasel Men fought with all the skill and bravery they could muster. They were deadly accurate with their slingshots and managed to pluck more than a few mercenaries off their bikes. However, their slingshots proved useless in close quarters. And although the Weasel Men's quickness allowed them to dodge most of the slashing knives, swinging chains, and smashing fists, they were outnumbered, smaller, and weaker. King Urabus and his first battalion raced to their aid, but they simply could not get to the battle fast enough. Before the King reached the gory battlefield, nearly all the Weasel Men lay slaughtered or mangled.

It was a devastating sight. But there was no time to mourn.

The first battalion established their line a short distance from the mercenary forces. Two lines of archers—one standing, one kneeling—prepared to fire. Prince Zotch the Itchy joined other eager swordsmen on horseback to the archers' left. Several others on horseback lined up on the archers' right. Behind them, the foot soldiers readied their swords, slings, and clubs.

The mercenaries regrouped and taunted the Royal Army with vile names and gestures. The King commanded his men to exercise patience once again and await his order. He knew each moment they waited brought the second battalion that much closer to their aid. The mercenaries pounded their weapons against their shields in a bone-chilling rhythm.

King Urabus held a hand up to his troops and shouted, "Patience!"

The mercenaries charged on their bicycles toward the first battalion's line.

King Urabus shouted, "Wait!" The closer the enemy advanced, the more accurate his archers would be. "Wait!"

The enemy's battle cries grew to deafening roars.

The King yelled, "NOW!"

CHAPTER SEVENTY-EIGHT:
Act Swiftly

Arrows flew. Horsemen advanced. Foot soldiers darted into action. Most of the arrows deflected off the mercenaries' helmets or shields. Another round of arrows zipped through the air. A mercenary took one to the throat. The archers advanced several yards, knelt, and nocked their bows. The enemies pedaled at breakneck speeds toward the line. But pedaling fast made it more difficult to hold up their shields. More mercenaries fell. The groups clashed. Horrible Rick's force jumped off their bikes and stabbed and clubbed at the Royal Army, who fought back just as violently.

Dennis, Lady Skulldigger, and Foggle-nogger remained safely at the swamp's edge. They witnessed Prince Zotch the Itchy flatten several mercenaries. They saw Mr. Dr. Rone wielding the sword with the grace and skill of a warrior half his age. Dennis observed the fighting with an unsettling sense of helplessness. Despite the obvious danger, he felt a bit like the lone classmate not invited to a birthday party. Or like a lifeguard watching a child drown. *Do something*. He looked around. Foggle-nogger covered his eyes. Lady Skulldigger appeared distracted. She gazed at the ground by her feet. Dennis assumed she also wished there was something she could do to help.

Horrible Rick's mercenaries outnumbered the Royal Army, and they were clearly well trained in hand-to-hand combat. However, the archers and horsemen gave King Urabus the upper hand. But not for long.

Dennis climbed a tree to get a clearer view. He was sickened to see how many dead and maimed soldiers littered the battlefield. Sir Ambrose had told him, *Only a child with a head full of misguided fantasies wants to go to war... the trick is knowing when to fight and when to remain peaceful.*

The mercenaries' numbers and savagery began to overwhelm the Royal Army. More and more of the King's men fell. Several retreated, including Mr. Dr. Rone and Prince Zotch the Itchy. The battle was over. The whole thing lasted but a few horrifying minutes.

The mercenaries celebrated their second victory and regrouped for the next.

Through the trees Dennis could see the Second Battalion—seemingly King Urabus's last hope—rushing to the meadow. He also spotted a snatching swooper returning over the horizon. This time no Rocknocerus loomed to swat it from the sky. This snatching swooper didn't carry any boulders. It flew around, surveying the battle scene. A black cape flowed behind its rider.

"It's Horrible Rick!" Dennis yelled. "Look!"

The snatching swooper circled above the fray once more. It dove, plucked a man off a horse, and shot up toward the clouds. The man clutched in its talons wore shiny boots and a white shirt trimmed with purple.

"He's got the King!" Dennis shouted.

Three archers nocked arrows and drew their bows before the snatching swooper could soar much higher. The first arrow pierced Horrible Rick's leg. The second shot hit the snatching swooper under its wing. It screamed and wobbled, and its erratic flight made for a difficult target. The third archer dared not shoot out of fear of hitting his King.

The Second Battalion stormed into battle. Foggle-nogger quivered with fearful excitement. But Dennis focused on the wounded snatching swooper struggling to fly. It succumbed to the pain over the woods and went down.

His great-grandfather's words played louder inside his head, *Sometimes it is our duty to fight... When something is evil—not just wrong or bad—it must be stopped... Act swiftly. Nothing is deadlier than a battle fought with hesitation and doubt.*

Dennis slid from the tree and ran. He dreaded what Horrible Rick would do. His determination to save King Urabus grew with every stride. He wished he had his great-grandfather's sword.

CHAPTER SEVENTY-NINE:
You Startled Me

Two mercenaries on bicycles raced away from the battlefront and toward the spot where Horrible Rick and King Urabus went down. They hollered and pointed at the sprinting boy. Dennis pumped his fists and knees faster and faster. Never had he run so fast. The mercenaries pedaled harder. Dennis reached the trees and sprinted down the rough, winding path. He hurdled a fallen tree, ducked a low hanging limb, and dodged drooping vines and mud puddles without breaking stride.

The mercenaries pedaled through or around, over or under the same obstacles, reaching a point where the path straightened between the rows of trees. They saw no sign of the boy, but a bleeding snatching swooper writhed in pain ahead of them. They accelerated.

A vine jerked taut across the trail, clotheslining the first mercenary off his bike. The hard landing knocked the wind out of him. The second rider ducked under and continued past. Dennis dropped the vine, stepped into the path, and picked up a baseball-sized stone.

He replayed Dr. Nolan's throwing instructions—*Twist your whole body and keep your eye on the target*—and hurled the rock at the biker. The rock beaned the mercenary on the back of the neck. His helmet flew off. He catapulted over his handlebars, hit the ground hard, and lay still.

Dennis hurried to the downed biker, who had yellowish blond hair.

Sebastian rolled over, rubbing the back of his neck. "Heard you found the old man."

"I did." A knife lay on the ground between them. They both spotted it at the same time. Dennis dove first and grabbed it.

Sebastian's eyes widened as Dennis raised the blade.

Nothing is nobler than avoiding unnecessary violence, Sir Ambrose had said. Dennis bit his lip and lowered the knife. Sebastian swayed on woozy legs, blinked, and gave his head with a quick shake. A twisted grin infected Sebastian's face as he pulled a second knife from his boot. "You're fighting for the wrong side, Denny."

"It's Dennis."

"Yep. I remember." He tried again to shake his head clear. "Just Dennis."

And as Sebastian brushed dirt from his scraped elbow, Dennis buried his foot into Sebastian's crotch.

The former superstar collapsed with a groan.

Dennis picked up the crashed bicycle and pedaled toward the snatching swooper. The dying beast's wheezed in agony. The boy stepped off the bike. With the knife, he snuck around the snatching swooper toward Horrible Rick's cursing voice.

He peeked around the giant bird and saw Horrible Rick tying a white cloth around his thigh where the arrow had hit. The snatching swooper oozed one last whine and died. Dennis sneaked another look. He did not see or hear the King.

The boy climbed atop the feathery corpse. He spotted Horrible Rick leaning against a tree and breathing heavily. Dennis crept forward and saw the King with his hands and feet bound, kneeling with a straight spine and his bearded chin held high.

"This is it, Lewis. Finally," Horrible Rick sneered.

"I am your father and your king. Failing to address me respectfully does not diminish my sovereignty," the King said. "It only reveals your smallness of character."

"Your sovereignty? My smallness of character? You really expect me to call you king? And Lewis, you stopped being my dad a long time ago. You disowned me, remember? You deprived me, your oldest son, my right to the throne. But it doesn't matter. Once I decode that precious Book of yours, and get rid of you, I will rule Croggerpooey. Me. Alone. King Horrick! Do you like Horrick? Sounds scarier, doesn't it?"

"You will never decode the Book."

"I don't have to. I'll make you do it."

"That will not happen."

"I think it will!" Horrible Rick limped over to his kneeling father and punched him. The blow stung, but failed to knock the monarch down.

"You test my capacity to forgive," King Urabus said.

Horrible Rick shook with rage. "You forgive *me*? You should be begging for *my* forgiveness! I owe you pain. And I will exact my revenge!" He leaned against the dead snatching swooper.

Dennis needed to do something fast. *If I can untie the King's feet, we can outrun Horrible Rick and his bad leg. But how can I reach the King without being seen?* Dennis dried his sweaty palms on his shirt and thought, *What would Sir Ambrose do? He'd kill Horrible Rick.* Dennis looked at the knife in his hand. *But I can't kill anyone, not even Horrible Rick. Maybe I can bean him with a rock.*

In his pocket was the stone Foggle-nogger had given him, but it was too small to do any damage. Before Dennis could sneak down the other side of the feathery corpse and grab some rocks, Horrible Rick picked up a thick, broken tree branch and swung a blow into his father's gut. The King folded against the ground. The bad son struck him again. The King let out a terrible moan. Then Horrible Rick unsheathed a dagger.

"Nooo!" Dennis screamed down the feathery slide with his knife. The landing stung his feet and knees. Horrible Rick pointed his blade at the boy. His evil eyes sparkled.

"Well, well, well," laughed Horrible Rick. "You startled me. No tickling for you this time."

The villain lunged with his dagger.

Dennis dashed to the side.

Horrible Rick grimaced as he circled with a limp and swung his blade a second time.

Dennis jumped back unscathed.

"You'll never catch me."

"I won't need to," Horrible Rick shrugged and turned to hop over to the King. "You will come to me." He held the dagger against the King's neck and glanced back to where Dennis had stood. But he wasn't there.

Horrible Rick glanced to his left, and a sharp pain flashed into his back.

"Awhh!" The knife was buried below his shoulder blade.

"I got you!"

"You? A boy?"

Horrible Rick grimaced as he strained and failed to reach the knife handle protruding from his blood-soaked back. He staggered and flung his dagger at Dennis, but it landed harmlessly in the dirt.

The boy grabbed the thick tree branch from the ground and held it like a baseball bat. "Here you go, Horrick!" The first swing smacked against Horrible Rick's bloody thigh. He fell. The second blow whacked his upper arm. Rick screamed, sounding much less than horrible.

Dennis used Horrible Rick's dagger to cut free the King's hands and feet. Then Dennis ran to fetch the bicycle. When he returned, Horrible Rick was gone. He had limped into the forest. Dennis propped the King on the handlebars and pedaled back to Black Burp Swamp.

CHAPTER EIGHTY:
We Must Obey

Foggle-nogger jumped with excitement as Dennis rode up.

"Think you might have one more spell in you?" he asked Lady Skulldigger, assisting the King off the handlebars.

She untied her pouches and sprinkled pinches of powders and herbs over his wounds while humming a little tune. Moments later King Urabus straightened up and smiled his thank you to the witch. Lady Skulldigger whispered something into the King's ear and he nodded.

"The battle?" the King asked. "How did the Second Battalion fare?"

"Heehee, we won!" yipped Foggle-nogger. "You won. Horrible Rick lost. Look!" What remained of the Royal Army, led by Prince Zotch the Itchy and Mr. Dr. Roger Whee Rone, approached the swamp's edge.

The weary soldiers congratulated each other. Foggle-nogger, listening intently to their battle stories, kept interjecting with "Well, braid my back hair!" and "Trim my ear hairs!" and "Ah, foggle-nogger!"

While Lady Skulldigger tended to injured soldiers, a figure was spotted running across the meadow toward the swamp. As he got closer there was no mistaking his magnificent ugliness.

"Unfeeo!" yelled Dennis.

"I made it! I tickled the snatching swooper's little throat thingy until he hocked me out. I survived!" Everyone greeted the good and ugly Unfeeo with hugs. No one seemed to mind the dead fish stench still clinging to him.

After the celebration, King Urabus wrapped an arm around Dennis. "You saved my life. I cannot fully express my gratitude."

Dennis smiled so wide he looked as though someone had stapled his cheeks next to his eyes.

Mr. Dr. Rone offered the Book to the King.

"Hold on to that a moment," the King said. "Perhaps it would be best if young Dennis Ponder remained."

"What?" Dennis asked. "You mean stay here?"

"You have proven yourself to be most valiant," the King said. "And Horrible Rick will be angrier than ever after this defeat."

Dennis looked to Mr. Dr. Rone for help. His teacher merely shook his head.

"Excuse me, sire," said Lady Skulldigger. "What about me?"

"You too have acted most unexpectedly. You have done much good rather well and I believe you have earned a second chance. I will allow you to cross over into Dennis's world."

"But sire, if I may be heard," Mr. Dr. Rone protested. "She killed Fred."

"Yes. And she has suffered for it and apologized. I forgive her and urge you to try as well. She may go, but not before I strip her of her magical abilities."

"My magic?" she asked.

"Wait a minute," Dennis interrupted. "I need to go home. I want to see my mom and friends."

"My boy," the King said, "I need you here a while longer."

"I don't want to stay."

Mr. Dr. Rone walked Dennis away for a private talk. "You mustn't argue with the King. Let me try to change his mind, but I can't promise you anything. This is his kingdom. We must obey his decisions."

Then Mr. Dr. Rone and King Urabus spoke privately at the swamp's edge. After several minutes, the King called Prince Zotch the Itchy over to join the discussion. Dennis watched intently, chewing on a thumbnail. Finally they appeared to reach an agreement. Mr. Dr. Rone waved for Dennis and Lady Skulldigger to come.

King Urabus spoke, "We will need our collective skills to stop Horrible Rick once and for all. That includes you, Lady Skulldigger and you, young Dennis Ponder. After Croggerpooey is safe, I promise to allow you both to cross over. Lady Skulldigger shall leave this kingdom without her magic; Dennis shall leave without any memories of his time in Croggerpooey. That is my decision. It is late. My men will pitch tents and we shall all rest here tonight. Tomorrow we hike to Castle Neede. There we will devise a strategy to get rid of Horrible Rick."

The King walked away.

"So how long will this take?" Dennis asked Mr. Dr. Rone.

"I can only guess how much longer you'll be needed here."

"It's not fair, you know. I did what I was told to do. I found you and got the Book back."

"Yes, you did."

"And why can't I keep my memories? You get to keep yours. How am I supposed to tell my mom and my friends about Croggerpooey if I can't remember anything?"

"You aren't supposed to tell them," Mr. Dr. Rone said. "Listen, it is better like this. Trust me, your friends wouldn't believe you anyway. This is beyond their imagination."

"I don't understand," Dennis said.

"You don't have to understand. Just believe. We'll talk more tomorrow. You and Foggle-nogger are sharing that tent over there. Good night."

When Dennis entered the tent, Foggle-nogger tried quite unsuccessfully to cheer him up.

"I'm sure it won't take a very long while to deal with that meanie. Besides, at least we get to be together a little longer. Do you want to read your story now?"

"No thanks," Dennis pulled the blanket over himself. "Maybe tomorrow." Before long, both Dennis and Foggle-nogger slept.

In the middle of the night, however, someone visited their tent.

CHAPTER EIGHTY-ONE:
You Deserve To Know

Dennis opened his eyes. Lady Skulldigger knelt beside him with her boney finger to her lips.

"Shh. Come. And bring Foggle-nogger's book."

Dennis and Lady Skulldigger tiptoed away from the tents and had a whispered conversation.

"You can go home," she said. "Right now."

"But you heard the King."

"Yes. But I have made arrangements."

"But I can't go against the King."

"You have done everything he's asked. All that was needed. You even saved his life. And now he won't allow you to go home? Who is he to say no to you?"

"But Mr. Dr. Rone…"

"He is waiting to send us back now just beyond those trees. Come."

Dennis knew something wasn't right. It felt like the witch had reverted to her devious ways. "Let me see Mr. Dr. Rone."

"Good! Yes, this way then."

They sneaked into the trees, careful to avoid the patrolling soldiers. There he was. Mr. Dr. Rone stood with the Book in his hands.

"Mr. Dr. Rone, are you sure this is all right?"

The man did not answer. He didn't even look toward Dennis. Even though only the stars and moon illuminated the scene, Dennis could see that Mr. Dr. Rone stood unnaturally stiff. His brown eyes seemed unfocused.

"What's wrong with him?" Dennis asked.

"He is under a spell."

"A spell? What are you doing?"

Lady Skulldigger rested her hands on Dennis's shoulders. "He will be fine."

"No, this doesn't feel right."

"Listen to me, Dennis. This is best for him and for us. Roger gets to do what he thinks is right—sending you home—without being responsible for disobeying the King. He can blame me. The King cannot punish him for something he could not control. You get to go home before the King destroys your memories. And I get to crossover with you."

"You just want to keep your magic," Dennis said.

"Yes, I do. But only to be safe. Only to use if truly needed. I have never been to your world. I need the ability to protect myself."

Dennis blinked and fidgeted. "This is wrong."

"What is wrong about going home?"

"King Urabus—"

"He is not your father. He is not even your King. Do not allow him to think for you. That is what the old Dennis would do. The Dennis that got bullied. The one that ran from danger. That is not you anymore. You can solve this problem. You can go home and be with your mother and friends. And you can help me. I knew it the first time we met."

"I don't know...."

"Think of your time in Croggerpooey. Meeting Foggle-nogger and your great-grandfather, Sir Ambrose. What you did to Sebastian. Don't you want people to know how you defeated that cowardly turd? The King will rip those memories away. You won't be able to tell anyone. Think of everything you have done here. All your accomplishments. You crossed the River of Snakes. You rescued Rone. You survived wolzelles! You saved the King's life! You, Dennis

Ponder, are a hero. But what good is being a hero if you cannot even remember it? It will be exactly as if you never did any of those brave acts. Is that what you want? Going home as a scared little boy? You are better than that now. You deserve to know how great you are. Do not allow the King to steal that from you. Do not give up. You can solve this problem. Let Mr. Dr. Rone send you home. The longer we stay, the more Rosie suffers. Going back now may save her life."

The boy had stopped fidgeting. After a quiet moment, he swallowed and slowly nodded his head.

Lady Skulldigger whispered into Rone's ear. He began turning pages until he reached page forty. He cleared his throat and began to read.

"Wait!" Dennis interrupted.

"What is it?" she asked.

Dennis remembered landing in Black Burp Swamp completely naked. He wanted to make sure he would arrive home with clothes on. Lady Skulldigger couldn't help but chuckle. She whispered into Rone's ear again. Mr. Dr. Rone flipped over a few pages, muttered a few foreign sounding words, and returned to the original passage. When the spell had been read, Mr. Dr. Rone closed the Book and waved an arm.

CHAPTER EIGHTY-TWO:
Dennis the Indomitable!

verything glowed whiter and brighter. The swamp and the rest of Croggerpooey faded away. The two travelers took a single step and found themselves out of the shine and in total darkness. Holding Foggle-nogger's book and Lady Skulldigger's hand, Dennis turned this way and that way through the black maze. Three times they had to double-back due to a dead end, but they finally reached the slight glowing outline of an elevator door.

Dennis pushed the familiar sideways arrow button. They waited in awkward silence. *Ding.* The door opened and in they stepped.

The elevator lurched back and shot up like a rocket. Lady Skulldigger fell to the floor. Dennis braced himself in a corner. Electricity tingled throughout their freezing cold bodies. The building pressure made their ears ache. The elevator rattled and swayed with a frenetic intensity. Tears and snot oozed out. They fought to keep from swallowing their tongues. And just when they couldn't bear it one millisecond more, it stopped.

Ding. The doors opened.

Next came an escalator, which ran as fast descending as its twin did going up. Both Dennis and Lady Skulldigger fell flat on their bottoms and laughed.

Outside the double doors, the familiar guard with wide, flaring nostrils held fast the chains leashed to the seven bad-breathed

Rottweilers. Dennis recognized the heavy cologne. The dogs wagged their tails at the sight of Dennis. However, they growled and pulled at their chains when they spotted Lady Skulldigger.

"It's okay," Dennis said. "She's my guest. Mr. Dr. Rone sent her." The guard tugged the dogs away, even the one intensely scratching behind its ear. "I know what happened. You did good well." He clanged a heavy bell hanging behind him. "Now everybody knows you're back."

It was daytime. Dennis and Lady Skulldigger practically skipped through Dizzy Whirled on their way to the exit. It was awfully tempting to stop for a cheeseburger or grab some cotton candy or popcorn, but Dennis didn't have any money and he wanted to get home as soon as possible. Once in the parking lot, an unexpected crowd engulfed them.

Frank, Glenn, Rinbombo, and all the Knight trainees—except Sebastian, of course—erupted in applause. Even the boys dismissed early from training welcomed them with loud enthusiasm. Dennis blushed.

Rinbombo boomed, "Dennis the Indomitable!"

The boys yelled back, "Dennis the Indomitable! Hip Hip Hooray! Hip Hip Hooray! Hip Hip Hooray!"

Miguel the Eager was the first to shake Dennis's hand. Both Brooks the Fidgety and Vance the Grinning high-fived him. Tom the Huge tossed Dennis into the air while Josh the Distracted watched an insect crawl by. Carter the Clever congratulated Dennis, and Matt the Mumbler said something indecipherable with a grin. Justin the Wise patted his back, and whatever Eric the Quiet said could not be heard. A toot sang from Donald the Flatulent's rear end, which Carlos the Quick easily evaded. And when Clayton the Smooth and Jack the Willing sandwiched Dennis in a hug, the cast on Jack's broken arm clubbed Dennis's back. Dylan the Dutiful made his way over on crutches and Jay Obie the Attentive broke out in a happy cowboy dance. Buddy the Enterprising gave Dennis a wink and a thumbs up. And Ziggy the Tearful well, you know, cried joyful tears.

Dennis saw Mr. Daffulion, with his stained tie and wide yellow smile. "Hyou did it, hyoung Mr. Ponder! Hyou really did it!" Then he added in a quieter aside, "Hyou most probably saved my career. Thank hyou so much."

"How's Mrs. Goodwyn?" Dennis asked Rinbombo.

"Still hospitalized. It was bad for a while there, but she's improved greatly the last day or so. I imagine seeing you will help." Then Rinbombo said in one of his so-called whispers overheard by nearly everyone. "Mr. Dr. Rone sent word. Although he isn't pleased about how you left, he understands why. He is worried about the witch. Keep an eye on her. Mr. Dr. Rone will do his best to get in touch with you as soon as he can. And Dennis, be careful with your memories."

Frank and Glenn drove Dennis and Lady Skulldigger home. As usual, the fast and swerving ride was full of screeching tires and blasting horns. But now it seemed more fun than scary. Dennis and Lady Skulldigger giggled and bounced around in the back seat the whole way. After another round of good-byes—this time with Frank and Glenn—Dennis took Foggle-nogger's book and walked Lady Skulldigger to the front door of Mrs. Goodwyn's house. He fetched the key from under the green flowerpot and handed it over.

"Thank you, young Dennis. Thank you so very much."

"You are welcome, Lady Skull…. You know, maybe I should call you something else."

She grinned. "Yes, please use my first name, Nhilossee. Nobody has called me that in many, many years. It will be good to hear it again."

"Okay, Miss Nhilossee."

She opened the door to her sister's house and stepped inside. Its cozy warmth relaxed her shoulders and smoothed another wrinkle. As Dennis started home, he saw Kimberly and Samir on the sidewalk.

CHAPTER EIGHTY-THREE:
Wow!

Kimberly waved, "Hey, where've you been the last few days?"

A few days? he grinned. *It's been a lot longer than that.*

Samir asked, "You go to a camp or something? Whatcha reading?"

Dennis looked down at Foggle-nogger's book. As he struggled with what to say, You-Know-Who came stomping out her door.

Bulldog shouted, "Where you been, you little creep?"

"I gotta go. I'll call you later!"

Dennis started to tell Samir he didn't have to run, but his words lost the race. Samir was already gone. Bulldog, with her eyebrows scrunched and fists clenched, was almost across the street now.

I got this. She's no worse than Horrible Rick. I saved the King.

"You better leave," started Dennis. But Bulldog shoved him into what was left of Mrs. Goodwyn's flowers. He dropped Foggle-nogger's book.

"Nice clothes, whatcha do, mug a garden gnome or something?"

"Leave him alone," Kimberly said.

"Mind your own business," Bulldog sneered.

Dennis stepped forward. "It's okay, Kimberly. Bulldog, listen, you better leave me alone."

"Shut up! I owe you one." She pushed him down. "And your fuzzy little friends aren't here to save you this time."

"Bulldog, I'm warning you. I'm not the same guy you remember." As soon as Dennis got up, Bulldog socked him right on the chin. He fell flat on his rear end and sat in total silence. Tiny colorful balloons floated and popped before his dazed eyes. He leaned back on his elbows and watched the balloons float and pop, float and pop.

"Stop it!" Kimberly yelled.

Dennis shook his head to clear away the balloons and thought he saw Sebastian and Enzol standing before him. He blinked twice before Bulldog and Kimberly came into focus, replacing the two images from Croggerpooey.

Kimberly rammed her shoulder into Bulldog's back. But she only bounced off. As Bulldog turned around to attack Kimberly, she unknowingly poised her rear end above Dennis. Without hesitation, he pulled his knees into his chest and shot his legs out straight with all his strength. Bulldog blasted through the air! She crashed tail-bone-first onto the sidewalk. Dennis and Kimberly looked at each other with wide eyes. Bulldog sat quietly where she had landed, still as a stone on the hard concrete.

Then she wailed, "WAAA-OWW!"

Dennis jumped to his feet.

Bulldog rolled a little one way and pushed herself upright. She hobbled across the street, rubbing her backside with one hand and wiping her eyes with the other.

"You're dead, Dennis Ponder," she hissed over her shoulder. "Hear me?" Her voice was thick with tears.

"I told you to leave me alone. I'm not the same guy!"

Bulldog paused in front of her house to spit. She sniffled and disappeared behind the slammed door.

"Way to go!" Kimberly celebrated. "Wow! She would've killed me." She brushed some dirt off Dennis's shoulder and said, "Thanks."

"You're welcome," said Dennis as he picked up Foggle-nogger's book. He spotted his new neighbor watching through Mrs. Goodwyn's old curtains. She gave him a slight nod.

Kimberly said something about getting home for violin practice and thanked him again.

Dennis pulled the black and green stone from his pocket and smiled at the thought of Foggle-nogger.

Then he ran inside and to hug his mother.

About the Author

J. Furey Hopkins teaches English to middle school students in California. He has a lovely wife and two marvelous children. When he is not writing or teaching, J. Furey Hopkins enjoys making his family laugh, wrestling with his dog, and listening to music. He often watches the goldfish and turtles play in his tiny backyard pond.

If this story made you smile, think twice, or turn the page when you should have been doing something else, please consider posting a book review. Mr. Hopkins would very much appreciate your nice words.